Chronicles of Leight

Book Three

I0576017

Dreambound Fae

By Evan Kelling

Chapter 1

I tapped my fingers rhythmically against the cold, metal table. The interrogation room was a dimly lit rectangle of gray brick and concrete flooring. The chain of my handcuffs ran through a metal loop welded to the table, giving me very little room to move my hands. The cuffs were uncomfortable as hell, making the skin under them raw and irritated.

"Harry Potter never had to put up with this crap," I muttered bitterly.

My first big job without my uncle breathing down my shoulder, and now I was stuck in a police station while people were in danger. It was far from fair and extremely inconvenient. But I couldn't blame Seattle PD either. What did I expect? That they'd just go along with my stories of wizards and Unseelie Fae? I scoffed at the thought. The mortal world was dealing with a classic case of denial, with no signs of recovery.

A door to my left clicked as it was unlocked and swung open. A woman came through. She was in her early thirties, maybe. Dark skin, short curly hair, and eyes that could stare into your soul, no magic required. She wore a maroon button-up under a police jacket and jeans, her pistol and SPD badge brandished so I could see them clearly.

"Detective Hart," I said, my mouth thinned into a line. I waved at her awkwardly, from the wrist up—no need to yank my chains. My wrists hurt enough as is.

Hart walked over to the table, taking a seat across from me. She dropped a folder onto the desk with a flourish of annoyance. She had not been my biggest fan over the last year. Who can blame her? Supernatural activity in Seattle has been steadily increasing over the previous year. And there was one person who seemed to turn up at every crime scene left behind by some paranormal nasty; me. Usually, I had my uncle to bail me out, or there wasn't any evidence to condemn me. But not this time. Nope, I'd been caught red-handed, or so it seemed.

"Mr. Leight, you've landed yourself in quite a bit of trouble this time," Hart said, with no sign of enthusiasm. Good ol' Detective Hart, a professional, through and through.

"Please, just Tobias," I said with a half-hearted grin. "Mr. Leight was my father's name."

"Now's no time for jokes, Mr. Leight," Hart said severely. "We found you with a body. The victim was drained of blood and mummified. Want to tell me anything about that?"

"It's a prop." I joked. "An old puppet of The CryptKeeper. Tales of the Crypt, you ever seen that show?"

Hart stared daggers at me, clearly unamused— tough room.

The detective was right, at least partially. Sure, she'd found me standing over a mummified body. But no, I didn't do it. Hell, I'd had a hard enough time keeping my lunch down when I'd entered the room. No, the thing that did this was one bad bastard. And I couldn't afford to be stuck here answering questions while it was still out there.

"Mr. Leight, I have multiple bodies and a police captain collecting sweat in his boots," Hart explained. "I don't have time for jokes, and neither do you. Work with me, and I can see about getting you a reduced sentence. Make my job harder, and you won't like what comes next."

I spread my hands and let out an exasperated sigh. "You want the story? Fine. But you're not going to like it."

Hart sat back in her chair, crossing her arms. She raised an eyebrow. "Try me."

I puffed out a breath. "You asked for it."

***

I really needed to practice running more often. I was way too out of shape for a guy who was constantly the target of bloodthirsty monsters. But there was no trial like a trial by fire. I ran through the halls of the abandoned hospital for all I was worth, clutching my prize under my arm. I heard the sound of splintering wood as the door I'd slammed behind me was blown off its hinges. I looked over my shoulder just in time to see two giant lupine forms bound out into the hallway and close in on me.

"Shit!" I cursed. I recognized them as cù sìth. They were large hounds, easily larger than an adult timber wolf. And boy, did they look unhappy. Their fur was a dark gray with patches of mossy green. Their tails were thin and whip-like, and even as they ran towards me, they flicked to and fro with alarming speed. Their golden eyes were locked onto me with a hungry stare.

I skidded around a corner and took off down the next hall, nearly tripping over some debris. As big and bad as they were the cù sìth didn't have the luxury of traction on the dusty, tile flooring. They slipped and fell over themselves in a tangled heap of furry limbs. It gave me some time to get some distance between me and them.

"Careful bucko, Scooby and Scrappy back there look hungry. And no one wants to be on a cù sìth's lunch menu." A voice came from the leather satchel I carried under my arm.

"Would you be quiet?" I snapped back. "Trying not to die here!"

"I really think I could help ya here." My satchel bound companion offered.

"Nuh uh, no way." I said breathlessly. "I might be fresh out of my apprenticeship, but I'm not that green. I don't make deals with Fae."

The voice scoffed, as if offended. "Well technically, I'm not Fae an—"

"Screw the technicality." I growled back. I jostled the bag a bit. "Now shut up, I'm trying to focus here."

I was about to take another turn when a dark shape leaped over me and landed in my path. The cù sìth stood in my path in a wide, threatening stance. I looked over my shoulder. Sure enough, its partner trotted up behind me and took a similar stance. They bared their fangs and let out a low growl. I'd been prepared for trouble when I'd gone on this job, but nothing prepares you for two faerie hounds trying to tear your face off.

I wore my sheepskin bomber jacket, which despite the heat wave Seattle was currently experiencing, was something I'd rarely leave home without. Summer may have only been a couple weeks away, but I'd be stupid to leave without the jacket. The leather that made up the outside of the jacket had been enchanted with a dozen different defensive spells that would offer me some protection against bullets, blades, and various offensive spells. It wasn't perfect, but it had saved my life on a dozen occasions.

Under it, I wore a magnetic baldric strapped to my chest. It allowed me to stow my polearm safely on my back. The magnets were strong enough to keep it there, but still allowed me to pull it off with ease. Good thing too because I was going to need it.

I draped the satchel's leather strap over my chest and pulled my polearm over my shoulder. Brandishing it in a defensive position across my chest, I turned so that I could keep my eyes on both of the cù sìth almost simultaneously. The two beasts stalked closer to me, heads low to the ground with their teeth bared. Their tails whipped around excitedly.

6

"Now, come on, guys. Can't we settle this like rational adults?" I asked, trying to keep my voice from shaking.

The beast to my left let out a sharp snarl in answer. I glanced at the left cù sìth for a second too long, and the one to my right pounced. I ducked into a roll in the direction the faerie hound had come from and spun on my knee to face the pair. The cù sìth who'd tried to jump me had already spun and rebounded towards me, followed closely by its companion. But now I had them on one side and lined up for my attack.

I spun my polearm once before pointing it at the pair. "*Kaze!*" I yelled.

A cyclone formed from the tip of my polearm and rushed forward to meet the two cù sìth. Their claws may have been good for gripping in dirt and stone, but they were no help to them on the tile floor of the old hospital. They tried to resist the winds, but were soon flung down the hall into a pile of old medical equipment. The beasts yelped on impact as various medical instruments buckled under them and crashed into them.

With my attackers temporarily incapacitated, I turned and ran in the direction I came, banking left in hopes of finding the exit. The faerie hounds wouldn't be down for long. cù sìth were resilient hunters and didn't give up easily. I was poorly equipped for a faerie encounter, being armed only with my polearm. Faeries were weak to salt and iron, and while my polearm was adorned with iron caps at the ends, it wasn't enough to do them serious harm. Which meant I'd either have to escape the beasts or kill them through raw firepower. Could I kill the cù sìth? Probably, but the effort would probably put me on my ass. My best bet was to make myself too much of an inconvenience and run away.

I heard the cù sìth bickering as they untangled themselves from each other and the debris they'd crashed into. It only took them a moment and before long, I heard the tapping of their claws against the tile floor. Man, these things were persistent. I considered my options.

Wind, I could fling the cù sìth around with air magic all day, but they were resilient, and I doubted it would do more than inconvenience them.

Fire, not a good idea at all; I'd stupidly left my charms bracelet at home. Without it, my control of fire magic was shaky at best, and this was a fairly old building. I didn't trust myself to not accidentally burn the building down.

Water, I'd been training in water magic and found I had a knack for it. Only problem was, Seattle was experiencing a heat wave at the moment, which left the air nice and dry. Most of the water I called up was moisture I pulled from the air. Without that moisture,

I'd have to conjure the water through my own magical reserves. I had perhaps one chance to use water magic before I severely depleted my energy reserves.

Welp, better make it count then.

I skidded to a stop and turned to face my pursuers. The cù sìth stopped about six feet away, trying to figure out what their prey was up to before proceeding. I spun my polearm once as I gathered magical energy. Water wouldn't be enough to deter these beasts, which meant I needed to put some extra oomph into my spell. An idea popped into my head. I grinned wildly as I prepared the spell.

I aimed my polearm at the beasts. *"Mizu!"*

A geyser of water flew through the air towards the cù sìth, flying in an arc towards them. I'd caught them off guard and I knocked the lead faerie hound into its packmate behind it. They fell in a heap of fur and claws and slid on the tile floor. Before they had a chance to recover their senses, I spun my polearm again, gathering my magic for the next spell. With a swift motion, I pulled the polearm back and away from the beasts.

"Págos!"

The spell reverberated through the air and sucked all the heat away from my surroundings, but specifically, from the water that drenched the cù sìth.

The water that soaked the beasts and the hallway surrounding them froze in less than two seconds, binding them. The ice bound them to each other and the tile floor, and they showed no signs of immediate escape.

"Hell yeah! Take that, Fidos!" I pumped my fist in the air. That took care of them, now I had to get out of here with the spoils of this little excursion. I deposited my polearm onto my back and started back down the hall.

***

I walked out into the morning sun with a sigh of relief. I'd managed to recover my quarry and escape two cù sìth before breakfast. I was feeling pretty good about myself right about now. That feeling of pride was quickly interrupted by a yammering sound coming from my satchel.

"Feckin' wizards, man! No respect or care for their elders!" The muffled voice yapped.

I sighed, ducking into an alley on the side of the abandoned hospital. I opened the bag and pulled out the thing my uncle had sent me to find. Upon first glance, it seemed to be an ordinary jack-o'-lantern. It had a stereotypical jack-o'-lantern face, two triangular eyes, and a zigzag mouth of jagged teeth. But that's where the mundaneness of it ended. A green light glowed from within, giving the pumpkin a strange, bottomless feeling to it. Like, the inside was much larger than the outside. Green flames twisted and coiled from the pumpkin's face in a seemingly annoyed fashion.

"You talk a lot for a pumpkin." I teased.

"I'm not a pumpkin, ya idiot!" The pumpkin snapped. "I'm an immortal spirit of power and knowledge, I'll have you know!"

"More like trickery and mischief, from what I've been told." I said simply. "Are you really—?"

"Jack of the Lantern, at your service." The pumpkin said smugly. The pumpkin tilted forward slightly of its own accord. It took me a minute to realize he was bowing. Jack straightened, his flames flicking upwards slightly. "I 'preciate you helping me out of that bind there. Those mutts got no manners and no respect for someone of my caliber."

"But...you're a pumpkin," I said, eyeing him skeptically.

"I am not a pumpkin, you dolt!" Jack spat. His flames writhed angrily. I held up my hands in a placating gesture, and he seemed to settle down after a moment. He sighed. "Seriously, you've heard of me right?"

His name was familiar, but I struggled to remember his tale. I sighed. "Just give me the Cliff Notes."

The pumpkin gave me a disapproving look—at least, I think he did. It was hard to tell, considering his face didn't actually move, but he seemed content to share his tale. "It's like this, ya see. Back in the day, I was something of a Robin Hood-type, ya know? Stealing from anyone and everyone, and giving what I stole to the people who wanted it more."

I eyed him. "Let me guess, you're the one who wanted it more."

Jack scoffed. "I mean, if it worked out that way, who was I to deny myself?"

"Uh-huh, have you actually read Robin Hood?" I asked him.

"I caught the first few minutes of the Disney film," Jack said. "Y'know, the one with the furries."

I sighed. "Okay, so what happened next?"

"Well, ya see, after a life of justified crime, I started getting the attention of the devil. And he didn't like how noble and good-hearted I was. So he came to drag my soul to Hell. But I tricked him ya see? I tricked him into making a deal wit' me."

The story was coming back to me. "You guys shared one last drink before you went off to Hell. You had no money, so you convinced this devil to turn into a coin for payment. Instead of paying, you decided to lock him up with a cross placed over him. It stopped the devil from returning to his true form unless he agreed not to take your soul."

"Hey, you're not as dumb as you look," Jack said backhandedly. "Anyways, after I died, the big man in the sky said Heaven had no room for me. Apparently, he didn't care too much for my choice in lifestyle. What a prude, that guy. Anyways, I decided I might as well go to Hell and party it up with my good friend downstairs. Except that no-good son of a bitch said he couldn't take my soul, on account of the deal we made way back when."

"So you were stuck, right?" I asked.

"Yep, and that cheeky bastard, the devil that is, gave me a stinking turnip that glowed with a green flame. He told me it would light my way as I wandered the Earth forever or somethin'." Jack finished.

"And somewhere along the line, you got yourself trapped in a pumpkin," I added, my voice laced with amusement.

"Uh huh, yep. Old habits die hard. I kept up my Robin Hoodery, and eventually pissed off some fae.

They thought it would be really funny to trap me in a pumpkin." Jack rolled his eye flames. "Couple hundred years go by, I get passed around from wizard to wizard. I know a lot of things, ya see? Wizards find me useful. And now here I am, stuck with another wizard."

I smiled at the poor spirit. Then I frowned. "Wait, what do you mean stuck?"

"An enchantment from the Fae, ya see." Jack began to explain. "Whenever someone, usually a wizard, recovers my pumpkin, it binds me to them and them to me. 'Penance for my mischief,' they said."

I sighed. "No one told me about any sort of binding."

"Either way, you're stuck with me, wizard," Jack said, his voice communicating a shit-eating grin. "Don't worry, after wandering around for so many years, I've learned a great deal about various things." You won't regret finding me, brother. Hey, I didn't catch your name, on account of the running we had to do from the faerie hounds."

"The running WE had to do?" I eyed the pumpkin. I let out a breath. "It's Tobias, Tobias Leight."

"Pleasure to make your acquaintance, Tobias," Jack said gleefully. "I gots a feeling we're gonna be good friends, buddy."

Somehow, I doubted that. The pumpkin was already getting on my nerves. And if the legend of Jack of the Lantern were true, I wasn't so sure I could trust him. I'd have to get him back to my apartment so my uncle could take a look at him. Maybe there was a way to weasel out of whatever enchantment had been placed on the pumpkin spirit. If not, maybe I could invest in some yappy spirit-proof earplugs. I pulled out my phone to call my uncle. My eyes widened when I saw the time.

I bolted down the sidewalk, stuffing Jack back in my satchel.

"What'sa matter? Is it the cù sìth?" Jack asked, his voice muffled once more by the canvas satchel.

"I'm late for work because I was too busy saving your ass!" I growled.

I was sick of running, and I was sick of Jack of the Lantern.

***

Thankfully, the coffee shop I worked at wasn't terribly far from where I'd found Jack. I still had to jog for ten minutes or so. But I made it, even if I was a bit late. The Grind was a craft coffee shop located in the downtown area. It was a haven for not just the bookworm crowd, but Seattle's magical community.

Wizards with minor talents made up most of the clientele, but we got all kinds of arcane customers.

As I walked in, I spotted a couple Ljósálfar, or light elves, sitting near the front window. They were each sipping on a steaming cup o' joe. Sitting in the far corner was a glaistig, a Fae woman with the bottom half of a goat. She sat with a mug in one hand and a book in the other. The Grind doubled as a library and had bookshelves lining the far walls. Even without considering the clientele, the coffee shop was a magical safe haven. An advanced veil far beyond my understanding kept a lot of the mundane crowd away. But even those who did find their way in would be completely oblivious to the supernatural patrons that often frequented the place.

Standing at the cash register was a good friend of mine, Remy. Remy was a wizard who mostly kept to themselves. They had mastered shapeshifting magic and often used it to change their body from male to female and back again, depending on where they found themselves on the gender spectrum that day.

Today, Remy was in their male form. In this form, they were a couple of inches taller than me. Their brown hair was styled into a short quiff with an undercut. A baby blue stripe streaked through the length of the right side of their head. Their clean-shaven face had a soft, but distinct jawline that reminded me of old marble statues. Their eyes were the color of caramel, making them look sharp and distinct against their slightly darker skin tone. Remy was of Hispanic origin, though I wasn't sure from where and they never mentioned it. They wore a black and white striped long sleeve and bleach-washed jeans under a brown canvas apron. Remy made eye contact with me and for a brief second, I felt the butterflies in my stomach go crazy. My face heated up, but I tried to play off. I raised my fist to my face and coughed before clearing my throat.

Remy crossed their arms and raised an eyebrow. "Tobias, you're late."

I regained my composure and hurried behind the counter. "Yeah, uh sorry. I had to deal with some wizard stuff."

"Wizard stuff?" Remy asked skeptically.

"Yeah, my uncle heard about some artifact that had ended up in an old hospital and sent me to find it." I explained. "Went smoothly until I got jumped by a pair of cù sìth."

Remy chuckled. "No wonder you look worse for wear."

"Gee, thanks." I muttered, setting my bag and polearm down on a shelf and pulling an apron off the wall.

"Is that coffee I smell? It's been years since I've had coffee! Pass me a cup!" Jack said, his voice muffled from the bag. I kicked the bag, urging the spirit to shut his trap.

Remy cocked their head at the bag, eyeing it skeptically. "Uh, what was that?"

I sighed. "New roommate."

Remy looked at me as if that didn't answer their question.

"It's a spirit bound to a pumpkin. I didn't have time to drop him off at home." I explained.

"Uh huh." Remy narrowed their eyes at the bag. Then they looked back at me. "Anyways, start on the dark roast. We need to get ready for the lunch rush."

"Aye aye, captain." I saluted before doing as I was told.

I started grinding coffee beans, ignoring Jack's occasional input on my coffee grinding technique. I wasn't sure how he was paying attention; the bag I'd stashed him in was completely closed. Every now and then, I caught myself stealing glances at Remy. I'd never found myself attracted to a guy before, or someone who was a guy part-time either. I wasn't opposed to the idea, but I hadn't had much time for dating during my apprenticeship.

I'd tried dating one of my best friends, Claire, after we'd gone to prom together. Well, sort of a prom. It was a bit impromptu and thrown together after we'd missed the actual prom. But wizard training had kept me extra busy once school was over, and Claire had gone off to college shortly after. So our budding relationship had sort of fizzled out. Now she was living it up at some fancy college. Claire had been pretty vague about what college she'd gone off to. Communication between us had petered off as well. Any conversation that got past more than one text was dry and she always seemed distracted.

Now, though, I was no longer an apprentice. Sure, I was still relatively new at this, but I was a wizard, through and through. I looked at Remy again. Maybe I could give the whole dating thing another chance. I wasn't getting any younger, after all.

My shift went by smoothly. I ground coffee beans and brewed coffee using the vintage syphon coffee maker. It was supposedly a more efficient way of making a purer cup of coffee. I wasn't sure whether it actually worked or not, but damn, it made a good cup of go juice.

I was just about to clock out for my shift when I felt my phone vibrate in my pocket. I frowned. I didn't usually get calls or texts. My phone was dryer than the Sahara. One of the few people who did call me was my uncle. I pulled out my phone. Sure enough, his face popped up on the screen.

I swiped on the screen and held it up to my ear. "Y'ello."

"Tobias, there's been an incident. Meet me at the Hotel Sorrento." My uncle said. The phone clicked.

I held the phone out, glaring at it. An incident? At the Sorrento? Whatever it was, it must've been serious. My uncle rarely called about some supernatural occurrence. Usually it was a text or two with minimal details, but this time he'd felt the need to call. I pulled off my apron and hung it on the hook where I'd first grabbed it. I grabbed my satchel and polearm, hastily heading for the front door.

"Hey, where's the fire?" Remy's voice came behind me.

I turned to them, frowning. "Sorry, my uncle just called. Something happened at the Sorrento."

Remy returned the frown. "Oh, well let me know if you need any help. You have my number, right?"

My face heated up again. "Uh, yeah. I'll text you later. Give you all the deets."

Remy smiled coyly. "Go get 'em, slugger."

I hurried out the front door, saving myself from further embarrassment.

Chapter 2

The Hotel Sorrento was an old, curved building and a cornerstone of Seattle's haunted history. The spirit of old Alice B. Toklas, a symbol of the LGBTQ+ community in Seattle and San Francisco and an advocate for recreational marijuana use haunted the place. Fun fact: She's credited with the creation of the weed brownie. She doesn't get nearly enough recognition nowadays if you ask me. It's said she still wanders the halls of The Hotel Sorrento to this day, even though she'd left Seattle before the place had been built. No one was quite sure why she haunted the hotel. But sightings were still reported, lights still flickered, and drinks were said to move of their own accord.

What a coincidence, then, that my uncle called me up to the very room where the paranormal activity was centered, Room 408. The room was well-furnished and had all the basic amenities expected in hotel rooms nowadays. A nice tv hung on the wall over the dresser, with a minifridge off to the side. There was a fancy gray easy chair sitting in the corner next to a desk. A door to my left led to the bathroom, no doubt it had a fancy shower in it. But the centerpiece of it all was the corpse laying in the bed.

The corpse was horrifying to look at. It had been mummified, its skin was gray and pulled taught against its bones. It had once been a woman, judging by the wide hip bones protruding against the weathered charcoal skin and the few wisps of long hair that remained. The smell was horrendous. I heaved once before running to the bathroom to empty the contents of my stomach into the toilet. I gagged and heaved as my lunch made its encore appearance.

"You finished?" My uncle's voice called from the room.

I spit into the toilet and wiped my mouth. "Yeah." I huffed. "Just give me a sec."

Once I'd regained my composure, I returned to the room. Bishop Leight appeared to be in his early fifties, but I knew he was far older. He wore a silk black dress shirt and matching slacks. He once sported a permanent five o'clock shadow, but it had grown into a slightly disheveled scruff of black and gray. His hair was cut short and had once been a faded black color with gray peppered in, but the last few years had been hard on him. The gray was starting to win the battle, overtaking the sides of his head and working on the top.

A few years ago, my uncle had been partially infected with vampire blood, beginning his transformation into a Blood Clan vampire. We'd been staving off the effects with potions and spell work, but it still took a toll on his body. Which is why we'd focused so hard on my training. It was also why I took care of a lot of the minor supernatural occurrences in the city.

The fact that he'd come here meant that there was something seriously bad going on. He leaned on an old, twisted staff of oak wood carved with magical runes that helped him focus his magic. He stared at the body with no expression, examining it with a cold, calculating look. I looked around, noticing the room hadn't been sectioned off with police tape. There were no crime scene markers or tarps. No red tape, nothing.

"Where are the cops?" I asked.

"I got the call first." Bishop said simply. "We have people in the police department that alert us to things like this. Gives us a chance to investigate before mortals get their hands on things. We only have a bit of time before the mortal authorities show up."

I cleared my throat, doing my best to keep my eyes off the mummified corpse laying in the bed. I did not want to look at the thing. It gave me the creeps. And the fact that something could do this to a body did not sit well in my mind. I'd be having nightmares about this for the next week.

"What the hell did this?" I asked him.

Bishop shook his head. "Not sure. Vampires, maybe." There was a hint of contempt in his voice when he mentioned vampires. Ever since becoming infected with their curse, my uncle had found a new disdain for vampires of all types.

"You ever seen a vamp do something like this?" I asked him.

"No, but the body's completely drained." Bishop said. "No blood, no remnants of a soul. And a thick aura of malignant magic all over it."

Gulp.

There were many flavors of vampire. Most notorious were the bloodsuckers, but there were also the Jiangshi. The Jiangshi were soul vampires from China, and until a few years ago, Seattle had been home to one of their factions. But save for a few stragglers, Seattle was basically Jiangshi-free. But Bishop had said the body was completely devoid of a soul. Even upon death, parts of a soul remained for a few days.

I frowned. What the hell could completely drain a person of both their blood and their soul? Nothing I wanted to meet, that was for sure.

Bishop gestured vaguely to the room. "Tell me, what do you see?"

I eyed him skeptically. Then I took a look around the room. First, the body. It's arms were splayed out by its head. Its empty eye sockets faced the wall. I couldn't see its legs, the body was covered by a couple of blankets from the waist down. The white sheets were spotless, save for some flecks of decayed skin that had come off the body.

"The person was asleep when they were attacked," I noted.

"Mhm, what else?" Bishop asked.

I narrowed my eyes, thinking. "No blood." I frowned. "And no signs of a struggle either. Whatever killed them, it did so without waking them up."

Bishop nodded. That was weird and definitely not something I'd expect from a vampire attack. The victim didn't fight back. Hell, it was likely they didn't even know what had been happening. That wasn't just weird; it was downright strange. Nothing about this rung any bells about the supernatural predators I'd read about during my training.

That's when I noticed something else.

I hooked a thumb at the door. "Any signs of a break in?"

Bishop shook his head. "Door was locked and intact."

I looked at the far wall, which was dominated by a large window with heavy curtains. "Window isn't broken either."

"So the question is, how did the attacker get in and out?" Bishop wondered.

I rubbed my face with one hand. "Man, this is giving me a headache."

A supernatural predator attacked and killed someone without leaving any signs of its passing. The corpse was withered and mummified, completely absent of its blood or its soul. And we had no apparent culprits. This job was going to be a challenging one for sure. I'd gone up against demons and vampires. I'd even had an encounter with an honest-to-God Bigfoot, but those had all been known quantities.

Even my uncle, in all his years of experience, seemed stumped.

"Looks like it's time to hit the books." I said.

"Agreed." Bishop tilted his head. "It's time to get home. We have a lot of work ahead of us." He headed for the door.

I stayed behind for a moment longer, taking a moment to absorb the scene just a little bit more in hopes that I'd be able to gleam something from this tragedy. Then I followed my uncle out the door and down the hall.

I looked back over my shoulder, to the infamous Room 408. The lights flickered in the hall. And for just a moment, I thought I saw an older woman in mid-20th-century garb standing at the far end of the hall.

***

There are a lot of cool things that come as part of being a wizard. Performing magic, obviously. Pretty cool. Fighting monsters and bad guys. Also pretty cool. Researching magic and monsters? Eh, less cool. I sat at a cluttered table in our small garage, reading from a tome that contained information on all kinds of supernatural beings.

The tome was organized in alphabetical order. I'd gotten through most of the B's when the stinging in my eyes started to get unbearable. I groaned, letting my head fall onto the book as I contemplated burning the damn thing. The page on goblins seemed to mock me, the mischievous-looking illustration grinning up at me.

I sat up, rubbing my eyes with one hand. So far, my research had revealed nothing. Nothing that could get in and out of a room without a trace while also mummifying a corpse.

I heard a muffled voice come from my satchel. I sighed. Jack had been piping up every so often, and he'd become increasingly more difficult to ignore. I huffed out a breath and reached down into my bag until I felt the soft but firm surface of the pumpkin. I pulled it out and set Jack down in front of me, the book between us.

"Sheesh, when was the last time you cleaned that bag, bro?" Jack complained. "Smells like a musty old cellar in there."

"You don't even have a nose." I pointed out.

Jack gasped, seemingly shocked by my accusation. The green flames flared. "I can't believe you'd say that. I'm very self-conscious about that, ya know!"

I rolled my eyes at the pumpkin. I still had to figure out how to get rid of him. I'd already tried throwing him in a trash can on my way home, but the stupid thing just showed up back in my satchel before I'd even made it home. I had no idea how the binding magic placed upon Jack's pumpkin worked, but it seemed that I was now stuck with him. I felt a pang of sympathy for all the wizards that had gotten stuck with him over the years. Even if Jack was as knowledgeable as he claimed, his personality alone made me want to throttle the trapped spirit.

A lightbulb went off in my head.

"Jack, you said you know a lot about magic and monsters and stuff, right?" I asked, trying to hide the excitement in my voice.

Jack's eye flames seemed to arch suspiciously. "Yeah, whaddaboutit?"

"Were you paying attention at all when I was at the Sorrento?"

Jack suspicion faded and I got a pleased vibe from him. Like I'd finally come around to the guy. "Yeah, sorta. I was in the bag so I was only listenin', but I got the gist. Classic case of a locked room mystery, amirite?"

I thought about that. He had a point actually. The only difference was we weren't dealing with a mundane killer. Whatever had killed the person in that room had been from my side of the street.

"Any ideas on what could've done it?" I asked him.

The pumpkin tilted, his flames receding quite a bit as he gave it some thought. Then he looked back up at me. "Was there a mirror anywhere in the room?"

I recalled everything I could remember about the room. Then I remembered. "In the bathroom. I noticed it when I yacked."

"Well that'll narrow down the suspect pool a bit then, boyo." Jack said.

I racked my brain, trying to remember the significance that the mirror could have.

Jack didn't bother waiting for me to work it out. "The reason there was no sign of a break-in was because the killer didn't have to."

"Oh, right. Mirrors can be used as gateways." I remembered.

"Exactly. A handful of supernatural nasties can use mirrors as passages between this world and The World Yonder." Jack explained.

The World Yonder was a strange and creepy place. Well, it wasn't just one place. The World Yonder was a collection of supernatural realms that was constantly growing, shifting, and changing. All kinds of magical beings called it home, the most notable of which were the Fae. The Fae of European folklore were something of a superpower in the supernatural world. Besides wizards, they were the most notable and strongest nation that we knew of. And if the killer was using mirrors to go between our world and The World Yonder...

"Jack, what are the chances that our killer was some sort of Fae?" I asked him.

Jack gave that notion some thought. "Well, only two things could get in and out of the room using a mirror without a trace. One of the Fae, or a wizard."

My gut said that a wizard didn't do this. The scene was too clean. "Let's assume it's a Fae then."

Jack nodded in agreement. "Only problem is, I've never heard of a Fae that could do something quite like this."

Well crap. Back to square one then. I was back to questioning Jack's usefulness.

"But, if I could get a look at the room. I might be able to pick something up." Jack suggested.

"So, you're suggesting we trespass on a crime scene?" I asked him.

Jack seemed to consider that for a moment. His flames fluctuated in a shrug-like motion.

I rubbed my eyes and then pulled out my phone to check the time. "Fine, we'll check out the crime scene after my shift tomorrow. Right now, I need some sleep."

Jack scoffed. "Sleep, I forgot about sleep. I don't miss it."

"Good for you." I muttered bitterly.

I rose to head to bed when Jack spoke up again. "What, are you gonna leave me here?"

I stopped at the door and eyed the pumpkin. "Yeah, don't touch anything. Night."

"I don't even have any hands!" Jack snapped back as I left the garage.

***

I found myself in a misty, dark expanse, completely devoid of any other detail. I looked back and forth but I couldn't find a single landmark or other noteworthy detail to help me determine where the hell I'd ended up. I took a couple steps forward, the sound echoing into the void.

Suddenly I felt the hairs on the back of my neck rose on end. A slimy chill crawled up my back and I spun around. I couldn't see into the void, but it felt as if something was stalking me. I got the sensation again and spun to face my stalker—still, nothing. Instinctively, I reached for my polearm, but it wasn't there.

I heard a rush of movement from behind. Before I could react, something hot and sharp slashed against the back of my leg. I gasped in pain and fell to a knee. My gaze darted back and forth, but whatever had attacked me had once again disappeared into the gloom.

"Who's there?" I called out in challenge.

Something laughed. It was a faint, mischievous snicker of a laugh. Something was toying with me. It was only then that I could hear the faint clicking of claws on the hard ground. But wherever I was, it was interfering with my senses. I couldn't tell exactly where the thing was.

Another flash of pain. I cursed and grabbed my bicep. A three-inch long cut had formed in my arm. I extended my arm, getting ready to let a spell loose. But there was nothing. No sensation of gathering energy. No familiar tug in my gut. Wherever I was, I was powerless.

"The man-thing meddles in affairs he knows nothing about." A slimy, raspy voice echoed all around me.

Something cut a deep gash into my stomach and I nearly fell over. "Gah!"

"If the man-thing values its life, it will find its trouble elsewhere." The voice warned.

A vague shape with glowing green eyes suddenly rushed out of the darkness. My instincts screamed but I couldn't move. My mysterious attacker was on me

before I knew it, and there was nothing I could do to
stop it.

Chapter 3

I shot up to a sitting position, gasping for air. I was in my room. I was safe. But why did I still feel an overwhelming sense of fear? Not the horror movie jump scare kind of fear either. Something far deeper, far more primitive. True fear.

What the hell had that been about? I'd had nightmares before. Hell, I'd confronted a Fallen angel in my dreams multiple times. But this was something else. It felt like I'd been in danger. I checked my body for the wounds I'd suffered in the dream. Sure enough, I was spotless. Not a scratch on me.

But it had felt so real.

And what had it said? It had warned me to stay away. Whatever had killed that hotel guest had just paid me a visit. And it didn't seem to happy that I was on its trail. I shivered, the residual fear fading into the recesses of my mind.

I scoffed indignantly. "No Freddy Kreuger wannabe is going to get the better of me."

I grabbed my phone from my nightstand. 3a.m. The witching hour, how appropriate. Resigning to the fact there was no way I was getting back to sleep after that encounter, I decided to get an early start to my day.

I pulled on some sweatpants, a hoodie, and an old pair of running shoes. I made my way downstairs as quietly as I could and headed for the door. Right before my hand touched the knob, I heard a familiar whine. I turned and saw my dog Scout peeking his head over the back of the couch.

To the average observer, Scout was a normal German Shepherd. But to those in the know, he was a ferocious but lovable hellhound in disguise. He was hell on wheels in combat, but he was also a sucker for a belly rub. Scout wagged his tail, his tongue lolling out happily.

"You wanna come along?" I offered.

Scout let out a quiet yip and hopped over the couch and trotted towards me. I pulled his leash out of a basket near the door and clipped it to him. I opened the door and we took off into the early morning.

I'd been working on my cardio since my magic career started. I wasn't going to be an Olympic athlete anytime soon, but I'd built up my endurance quite a bit. It came in handy when you had bloodthirsty monsters on your tail. Scout and I took off down the sidewalk along the main road at a brisk, steady pace.

The early morning air was cold and crisp, but not uncomfortable. I prefer cold and rainy weather, which makes Seattle the perfect stomping grounds for yours truly. At least, most of the time. Seattle, and Washington as a whole, had been experiencing a steady increase in hotter and dryer weather during the day time.

It had been steadily getting hotter over the last few years. I thought about it for a moment. In fact, it had first started when I'd thwarted a Fae plot to conceive an army of super vampires. But surely it was a coincidence, right?

I gave the idea some more thought. It could be a coincidence, but coincidences were rare when it came to the magical side of things. A crucial detail taunted me from the edge of thought. Something I should know from my studies. It was something I'd have to brush up on later, maybe after my run.

As we ran, I noticed Scout acting strangely. Usually when we run, his only concern is the running itself. He would pant happily, only looking ahead of him. But his ears were up, head on a swivel, and he almost seemed to be holding his breath. The fur along his spine stood on end, and I could barely detect a low rumbling in his chest.

Something had Scout on alert, and that made me nervous as hell. I kept running, not wanting to tip off any potential spooky predators lying in ambush. I was woefully unprepared for any encounter with the supernatural. I had none of my magic paraphernalia with me, which would make it far harder to focus my magic. Scout was more than enough to scare off most of the supernatural predators that called Seattle home, but clearly whatever was stalking me didn't get the memo.

The sound of flapping wings was my only warning. Scout let out an alarmed bark and I had only a split second to react. I dropped his leash and dove to my left. Something crashed into the ground where I'd been only a moment before. I felt shards of concrete whiz passed me, leaving me with several small cuts on the back of my hands and my face.

I fell into a roll and quickly rose to my feet, pivoting to face my attacker. For a second, it was hard to make out the creature in the darkness. But as my vision adjusted, I was able to make out what had just tried to crush me into the concrete. The thing was vaguely humanoid and covered in black feathers. It had three large talons for fingers and four for toes, with one on the back of its foot. Black avian wings extended from its back and acted as a cloak. It had a large curved beak and where its eyes should have been, were empty sockets that were black as night.

I'd seen this thing before in the tome I'd been flipping through the night before. But for the life of me, I couldn't remember what it was. I didn't have time to ask the thing politely, because the raven-man was already charging after me. It lunged at me with its gleaming talons reaching for my throat. I threw myself out of the way again, feeling its talons graze my sweater as I dove.

I tumbled less than gracefully, scraping along the asphalt of the road. I scrambled to my feet as the raven-man gathered itself. Man what was this thing called? It was something like... rat crap? Cat trap? No, those obviously weren't right.

"What did I do to deserve a visit from Tweety Bird's bigger, more emo cousin?" I taunted. "Did I win a contest or something?"

The raven-man squawked angrily. I gave the monster a wicked grin, trying to hide my fear and keeping the thing's attention on me. Sure, I didn't have my polearm or my charms bracelet, but I did have...

The raven-man had made a big mistake by focusing so intently on me. It had completely disregarded my running partner. A giant, muscular shape backhanded the raven monster from behind. The raven cawed in pained surprise as it flew into a nearby streetlamp. The sound of shrieking metal tore through the night as the streetlamp folded in on itself around the raven creature.

Scout stood where the raven had once been, in his full hellhound glory. His general build was reminiscent of a bulldog, only ten times the size. His coal-colored skin was rippling with muscle, his forelimbs reminding me of classic bodybuilders. His front paws had shifted completely into giant hands with sharp claws that matched his mouth full of mismatched sharp teeth. A line of flames ran down the length of his spine.

Scout planted his feet and let out a roar of challenge. I let out a whoop of excitement, pumping my fist in the air. "Good boy!"

More wrenching metal drew our attention to where Scout had launched the raven. It tore itself free of the twisted, deformed streetlamp. It took a wide stance, flaring its wings as it returned Scout's roar with its own defiant battle caw. It was way more intimidating than I made it sound, I swear.

I suddenly remembered the creature. I snapped my fingers, pointing at it. "Ah! You're a nachtkrapp, aren't you?"

The nachtkrapp cawed again, seemingly in confirmation of my guess.

Nachtkrapps were a type of German fae, raven spirits of death and disease. In ye olden times, they were notorious for kidnapping children. They also were said to have shapeshifting and shadow magic abilities. Nachtkrapps were supposedly extremely rare in the United States, so what the heck was one doing here?

The nachtkrapp and Scout charged each other simultaneously. They collided in the middle of the street, creating a shockwave of pure kinetic energy that threatened to sweep me off my feet. Scout tried to bite at the nachtkrapp, but the raven fae was strong and kept Scout's jaws at bay with its strong talons. I was surprised at the nachtkrapp's strength. Despite Scout having a few hundred pounds over the fae, it was still strong enough to hold him at bay, and then some. The nachtkrapp's stance shifted, and it threw Scout over its shoulder and into a brick wall that bordered the sidewalk.

Scout yelped as he collided with the wall. It crumbled around him, burying him in rubble. Not a second later, Scout burst out of the rubble with an angry roar. With the nachtkrapp momentarily distracted, I made my move. I rushed the creature, preparing to attack. My options were limited, without my foci, but I'd make do. Magic was only one tool in my repertoire. This thing was roughly human shaped, so perhaps it shared some of the same weak points. Either that, or I was going to do something very foolish and embarrassing.

The nachtkrapp turned, having realized I was on the move. But it was a second too late. I dropped to a slide, aiming between the thing's legs. As I slid, I pulled my fist back and let loose. My aim was true, and I hit the thing right in the crotch. I slid under and passed it as the nachtkrapp let out a pained caw.

"Huh, can't believe that actually worked." I said, rising a few feet away from behind the nachtkrapp. I'd caught the fae off guard.

Anything from the supernatural world never expected wizards to resort to basic physical combat. They always expected us to sling fire around or something. A tradition of sorts that the nachtkrapp kept alive, obviously. It doubled over in pain, leaving it open to attack.

Scout saw the opportunity, bellowing a mighty roar as he pounced on the nachtkrapp. My attack had stunned the fae, but it was far from defenseless. Before Scout could land, the raven's wings flared and tendrils of shadow emerged from underneath. They wrapped around Scout and held him high in the air, giving him no leverage to use his strength against the bindings. Scout growled and snapped at the tendrils, but wherever he struck, his jaws went through the bindings like they weren't even there.

The nachtkrapp rose to its feet, still holding Scout suspended in the air and stared me down. I stuck my tongue out indignantly. This was enough to rile up the raven fae and with a twist of its body, it threw Scout at me. My eyes widened and I had only a moment to react.

I aimed my hands at the ground. "*Kaze!*"

Wind propelled me eight feet into the air just in time. Scout hit the ground and tumbled passed me. The poor hellhound yipped in pain as he rolled uncontrollably. I landed hard on my ass, and I knew there'd be an unflattering bruise as a result. No time to worry about that though. I looked up to see the nachtkrapp had rose high above me, flexing its talons in preparation for a killing blow. I needed to put this thing down, or at least scare it off. But without my foci, the only offensive magic I could use reliably was wind. Fire and water would have unpredictable results.

I aimed my open palm at the airborne nachtkrapp and shouted, "*Kaze!*"

Wind rushed up at the nachtkrapp. Its wings did what they were built for and caught the updraft I'd created. The nachtkrapp flew higher into the air, tumbling out of control high into the sky. As my wind died, it began to fall back down towards the hard asphalt. Hopefully I'd disoriented it enough, and it would hit the ground hard. Hopefully enough to immobilize it, or at least scare it off.

But I'm never that lucky. When it was about twenty feet above the ground, the nachtkrapp righted itself in midair and flared its wings. It caught just enough air to allow it to slowly descend and land unharmed. Its chest heaved as it stared me down from about twenty feet away. I matched its stare, trying to look way more badass than I felt at that moment. By the way it was breathing, I knew I'd made it expend way more energy than it had expected to. Or at least, Scout did. I'd been playing support.

Speaking of, Scout had evidently recovered from his tumble down the street. The hellhound lumbered up next to me. I placed a hand just under his shoulder, thankful for the hellhound's presence. If he hadn't been here, I'm not sure I would have lasted this long in a fight.

The nachtkrapp's empty eye sockets radiated pure malice towards me. This thing was an apex predator where it came from, and I'd embarrassed it. It stood as if it was preparing to charge again, but if I was reading it right, it knew it was currently at a disadvantage. But the thing seemed determined. It braced itself to charge, flaring its wings and extending its talons.

I tensed, bracing myself for the rush.

Then the nachtkrapp stood up straight, cocking its head to glance over its shoulder. I eyed it suspiciously. After a moment, it nodded and faced me again. With one more scornful stare, the nachtkrapp folded its wings around itself and simply melted into a puddle of shadow on the ground. Another second passed and the puddle of shadow seemed to dissolve.

The nachtkrapp had retreated. But what had it done there at the end right before it disappeared? I glanced around my surroundings then stared at where the nachtkrapp had vanished.

"What the hell was that about?" I yelled into the abandoned street.

***

"A nachtkrapp, huh?" Bishop said, almost skeptically.

"Uh huh. Damn thing jumped me out of nowhere." I answered. "If Scout hadn't been there, I would've been bird food."

After my encounter with the raven fae, I'd rushed home before I got caught up by the authorities, who'd certainly been made aware of the commotion. I shook Bishop awake, which wasn't hard to do. He had always been a light sleeper. After he had a chance to wake up and get some coffee in him, I'd explained what had gone down during my early morning jog.

"There's something else," I said. "The reason I was out so early, I had a nightmare."

Bishop took another sip and listened intently.

"It wasn't like a normal nightmare. It felt as real and vivid as the conversation we're having now." I explained. "There was something stalking me under a shroud of darkness. It struck at me, and the wounds hurt for real. And it left me with a warning. It was trying to scare me off of this case we're working."

Bishop eyed his coffee in contemplation. He stood there like that for several long seconds. Then he downed his coffee and set the mug on the counter. "I had the same dream."

My eyes widened. "You did?"

Bishop nodded gravely. "I was willing to chalk it up as an isolated incident. But it seems something paid us a visit last night."

"What was it?" I asked.

He shook his head. "Not sure. But that's what we're going to find out."

Bishop made his way over to the door that led to garage and left the room. A moment later, I heard his voice from behind the door. "Tobias, what the hell is this?"

Oh, right.

I went into the garage, where I'd left Jack's pumpkin sitting on the center table. As I entered, Jack's inner flame blazed to life, and he turned to address me.

"Master Toby! What a pleasure, sir!" Jack tilted himself in a bow. He spoke with an awful British butler voice.

I facepalmed, dragging my hand down my face. I let out a sigh. "Sorry, with all the excitement from yesterday, I forgot to introduce you to my new problem."

"Funny way to say 'best buddy' if you ask me," Jack muttered dejectedly.

Bishop's eyes lit up with a faint purple color, indicating he was using his wizard's senses. He stared intently at Jack, examining him in the arcane spectrum. After a moment, the light in his eyes faded as they returned to normal.

"This is the artifact I had you recover?" Bishop asked.

"Uh huh. His name's Jack." I explained.

"Jack of the Lantern, at your service," Jack chirped, recycling his introduction from the day before.

Bishop huffed out a breath. "Yes, I know who you are."

"My reputation precedes me." Jack's flames flared out into a grin.

I didn't have the heart to tell the poor guy that that wasn't always a good thing. Bishop walked over to the pumpkin, picking it up by the stem, which was still attached. He stared into the green flames coming from Jack's eye holes. Then he set Jack back down in the same spot.

"He's a troublesome one, Tobias," Bishop said. "I'd tell you to get rid of him, but I already noticed the binding enchantment on him. You're stuck with him, at least for now."

"Yeah, I know. Honestly, I've already made my peace with it." I said. I scratched my head. "I was actually planning on putting him to use."

Bishop arched an eyebrow.

"Jack's a spirit who's been around for quite awhile." I explained, even though I knew he knew that.

"If we take him to the crime scene, I'm willing to bet he can spot something we didn't."

Bishop considered that for a moment. "Very well."

I smiled. "Sweet, I'll take him by the Sorrento after my shift."

Bishop held up a hand. "Just don't get caught sneaking into a crime scene. I'm not bailing you out."

"I won't. Scout's honor." I promised.

"In the meantime, I'll work my connections with the fae. I have a feeling they're linked to this somehow." Bishop explained.

"Oh what gave you that idea?" I asked. "Was it the cù sìth that tried to eat my face? Or the nachtkrapp that almost crushed me into paste on the sidewalk?"

"Don't get smart with me." The old wizard muttered. He wandered back inside.

Alright then. I had a few hours before work. After my run-slash-evil monster encounter, I was ready for a cat nap. I'd get some shuteye, freshen up, brew some coffee, ask out Remy, solve a spooky mur—

Ask out Remy? Why had my subconscious thrown that out at me now of all times?

Maybe because for the first time in the last few years, your life was in clear and present danger, you dolt. I thought.

Sheesh, no need to be so harsh. I thought back at myself.

I decided it was better not to mentally bicker with myself when I could be snoozing. So I updated Jack on the plan for the day and headed back to my room. I could hear Jack whining at once again being left alone to his own devices.

"But Dad!" He whined. "I don't wanna go to work with you! I wanna investigate a murder…"

I sighed. The spirit of the pumpkin was going to take a lot of getting used to.

***

I awoke from my nap just in time to get myself ready for the day. I freshened myself up and gathered my gear. I packed a few odds and ends into my satchel, along with Jack's pumpkin. I tucked my baldric and polearm in there as well. My polearm didn't quite fit inside, so it stuck out at an angle. It'd be fine in there for now. I made sure to put on my charms bracelet before I left too. I wasn't going to be caught without it for a third time.

I made my way to the front door and just before I touched the knob, Bishop stopped me.

"Oh by the way, the mechanic called." He explained. "Your car should be ready later today."

I beamed. "Sick, I'll pick it up after my shift."

"Should save you a whole lot of walking." Bishop said.

"Alright, I'll see you later." I said, opening the door and walking out.

"Be safe. Don't do anything stupid." Bishop said, lowering himself into his chair.

"Who, me?" I smiled knowingly.

***

I made it to The Grind with only a few minutes to spare. Remy stood behind the counter, in their usual spot. They were in their feminine body today. A lot of their features transferred over quite nicely. Now a couple inches shorter than me, Remy wore their hair in a high ponytail. The blue streak in their hair flowing nicely from their forehead to the end of the tail. They wore a navy crop top with long sleeves. Their high waisted jeans making up for the lack of coverage from the shirt. Remy, in either of their forms, had an appealing, athletic build with very little body fat. I had no doubt they could bench press me with only a modest effort. In either body, their arms had a fair amount of muscle to them.

I wasn't terribly out of shape or anything, but my noodle arms and slightly pudgy stomach was something I couldn't help but compare to their near Olympian physique.

Remy gave me a warm smile as I entered. "Hey Toby." They cocked their hips to the side as they greeted me with a wave.

"Uh, hi," I said, waving stiffly.

They aimed a pointed gaze at my bag. "Seems like you're quite prepared there."

I lifted my bag off my shoulder as I went behind the counter, setting it down in its usual spot. I also took off my jacket, folding it and placing it on top of my bag. "Yeah, I got some investigating to do after work today."

Remy looked up thoughtfully, placing their finger on their chin. "Want some company?"

I eyed them, playfully suspicious. "You want to come along? On my spooky murder investigation?" I pulled on my apron, tying it as I spoke. "I thought you kept clear of Order business."

Remy shrugged. "Well yeah, but it wouldn't be so bad if I was tagging along with you." They held their hands behind their back, leaning forward and giving me a playful look.

I blushed, my face heating up like I was standing in the middle of a volcano. I cleared my throat, scratching my nose. "Uh, yeah sure. That'd be cool. I could use some backup."

"It's a date then." Remy winked. "Now get to work, we have customers."

Remy turned around and addressed someone waiting at the counter. I turned to face my workstation, ignoring the heat in my cheeks. Get a hold of yourself, Tobias. It wasn't literally a date or anything like that, Remy was just offering to come along to make sure you didn't get yourself killed.

My shift went by pretty smoothly, I only spilled coffee on myself a couple of times. I noticed I was only so clumsy whenever I was on shift with Remy. There was just something about them that turned my brain into mush.

Meanwhile, Jack would not shut the hell up. He kept yapping about anything and everything that came to mind. He talked a lot about the nachtkrapp and how lucky I'd been to survive the encounter, even with Scout the hellhound to act as my bodyguard.

"I'm telling ya, something wasn't quite right with that old bird." Jack said, his voice muffled from my bag.

"What do you mean?" I asked.

"Nachtkrapps are some of the deadliest of the Unseelie fae." Jack explained. "They have a startling level of control over their magic, allowing them to morph into and control shadows and they can even turn into a flock of ravens that shred through their victims. And that's some of their least deadly talents."

I considered that for a moment. "It did mostly use physical attacks to fight. It only used its shadow magic to momentarily restrain Scout. And then to escape."

"From what you told your uncle and I, that nachtkrapp wasn't acting normal," Jack said. "Fae are weird, but they're pretty consistent. Unless..."

"Unless what?" I eyed him. My hand slipped and I spilled a bit of hot coffee on my wrist. I hissed in pain and set the pot down to dab my wrist with a towel.

"Unless someone was issuing commands. Controlling it." Jack explained.

I chewed on that for a second. "Right before it left, the nachtkrapp looked over its shoulder."

"Could've been communing with whoever was controlling it." Jack's tone indicated a shrug.

"And who can control a nachtkrapp to use as a hitman?" I asked, pouring some coffee into a mug and passing it to the customer waiting at the counter. They gave me a strange look, and I smiled awkwardly.

"Another fae, perhaps. But they'd usually just issue a command and let the subordinate carry it out." Jack said skeptically.

"Anyone else?"

Jack didn't say anything for a moment as he considered that. "Could be a mortal."

"A mortal? As in not a wizard?" I asked.

"It's not unheard of. Humans have been making all kinds of deals with fae and demons for centuries. Anyone can make a bargain with the fae if they're willing to pay the price."

"It doesn't make much sense though. The nachtkrapp, the cù sìth, and the possible fae killer. That makes three, maybe four, hostile fae in Seattle. And I'm on their radar. What's the likelihood that a mortal has made a bargain with four separate fae?" I pondered.

Jack considered that. "Very, very, very, very, very, VERY unlikely."

"Then who else?" I asked.

Jack didn't have a chance to answer me. Someone planted their hand firmly on the counter. I jumped in surprise, nearly spilling hot coffee on my hand again. I looked up at the customer. And I kept looking up, and up, and up.

The man was nearly nine feet tall, wearing a maroon hoodie with a forest green t-shirt underneath. There was a silver Celtic knot symbol emblazoned on the right side of his hoodie. He wore his long rust red hair back in a man bun that transitioned smoothly into a beard that flowed down to cover his neck. I recognized him before my eyes locked with his glowing golden ones.

"Hello Tobias," Lugh said.

Chapter 4

I sat across from the Celtic god of justice and light on one of the old, comfortable couches we had at the coffee shop. I took a long sip from my mug and set it down on the coffee table. Lugh sat across from me, sipping his coffee slowly. He smacked his lips a couple of times as he eyed the brew, as if he were meticulously picking it apart in his head. The Celtic deity seemed to be in no rush.

I leaned forward, with my elbows resting on my legs and I glared at Lugh. He seemed to be completely oblivious. My leg started shaking as Lugh took his time with his drink. I cleared my throat, hoping to get his attention. Again, I got no reaction from the god.

Finally, I spoke up. "I have a phone, y'know?"

No response, he kept on sipping his coffee.

"This is the third time in about three years that you just show up, unannounced." I continued. "You could try shooting me a text, at the very least. Before you waltz into my workplace, all mysterious-like."

Lugh tilted his head back, pouring the last of his coffee down his gullet. He sat the mug down on the table, making a satisfied sound. He patted the corner of his mouth with a napkin, wiping away a drop or two of coffee that he'd missed.

"Very good brew, Tobias." Lugh said, finally. "Much better than the last time I was here."

"It was my first day." I said defensively.

Lugh held up a placating hand. "Right. Well, you're probably wondering what I'm doing here."

"Yeah, for the last ten minutes or so." I said grumpily.

Lugh smiled, knowingly. "Yes, well. No doubt you've noticed the increased fae activity in the city recently."

"Almost got my face chewed off by a couple cù sìth. And then a nachtkrapp jumped me and my dog late last night. Or early this morning, depending on how you look at it." I explained.

"Mhmm," Lugh grunted. His golden eyes seemed to stare straight into my soul. "Do you remember that talk we had a few years ago?"

How could I forget? Lugh had made his first appearance right after I'd thwarted a plot to make a legion of uber vampires. He'd appeared in my uncle's apartment late one night because he wanted to warn me of what was coming next.

"You told me something was being set in motion. That Medb's plans to make her own personal vampire army was just one aspect of what's to come. That one day, I'd need to be ready."

Lugh grunted in confirmation.

I eyed him warily. "Are you saying today's the day?"

Lugh just looked at me knowingly.

"So what am I supposed to do?" I asked. "What can you tell me?"

"All I can tell you is, stay the course." Lugh said.

"Stay the course? That's it?" I sputtered, absolutely baffled.

Lugh nodded. "You're on the right path. Continue as you are."

"You came all the way from Ireland just to tell me that?" I growled. "You can't tell me who's sending these fae after me? Matter of fact, what can you tell me about the thing leaving behind mummified corpses?"

Lugh held up his hands in surrender, rocking back slightly. Then he leaned forward, his golden eyes flashing. "Remember Tobias, not only am I a god, I'm a member of the Tuatha Dé Danaan, progenitors of the fae as a whole. There are rules to what I can do, what I can say. I'm pushing my limits by doing this much."

I scoffed. "Well pat yourself on the back. Your cryptic guidance has really changed my life."

An angry fire flared in Lugh's eyes. "Watch yourself, boy. I may come off as a casual and laid-back sort of god, but I will not tolerate disrespect, especially when I'm going out of my way to help you."

My own temper threatened to rise up, but I fought it down. I'd get nowhere if I started mouthing off to a Celtic deity. "I'm sorry, Lugh. I meant no disrespect, this is just frustrating."

The anger faded from Lugh's eyes and he seemed to relax. "Well you'd better start getting used to it, kid. As far as dealings with the fae and Tuatha go, this is pretty tame."

I grunted, crossing my arms as I sat back in the couch.

Lugh rose from his seat and I quickly followed suit. He extended his hand to me. "You're doing well so far, Tobias. I've seen many a wizard, sorcerer, and druid in my days. I know potential when I see it. And I'm not the only one who's noticed."

I put my hand in his, firmly shaking his hand. "Wait, who else has been keeping tabs on me?"

Lugh smiled knowingly, taking his hand back and he started walking toward the exit. He carefully maneuvered around the low-hanging lights. Then he stopped at the door and looked back at me. "One more thing. Remember your family, Tobias. Family is the key. And there's not many families that compare to mine when it comes to drama."

Then he ducked through the front door and turned the corner. I walked across the room to glance outside. But by the time I got there, the Celtic god of nobility had disappeared.

Family? What the hell was he talking about? The only blood I had left was Bishop. My parents had died in a fire when I was very young. Once upon a time, I'd believed it to be an accident. But in reality, they'd been murdered. By exactly who, not even my uncle knew. The leading theory was that followers of the Fallen angel Azazel were the culprits, but no one had ever been caught. I had no other family. No siblings, cousins, or grandparents to speak of. So what Lugh was on about, I hadn't a clue.

I turned in time to see Remy walking up to me. They had taken off their apron and let their hair down. "I meant to give him a punch card before he left."

I chuckled. "You were going to give a Celtic god a punch card? Buy ten coffees, get the eleventh for free?"

Remy shrugged. "I mean, if he's going to be making regular appearances."

"Fair enough." I said. "Ready to go?"

"Uh huh."

"Let me just grab my stuff and we can go." I said. "Gotta pick up the Bee before we head to the Sorrento."

Remy smiled. "I finally get to ride in that car of yours, huh?"

I cleared my throat, quickly running behind the counter to grab my bag. "Uh, yeah. It's finally out of the shop. Good thing, too. I was getting sick and tired of walking everywhere."

Remy shrugged. "I dunno, it was doing good things for your glutes." They gave me a devious smile.

My face heated up like the sun and I rushed passed them out the front door. I heard Remy let out a mischievous giggle before following close behind me.

The fact that Remy's teasing jabs made me far more nervous than Lugh's anger. But I wasn't going to tell them that. We headed down the sidewalk towards the mechanic's garage so I could finally retrieve my noble steed.

***

Last year, after I had to borrow a friend's beat-up old Volkswagen Beetle, I decided I needed my own wheels. I saved up some cash and convinced my uncle to match it. And that's how I got my 1969 Dodge Super Bee. The car wasn't in the greatest condition, but at least it looked cooler than a Beetle. A good majority of my funds went into getting the car in semi-working order.

The Bee growled defiantly as we rolled down the street. The car had personality and it was reliable, and it showed a stubbornness to run despite its age and condition. It had been freshly painted a bright yellow with a black hood. It wasn't even close to being inconspicuous, but that's just how I liked it. Bright and loud, like me.

"Be honest, you just wanted a car that looked like Bumblebee the Transformer." Remy said, as they eyed the base of the steering wheel. They had a satisfied look on their face as they listened to the engine grunt and roar.

I scoffed indignantly, placing my hand on my chest in a faux-shocked fashion. "How dare you accuse me of something so childish?"

Remy raised a doubtful eyebrow in an "Are you kidding me?" look.

I focused on the road ahead of me. "The used car lot had sold their only Camaro earlier that day," I admitted.

They snorted and giggled. "Man Tobias, you are such a kid, you know that?"

"Hey, I've tangoed with demons, vampires, and a skinwalker. If I want to get a car that resembles a giant robot, then I think I'm entitled to." I said pridefully.

Remy threw their hands up in surrender. "Fair enough." They said. "So where are we headed?"

"The Sorrento," I said. "It's where the body was found. Jack thinks he can help narrow down the suspect pool if he can get a good look at the room."

"Hey, I know I can!" Jack's voice came from the back seat.

I'd pulled him out of the bag because he wouldn't stop complaining about how cramped my satchel was. His pumpkin sat in the seat behind Remy's. Despite his protests, I'd insisted on buckling him in. The strap sat awkwardly over his carved mouth. I had to convince him to stop pretending his voice was muffled due to the seatbelt.

I ignored the pumpkin, focusing on Remy. "Were you ogling my car, by the way?"

Remy, who was still ogling my car, turned their attention to me. "I wasn't ogling your car. You don't ogle at cars."

"Well, you definitely were." I accused as I made a right turn.

"Don't be jealous of your car, Tobias," Remy said teasingly. "It's unbecoming of you."

I sputtered. "Jealous? Please."

"Oh yeah, you're totally jealous of the car, dude," Jack added helpfully.

"I'm instituting the quiet game until we get there. Losers get their pumpkin tossed out the window." I growled.

"That seems oddly speci—" Jack began.

I cut him off. "Quiet game!"

Remy crossed their arms, a knowing smirk on their face as they sat back and let me drive in peace. I was not jealous of the Bee. The thought of that was just ridiculous. I was not going to allow myself to be teamed up against in my own car. Especially when one of the perpetrators was a freaking pumpkin.

After a few more turns, we arrived at the Hotel Sorrento. I parked the car and reached into the back to grab Jack and my satchel. He screeched several protests in a language I didn't know as I stuffed him back in the bag. I wasn't about to get questioned by hotel staff about my talking, flaming pumpkin. I bopped him on top of the head and he finally pipped down. Remy exited the car after me and I made sure to lock it.

"So the two of us," Remy paused for dramatic effect. "going into a hotel together."

"Would you stop it?" I grunted in denial as I headed for the front entrance.

Something a lot of people fail to realize, if you act like you're supposed to be somewhere then most people will take it at face value and leave you be. So Remy and I walked straight into the hotel and headed for the elevator. The elevator dinged and we entered. Remy hit the button for the fourth floor and we waited as the elevator began its upward trek.

For a moment, neither of us said anything.

"Tobias, when are you going to ask me out?" Remy said simply as they watched the floor numbers change on the small screen above the door.

I coughed in surprise. "Uh, excuse me?"

Remy crossed their arms and turned their attention to me. "You're not exactly subtle, Tobias. I see you staring at me at work. And you don't have the best poker face. You get flustered if I even look at you funny."

I stared straight ahead stubbornly. "I don't get flustered."

"You really do. It's cute, though." Remy smiled.

The elevator dinged and the doors slid open. We walked out and I took the lead as we headed to Room 408. The hallway was empty and quiet, which left me with little opportunity to deflect.

I sighed, my cheeks flushing. "Sorry. It's just the last time I went out with someone, she left. And our relationship, platonic and otherwise, fizzled out hard. I barely hear from her anymore."

Remy frowned. "So what? You're just going to push away any opportunity you get for happiness?"

I made a shooing motion. "No, of course not."

"Then?" Remy cut me off and planted their feet, blocking my way to the room.

I threw my hands up, looking at the ceiling as I realized this was a losing battle. Even for someone as stubborn as me. I took a deep breath and looked Remy in the eye. "Do you..."

"Uh huh?" They said, urging me to continue.

"Want to go out sometime?" I said.

Remy smiled. "That wasn't so hard, was it?"

I rolled my eyes. "You're impossible."

Remy turned and resumed walking down the hallway. I followed closely behind. "The answer is yes, by the way. I'd love to go out with you."

Chapter 5

We stood outside the door to Room 408. A notice on the door marked it as a sealed crime scene. There was more tape over the seam of the door, making it impossible to go inside without breaking the seal.

"Huh." I grunted.

Remy raised an eyebrow. "What is it?"

"I've never broken into a crime scene before." I said simply.

"And you're worried about being caught?"

"Yeah. We weren't exactly stealthy coming in here and they're definitely going to notice the broken seal once we go in." I said, hesitation painting my words.

Remy shrugged and smiled. "Well if it makes you feel any better, I've kept us under a veil since we pulled into the parking lot."

My eyebrows climbed up my forehead in surprise. "You have?"

Remy nodded, winking. I'd never seen Remy's magical abilities first hand, so I was never quite sure of their skillset. But they'd been maintaining a veil this whole time and I hadn't even noticed. That either spoke highly of their magic or poorly of my observational skills. Probably both.

"So as far as anyone is concerned, some clumsy maid wasn't paying attention and opened the door?" I suggested.

"How clumsy of that maid." Remy said.

I grinned broadly and turned my attention back to the door. I reached for the door handle, then hesitated for a moment. Thanks to Remy's veil, no one could see us. Security camera footage would be distorted and useless as well. But fingerprints were another story.

I opened my satchel and reached inside. I found what I was looking for and pulled out a box of latex gloves. Usually, I used them when handling sketchy materials for potions or complex magic rituals. I took a pair out of the box and held it over to Remy. They took a pair of gloves and pulled them on. I deposited the box back in my satchel and pulled my own gloves on.

Okay, now I was ready to trespass on a crime scene. I grabbed the door handle and turned. The handle offered no resistance and the door remained closed despite my efforts to open it. I frowned at the handle and tried again. Same result.

"It's a hotel door, dummy. It needs a keycard." Remy explained to me like I was five.

I scowled at them. "I know that."

I didn't have a keycard, but I had the next best thing. I held my open palm over the door handle and focused a tiny bit of magic into the mechanism. With a whispered word, my magic rushed into the lock and gently slid it open. I grabbed the handle and pushed the door open, tearing through the tape that sealed the door.

I bowed slightly and gestured into the room. "After you."

Remy let out a low laugh. "What a gentleman."

Remy entered the room first, and I followed closely behind. The police had removed the body and replaced it with a rough tape outline. Which didn't matter much, since the body had curled in on itself upon mummification. There was a dark stain on the sheets, left behind from the body.

The stench of death still permeated in the room. I gagged, holding my hand to my mouth. I swallowed, steeling my nerves. I looked to Remy. They held the back of their hand to their nose, trying to stifle the smell. At least I wasn't alone on that front. I cleared my throat and walked past Remy. I reached into my bag, finding the newly familiar shape of Jack's pumpkin and pulling him out.

"Hey, watch the stem!" Jack hollered.

"Keep it down." I snapped.

I set him down on the bed, facing the dark stain. The pumpkin's eerie green flames flared in surprise as he saw the stain. I crossed my arms, waiting for him to say something.

"Well?" I beckoned.

The pumpkin spun of its own accord to face me, his flames twisted into a frightened expression. "I dunno what this thing is man, but it's one nasty customer."

"What do you mean?"

Jack turned back to the stain, the light from his flames dimming slightly. "The psychic residue left behind 'ere is absolutely disgusting. It's slimy, evil magic."

I widened my eyes at that. From what I remembered of his legend, Jack was a crook in his past life and morally ambiguous at best. For him to call something evil said a lot about whatever this thing was.

I turned to Remy, who looked just as disturbed by Jack's revelation.

"What else can you tell me about this thing, Jack?" I inquired.

Jack grumbled as he took in the scene. He turned around a couple of times to take in the room. He mumbled to himself as he took in details that were invisible to me. He made a tongue-clicking noise and finally turned back to face me.

"Nothin'," Jack declared.

My mouth dropped open in disbelief. Remy let out a sputtering sound.

"What do you mean...NOTHING?" I growled.

Jack shifted in a faux-shrugging motion. "I ain't never seen nothin' like this, man. I dunno what to tell ya."

My body spasmed in anger as I tried to find the words to encapsulate my anger. I reeled towards the pumpkin, grabbing him roughly and brought his face to mine. "You said if I brought you here, you'd be able to tell me something!"

"Hey hey, watch the merchandise! And I said I *might* be able to tell ya something!" Jack snapped defensively.

I let out an angry and distressed noise as I struggled to string together a rational thought. After another second of angry sputtering, I opened my bag and stuffed Jack back inside ungraciously. Jack let out a string of curses as I stuffed him inside and zipped the bag up.

I slumped against a wall and sighed heavily. Remy walked over to me, a look of concern on their face.

"You okay?" They asked.

"No, I was really hoping I'd catch this one early. If I could figure out what it was, I'd be one step ahead on how to fight it. I put my faith in that damn pumpkin, like an idiot, and he let me down."

Remy frowned thoughtfully. "I know it's frustrating. But, it's not like you've lost. We can still find this thing and stop it. Jack was just one possible avenue of learning more about it."

I turned to them. "We, huh?"

Remy's frown reversed into a smile. "Of course, I'm here for the long haul. Plus, without some backup, you're bound to get yourself killed."

A lightbulb went off in my head. "Good, because I'm gonna try something."

I reached into my bag, ignoring a rueful stare from Jack. I pulled out a box of rock salt, a clump of sage bound with twine, and a lighter. Remy eyed me skeptically as I started dumping the salt out into the shape of a circle. Once I finished laying out the circle, I knelt down in the center.

"What are you doing?" Remy asked.

"Officially, there were no witnesses to the murder," I said as I lit the sage with my lighter. "But that might not be entirely true."

I tucked the lighter in my pocket, holding the burning sage with my other hand. I pulled the glove off my free hand with my teeth and touched two fingers to the line of rock salt. I closed my eyes as I whispered a word and eased a bit of magic into the salt. An inaudible hum of power began to buzz against my arcane senses. I tried to focus on the spell I was putting together, but there was a nebulous haze that kept brushing against my senses. It took me a moment before I realized what it was.

I opened one eye and glanced in Remy's direction. "I'm gonna need you to drop the veil."

Remy gave me a skeptical look. "But, then anyone could see us."

"I know, which is why you're going to keep a look out." I flicked my head toward the door. "I need to focus to make this work, and your veil is making it hard to think."

Remy stuck their tongue out at me, but did as I asked. The hazy feeling produced by the veil suddenly ceased as Remy crossed the room to peek their head out the door.

I closed my eye again and started mumbling nonsense words as I focused on the spell. If I did this right, I might be able to get some sort of clue as to what had killed the hotel guest. If I did this wrong...well, I didn't want to think about that. So I focused on the string of faux-Latin words I was mumbling. I felt my magic empowering the words with each syllable, until I finally said:

"Alice B. Toklas, I beseech thee. Appear before me now, so that you may help me in the task set before me." My words reverberated with a silent, tangible energy.

Subtle tendrils of power flowed out of the salt circle and into the hotel, rushing down the halls as they seeked their target. I felt my magic make contact with something. It reacted nervously, carefully inspecting my power for any ill will it may have harbored. I tried to instill a sense of honest curiosity and gentleness into the energy. I wanted the ghost to know I meant no harm to her or her demesne. I just needed any answers it could provide.

A rush of cold air filled the room. I shivered, but kept my focus on my intent. Any doubt or nervousness could spook the spirit. And it would be unlikely to answer my call a second time. I opened my eyes just as the transparent form of Alice B. Toklas coalesced in front of me.

The room had darkened, the only light coming from her shimmering form. She wore a black tweed jacket with a striped scarf, and a brimmed hat with a lot of lacey ribbon and frill. Alice stared at me with a blank expression, saying nothing. She stood outside of the salt circle, I resisted the urge to let out a whoop of excitement. I'd never performed a séance in earnest before, and I hadn't been sure it was going to work. Alice's unblinking stare bore into me. I wasn't frightened by her by any means, just deeply unnerved.

"Thank you, Ms. Toklas, for gracing me with your presence." I said politely.

"What brings you here, child?" Alice said, in a kind but firm voice.

"I seek answers for what transpired here. Someone was killed in this very room." I explained. "You've resided in this hotel for decades, specifically in the area surrounding this room. I was hoping you could tell me something, anything, about the thing that killed the person who had been staying in this room."

Alice's blank expression contorted into a troubled frown. "It was a dark thing. Something that did not belong on this Earth."

"What did it look like?"

"Like a monster. A slimy, emaciated creature." Alice's voice quivered as she spoke. "It crouched on the poor woman as she slept. She cried out as if she suffered from a horrible nightmare. The creature crouched and fed. It wasn't long before she was gone, reduced to a husk."

I frowned. She was getting nervous. I needed her to stay focused. "I need more details on the creature. What it looked like, where it came from. Anything you can tell me."

Alice's voice rose to a wail. "It was horrible! Slimy skin and a skeletal figure, it dug into her soul with its claws! It cackled and screamed as it consumed her!"

The temperature in the room dropped by several degrees. My breath came out in a frosty cloud. The lights began to flicker. A gust of wind rushed past me and threatened the integrity of the salt circle I'd set up. Alice wailed in terror and I realized I'd made a mistake. A ghost's emotions were unstable at best and whatever the spirit of Alice B. Toklas had seen was so horrible it was sending her into a twister of fear. I had only a second to make a decision.

With an effort of will, I broke the circle. "Alice B. Toklas, I release you! Return to your quiet dwelling where you may rest and recover!"

With the magic of my circle released, Alice B. Toklas let out one final wail before she dissolved into mist. The lights in the room flickered on and returned to their full brightness. The biting cold air faded back to a normal temperature and the jitters left my body.

I rose from where I sat, blowing out the embers that still burned on the clump of sage. I deposited my supplies into my satchel as Remy hurried to my side. They looked at me with concern as I zipped up my bag.

"What the hell was that about?" Remy asked.

"I'm not sure." I scowled as I thought about the encounter. "Whatever was in this room, it scared the hell out of Toklas' ghost."

"So, what happens now?"

"Toklas didn't give me much, but she did give me some details on what this thing looked like and maybe how it killed the woman who'd been staying in this room. I'm gonna see if I can cross-reference what she told me and see if it matches anything on record." I explained, still trying to wrap my head around the encounter.

Remy considered that for a moment. "Well, could it wait a couple of hours?"

"Uh, why?" I asked.

"Well, you did ask me out on a date." Remy reminded me. "And the night's still young."

"You want to go on our date right now? After visiting a murder scene and watching me commune with an undead spirit?" I asked half-rhetorically.

"I mean, it'd be like a pre-date. Something small and simple, no biggie."

I gulped. No biggie, right. Just something small. We could get coffee. No, we worked at a coffee shop. We drank plenty of coffee. Maybe ice cream?

"Sure, let's head down to the car and we can iron out the details." I said, feigning an air of confidence.

Remy winked. "Come on then, wizard boy."

They wrapped themself around my arm and led me out of the room. We headed back down the hall towards the elevators. I pressed the down button and we waited. The elevator dinged and the doors slid open.

My entire body stiffened as two individuals emerged from the elevator. The first was a uniformed police officer, a serious expression on his pale face. He was tall with boring features, completely unremarkable. The second was a black woman a few inches shorter than me. She had severe features and short curly hair. Her eyes were a dark brown, but something about them seemed to stare right into my soul as she made eye contact. She wore a police jacket over a gray button-up. Her SPD badge was hooked onto her waistband where it could easily be seen.

I gulped.

"Evening, officers." Remy said politely. But I detected a hint of nervousness to their voice.

"Detective, actually." The woman said. "Detective Hart. Now, if you'll excuse us."

I stepped to the side, pulling Remy with me. "Sorry detective, we were just heading out."

Detective Hart and her companion said nothing further as they walked past. They headed down the same hall we had come from, a knot twisting itself in my stomach. We had to get out of here, and quickly.

I pulled Remy into the elevator and pressed the lobby button repeatedly until the door finally closed. Neither of us said anything. In our eagerness to go to our pre-date, I'd neglected to have Remy throw up another veil for our exit. There was no doubt the detective was headed to Room 408, which we'd illegally entered. The same room where I'd laid out a circle of salt to commune with the spirit of Alice B. Toklas.

We'd been as careful as we could be, right? We'd worn gloves and hadn't touched anything besides the salt circle itself, which they wouldn't be able to link back to us. Right? The elevator dinged as we arrived at the lobby. Remy and I walked at a brisk pace, keeping our eyes down as we hurried back to the car.

Neither of us said anything until we were safely back in the car. I puffed out a long, anxiety-ridden breath. "Sheesh."

"That was a close one." Remy said.

"I'm sorry, I should've been a bit more careful. I wasn't thinking straight." I apologized.

"Don't be sorry. Hey, they probably won't even think to connect us to the breached crime scene." Remy reassured me. "Clumsy maid, remember?"

"Right. Yeah, right." I said, not sure who I was trying to convince more.

"So, where are we going?" Remy asked.

"Huh?" I shook my head, trying to shake off the frightened daze.

"Our pre-date, remember?" Remy reminded me, an amused look painting their expression.

"Oh, right! Umm..." I started to brainstorm ideas.

That's when my phone rang.

I let out a series of muttered curses as I struggled to pull my ringing phone out of the confines of my jeans. Remy giggled at my struggle. I finally pulled my phone out, Bishop's name was displayed on the screen. I straightened my expression, clearing my throat as I answered the phone.

"Hey, Unc. What's up?" I said.

"Tobias, another body has been found." Bishop said in between coughs.

I sighed. Supernatural predators had the worst timing. "Where?"

Bishop gave me the address. I frowned at the sound of his voice. He sounded strained, and he couldn't get two words out without choking out a cough.

"You okay, Bishop?" I asked, concerned.

"Yeah, I'm fine." He grumbled. "Can you handle this one on your own?"

I nodded. "Yeah, I got it covered. No problem. Get some rest, okay?"

Bishop hung up without responding. I held my phone in front of me, frowning. I turned to Remy, who was patiently waiting for the details.

"That was my uncle. He said another body's turned up." I explained.

Remy nodded, hurriedly. "Okay, let's go then. I've got your back."

I gave them an apologetic look. "I'm sorry, look's like our pre-date's going to have to wait."

Remy gave me a reassuring smile. "It's no problem. We've got a monster to catch."

I grinned as I shifted the car into gear and made our way into traffic. The Bee roared as we drove down the street and headed towards our second murder scene of the night.

Chapter 6

The address Bishop gave me was for an old apartment building on the outskirts of the city. It was the less savory part of town. Even as an experienced martial artist and wizard, this wasn't the kind of place I wanted to hang around for long, especially as night settled in. Weeds sprouted from the cracks in the parking lot, and the painted lines were so faded I wasn't exactly sure where to park. I eventually decided to park under the lone, flickering parking light and stepped out of the car. Remy followed closely behind me as I approached the building.

I double-checked the address that Bishop had provided before heading up a set of old stone stairs. My steps echoed against the stone, bouncing off the walls. As we reached the top of the stairs, I glanced around and frowned. The place had seen better days.

Everywhere I looked, I saw barred windows, chipped paint, and suspicious stains in the concrete.

"What apartment is it?" Remy asked.

"Unit 211," I answered. I started walking down the hall, looking at each door. Metal numbers were nailed into each door, marking them.

"Tobias, wait," Remy's voice called from behind me.

I stopped and turned on the spot to look back at them. Remy pointed to a door and I walked over to investigate. It was a good thing I'd brought Remy along, because my oblivious self walked right past the apartment I was looking for. To be fair, the numbers had fallen off the door long ago. The only evidence that this was Unit 211 was the faded impression of the numbers on the door.

I put on a fresh pair of latex gloves and tried the door. This time, the door was unlocked. I pushed the door open, the hinges squeaking loudly, and I stepped inside. The apartment was cloaked in a layer of darkness, making it hard to make out any details at all. I pulled my polearm out of my satchel and held it out in front of me.

I channeled my magic into the polearm and whispered a word. After a moment, an orb of light appeared at one end of my weapon. With a gentle flick of my wrist, the orb floated lazily into the air and began to brighten. After a couple of seconds, the orb illuminated the entire room. The interior of the apartment was just as rundown as the exterior, if not worse. The carpet was stained beyond repair. Trash and debris was littered everywhere. I made careful note of needles, crack pipes, and other drug paraphernalia spread around the room.

There wasn't much in terms of furniture. A low-rise coffee table sat in the center of the living area, where a lot of the drug paraphernalia was strewn about. Several old couch cushions were spread around the room as well.

The kitchen was to my left, but there wasn't much to see there. Whoever lived here, they owned no appliances whatsoever. An investigation of the cupboards revealed they owned only a handful of plates and utensils. The only food items were random boxes of snacks, nothing substantial. The apartment reeked of death, but our investigation of the entryway hadn't turned anything up so far.

"Whoever lived here wasn't exactly an upstanding member of society, were they?" Remy mumbled.

"No," I agreed. "but that doesn't change anything. No one deserves to die. Especially not like this."

"That's not what I was saying," Remy said. "I'm just saying, maybe the killer is going after people who wouldn't be noticed or missed."

I frowned. "Then why kill someone at a famous hotel?"

Remy shrugged. "Not sure. Maybe because they were from out of town? It'd probably help if we knew more about who they were."

I nodded in agreement and filed that idea away for later. "Come on, let's check the bedroom."

I walked towards a door on the far side of the room. It was cracked open slightly, and as I approached, a renewed waft of death assaulted my senses. Covering my nose, I flicked my polearm towards the floating ball of light, beckoning it to follow me into the bedroom. As it approached, the details of the room were revealed to me. The carpet was in a similar condition to the living room, stained and torn by years of neglect. There was no furniture except for a bare mattress and pillow in the middle of the room.

The corpse was in a similar condition to the one I'd seen at the hotel, except this one was partially clothed. It wore a peach-colored bra and cotton pajama shorts on its slender form. Her skin was dried and blackened, tight against her bones. Her arms were wrapped around her, skeletal fingers gripping her shoulders.

Her head was arched back, and her mouth was open wide as if she'd been screaming.

"This is horrible," Remy whispered.

That's right, Remy hadn't seen the last body. Even though I had, I'd had to brace myself against the site. Otherwise, I'd be spewing chunks all over again. Even now, my stomach quivered uncomfortably, and I had to fight to keep my composure.

"I know, which is why I plan to catch the thing that's doing this," I responded. "Give me a moment to take a look around. Watch my six."

I took a deep breath and then allowed my awareness to slip into my arcane senses. A thick haze of dark, sickly energy permeated around the room. It manifested itself as a blanket of black fog that snuffed out all traces of light. In this view, even the ball of light I'd created had been dimmed to almost nothing.

I turned my attention to the body. The body looked as it did in reality, except for the glowing green veins that traced its form. They pulsed and flowed like a disgusting slime. It took me a moment to realize what I was looking at.

"What do you see?" Remy called from the door.

I smirked. "I think I've got this thing's number now."

"What do you mean?" They asked.

I said nothing as I approached the body, making sure to switch from my arcane senses back to their mundane counterparts. I reached inside my satchel and pulled out a pocket knife and an old bandana I'd worn for a school spirit day or something years ago. I took a deep breath before I got too close and held it, kneeling down before the body. I grabbed its wrist, flicking the knife open. I pressed the knife against one of the corpse's fingers and with a small effort, sliced cleanly through it. Flakes of decayed skin flew off and scattered around me. I placed the severed finger into the bandana and wrapped it up carefully, tying the ends tight so that it couldn't fall out.

I stepped passed Remy into the front room, where I released the breath I was holding. I took several deep breaths, pulling the rancid air into my lungs.

"Did you just...?" Remy began.

"Cut off a corpse's finger. Yep." I confirmed. "The corpse is teeming with traces of our killer's magic. It's an ugly, disgusting energy. I haven't seen anything quite like it."

Remy didn't say anything as they thought through the potential uses for the severed finger. I knew they figured it out when their eyes lit up. "You're going to track it."

I smiled wildly. "Sure am. This thing's killing spree ends tonight."

***

I wasn't going to take any risks in tracking the killer down, so I opted to use a complex tracking spell. A simple tracking spell involved the use of one object and imbuing it with magic so that it acted as a sort of compass that would lead a wizard back to the source.

In the past, I'd used a bullet that someone had shot at me for a simple tracking spell, and it led me back to where the gun was at that moment. The gun and bullet had a very concrete relationship, so the simple tracking spell was all I needed.

But in this case, I didn't have a link that was as direct. I was using a victim's body part to track down their killer. So a more complex, ritual tracking spell was necessary to find our culprit. Which meant I needed some supplies.

Luckily, there was a convenience store near the old apartments that would have everything I needed. I took a few minutes in the store to gather my supplies. It was a seemingly random and meaningless collection of items, but they were vital tools in my mission. I paid the clerk at the register and hauled my paper bag of ritual objects back to where Remy was waiting.

They waited patiently in an alley across the street from the convenience store. Luckily, there weren't a lot of pedestrians out tonight, or I would've been more worried about Remy loitering by themselves in a seedy neighborhood as the sun was setting. Don't get me wrong, it wasn't Remy I was worried about. It was any poor sap who thought they'd be an easy victim of whatever nefarious schemes they had in mind. Remy was a powerful wizard; I knew that from their ability to shapeshift. It wasn't a skill for lightweights. Remy could take care of themselves.

Remy stood there, arms crossed. "Did you get your shopping done?"

"Yup," I said through a mouthful of candy bar.

They gave me a suspicious look that I politely ignored. I knelt on the ground as I unpacked my bag of goodies. A complex tracking spell like this requires seven components. First was the compass item, which would be what the spell would empower to lead me to my target. Pickings were slim at the mini-mart, so I'd had to settle on a rubber ball.

Next was the major focus, or the object with the most significant connection to our target. That was the corpse's finger. It belonged to the victim and still held a trace of our killer's magical aura.

Finally, were the five minor foci, which were directly tied to my own senses. These were used to draw a connection between me and the major focus, which was, in turn, connected to the compass item. For smell, I'd purchased a pack of cheap cigarettes. I'd never cared much for the smell of cigarette smoke. Which was appropriate, since I didn't care much for our killer either. For taste, I'd bought a bag of chocolate peanut butter candies. I was a sucker for chocolate and peanut butter. For sight, I'd bought a cheap pair of sunglasses. They were a simple pair of sunglasses with a black frame and black lenses.

For touch, I'd had to go a bit abstract. Usually, it was about the texture of an object. But again, my choices were limited so I'd gotten creative. I pulled out a Rubik's cube, something you had to touch a lot to solve. Finally, for sound I bought a toy rocket ship that made an incredibly annoying noise when turned on.

After unpacking my spell components, I reached into my bag to pull out a thick piece of blue chalk. I cleared a section of concrete of any dust or debris and then drew a two-foot wide circle with the chalk. Within the circle, I drew a five-pointed star, completing the pentagram. Carefully, I placed the rubber ball and the finger in the center of the star.

Then I took out one of the cigarettes, lighting it with a cheap lighter I'd picked up as well, and set it at the farthest point of the star from me. Then I placed the bag of candy, the sunglasses, the Rubik's cube, and lastly, the toy rocket. I made sure to turn the rocket on, and it began to screech loudly with futuristic sound effects.

"You know, to anyone else, you'd look like a madman," Remy pointed out, amusement in their voice.

I cocked my head back, grinning. "And what do I look like to you?"

Remy smirked. "A madman. But an adorable one."

I turned back to the circle, shrugging. I could live with that. I touched two fingers to the edge of the circle, willing energy into it. There was an inaudible snap of energy as my magic empowered the circle, sealing it off from foreign energies. Then I began the spell.

I'd been gathering my magic since I'd finished drawing the circle. It swirled within the circle, completely invisible as it swirled and twisted within the circle. I closed my eyes, focusing on the spell and my intent for it. I felt a tug in my gut as the magic reached out into the world, seeking my target like a fishing line in a deep, vast lake.

Something stirred in the void as my spell grazed it.

"There you are," I muttered.

I willed the spell to coalesce and tag the killer. I felt it swirl around my unseen target, preparing to bind to the killer. A wave of nausea hit me, and suddenly, the thing's presence rushed away. The thing had detected my spell, and it was on the run. I swayed but kept my focus on the spell. I wasn't sure if the thing knew exactly what was happening or if it was like an animal reacting to unknown stimuli. I gritted my teeth and urged the spell to pursue my target. I felt a rushing sensation as the spell closed in on the killer. The thing was fast, but my magic was moving at the speed of thought. Trying to outrun it was pointless.

Finally, I felt the spell sink in, wrapping around my target and pulling taut as the connection was solidified. I opened my eyes, letting out a gasp of air and falling back on my ass. I wiped my brow and realized it was slick with sweat.

"You okay, Tobias?" Remy asked. "You were shaking."

I nodded breathlessly. "Yeah, whatever this thing is, it tried to outrun my tracking spell. I had to put in more energy than I expected to get the spell to latch on."

"So you got him?"

I smiled broadly. "You bet I did."

I stood up and started putting everything away. I wrapped the finger back up in the bandanna and put it back in my satchel, along with the chalk. Everything else, save for the rubber ball, went back in the paper bag. I made sure to put my baldric on under my jacket, placing my polearm on my back, where the baldric's magnets held it in place. I pulled on my satchel and grabbed the rubber ball. Remy rolled the paper bag up until it was a fraction of its original size.

"Ready?" I asked.

Remy nodded.

I gave the rubber ball an underhanded throw towards the alley's exit. Upon hitting the ground, it bounced sharply to the left, completely ignoring the laws of motion. It continued to bounce down the sidewalk under its own power, and was threatening to leave us in the dust.

"Come on, we've got a killer to catch." I said, taking off at a brisk pace in pursuit of the rubber ball.

Chapter 7

The ball was apparently in a hurry. Remy and I had to jog at a steady pace just to keep up with it. It took a sudden left and I nearly tripped over myself as I pivoted to follow it. Remy was close behind me. Luckily for us, night had fallen and there weren't many people out and about to witness two idiots chasing after a rubber ball.

We followed the rubber ball as it bounced into a motel parking lot. As I took my first step into the parking lot, my blood went cold. I felt a slick and slimy energy crawl up my spine. I felt like doubling over and throwing up. I swallowed, reeling in my composure.

"You feel that?" I asked over my shoulder to Remy.

Remy gasped. "Yeah, I think we're in the right place."

The ball hadn't stopped for us and had already crossed the parking lot. It flung itself repeatedly against the first door of the motel's rectangular building. No one was around. All the rooms were dark, including the one that the ball was desperately trying to break into. The only light came from the office, which was on the far side of the motel, away from the room we needed to get into. I started walking towards the room, only a hundred feet away.

"Remy, veil us," I whispered.

Remy hissed out a word and I knew they had already brought up the veil around us. I'm not sure how much help it would be against a supernatural killer, but at least it was unlikely anyone would notice us breaking into a hotel room. As we got closer to the door, I stumbled as the sickly energy grew thicker and resisted against our approach.

Remy coughed. "Tobias, what is that? It's pushing against my veil."

I cursed. "I'm not sure. I've never felt something quite like this."

"I'm going to have to drop the veil. Whatever this aura is, it's pushing back and making it difficult to keep up the veil." Remy explained through gritted teeth.

I cursed again. "Fine, drop it. We'll have to move quickly."

They did so, and I felt the sickly aura's resistance lessen a bit. Now it was only a minor inconvenience. I knelt in front of the door and pulled my polearm off my back. I held my free hand up to the door's lock. I whispered the incantation for my lockpicking cantrip and the door clicked open.

I turned to Remy. "Ready?"

Remy nodded, pulling a thin ivory wand from somewhere behind them. I had never seen Remy's magic tools before. The wand was slender and carved with small runes, about a foot in length. They held it at their side, ready to unleash deadly magical power.

I held up my hand, counting with my fingers.

One...

Two...

"Three!" I yelled and burst through the door, polearm at the ready.

I charged into the room and only had a second to take in what I was seeing. That second felt like an eternity as I took in the revolting sight. The creature was humanoid, but that's where the resemblance ended. Its skin was covered in splotches of gray and black and was slick with a slimy film. Its arms and legs were far too long, while its torso was too small. It had long, thin bony spikes extending out of its spines. The creature's long claws had sunk into the sleeping figure's chest. It's not like it had slashed into the victim, but as if the creature's claws were melting into them. It had a bald, oval-shaped head with needle-like teeth and dark, sunken eyes with bright white points. It reared its head back, letting out a sound that was somewhere between cackling laughter and the roar of an engine. I'd never seen anything like it.

I could feel the transfer of energy as it fed on its prey. I shook off the momentary shock and leveled my polearm at it. I twirled it once, gathering up my magic before aiming it again and shouted "*Kaze!*"

Wind swirled forth, rushing towards the unknown creature. Loose papers and articles of clothing were swept around me as the wind collided with the monster. The wind lifted it into the air and flung it against the far wall.

"Remy, get them out of here!" I said, gesturing to the stirring motel guest.

Remy wasted no time, rushing past me to help the poor woman up and out of the room. The poor woman was confused and disoriented, but I could see the fear on her face. Remy pulled her along, urging her to follow them.

The creature rose just as Remy and the woman had left.

"You are one ugly son of a bitch. You know that, Smeagol?" I spat, then considered the quip for a second. "Hmm, more like Smeagol's ugly cracked-out cousin."

The monster didn't care for my banter. No doubt it wasn't very pleased that I'd interrupted its meal. The creature let out a chortling roar, displaying its claws in an intimidation display.

"I'd say you aren't the ugliest, scariest thing I've fought in awhile, but I'd be lying. So take that for what it is." I growled, holding my polearm up in ready position.

The creature roared again and lunged for me. I didn't want to risk it getting out of the room, so instead of ducking, I held my polearm across my body in an attempt to catch the blow. The creature crashed into me and sent me tumbling backward. It slashed at me with its claws, but my bomber jacket's defensive spells deflected the claws easily. The force from the blows still didn't feel great, but at least I wasn't gutted yet.

With a jerk, I hit the thing across the face with one end of my polearm. It shrieked in pain and I hit it again. It roared two inches from my face, but in doing so it had removed a bulk of its weight from my core. I huffed a breath and wrapped my legs around its torso, bending awkwardly to do so. With all my might, I flung my legs down, dragging the creature along and slamming it into the ground. I rolled and came up on my feet.

I had a kneejerk reaction to let loose some fire magic, but I stopped myself. I had to assume the motel was full of innocent, sleeping bystanders. Fire magic could get out of hand very quickly in the old, rundown motel.

The creature moved around in an insect-like fashion, scuttling around until all its body parts were untwisted from each other and rose from its full height. It looked sickly and emaciated, but it was a farce. This thing was strong, fast, and deadly. And I had the sneaking suspicion that it could handle itself just fine in a fair fight.

It lunged at me, slashing me with its claws. I backpedaled awkwardly to avoid its blade-like claws and fell into the cheap dresser. It saw its chance and jumped on top of me. Instantly, I felt the nausea I'd been feeling intensify. It crouched on top of me, pinning me painfully to the dresser. It's drooling mouth less than an inch from my own and I suddenly felt my strength begin to drain away. My vision blurred and I felt my head loll to the side heavily.

I couldn't focus. I couldn't see. I wanted to call up my magic but whatever this thing was doing, it made whatever spell I tried to focus on slip out of my grasp. I heard a clatter as my polearm slipped between my fingers and hit the ground. I heard its chortling laugh, it sounded far away. Darkness began to creep in from the corners of my vision.

The creature had me right where it wanted me. I'd lost the fight and now it was going to eat me. I'd end up like the other corpses I'd found. And there wasn't a damn thing I could do to stop it.

"*Lumieros!*" A voice rang out, crystal clear in my hazy mind.

There was a flash of light and the creature's weight vanished from my body. I slumped to the floor, groggy and disoriented.

"*Lumieros!*" The voice bellowed again.

I got a better look this time as my vision began to clear. A bolt of pure white light rocketed into the room and struck the creature, which had fallen into the back corner. It shrieked in pain and fury as the light struck against its dark, slimy flesh.

Remy stepped into the room, wand pointed directly at the creature's crumpled form. I struggled to my feet, fumbling for my polearm. I grabbed it with clumsy fingers and used the dresser to pull myself up to my feet. I held my polearm shakily, aiming it at the creature.

To its credit, the creature recognized when it was outnumbered. It looked from me to Remy and back to me. It righted itself, standing on all fours in an awkward stance where its rear end was raised higher and it held its head low. It galloped across the room, bouncing off the bed. I turned to track it, ready to unleash another magical strike. But it ignored us entirely and dove headfirst into the mirror hanging on the wall nearest the door. The mirror's surface rippled like water, shimmering with an eerie light as the creature dove through.

When it was gone, the mirror's surface returned to normal and the light faded away, leaving me and Remy alone in the trashed motel room. I panted heavily, staring at the mirror and then looking towards Remy. Now that the danger had passed, Remy's determined expression melted away to reveal a look of fear and anxiety.

"Are you okay?" Remy hurried over to me, depositing their wand into their pocket.

Remy helped me steady myself as I placed my polearm on my baldric. I took a few deep breaths, shaking off the remaining nausea and haze that clouded my mind. "Yeah, I'm fine. Just a little woozy. That thing was strong."

"And ugly as hell," Remy added.

"That," I agreed.

I walked over to the mirror, inspecting it closely. There was nothing special about it. Just an ordinary mirror. But Jack had said that only two things could use the mirror as a doorway, a wizard or one of the fae, and that thing was no wizard. At least, I hoped not.

"What was that thing?" Remy wondered, watching me.

"Pretty sure it was a faerie," I answered, still staring at the mirror. I turned to face them.

"Never seen a fae that looked that messed up," Remy said.

"I know, neither have I. Not even in Bishop's bestiary," I said. "But I don't know what else could have escaped through the mirror."

"So now what do we do? You're not thinking of tracking it down again for round two, are you?"

"If you asked me a few years ago, I would've definitely said that we had to find that thing now and take it down." I said. "But we caught it by surprise and it still nearly killed me. We don't know enough about this thing to fight it head on."

"So what are you going to do? Research? You already said you've never seen that thing in your uncle's book." Remy pointed out.

"My uncle may not have any information on this thing," I said. "But I know someone who might."

***

Remy and I made sure that the woman from the motel room was alright. She seemed rattled, but we'd gotten there just in time. That strange fae monster didn't have a chance to sink its claws into the poor woman's soul.

Evidently, the commotion had woken someone up and SPD was called. They showed up while checking on the poor woman. They then called paramedics to have her checked out after she said someone had tried to assault her in her room. An officer took Remy off to the side to question them. Which left me alone with the charming detective I recognized from the hotel.

Detective Hart frowned as she approached me. "Haven't I seen you before?"

I tried to give her a pleasant smile. "I got lost when I was a kid. They put my face on a bunch of milk cartons."

Hart's frown deepened. She pointed at me, thinking. "I remember you now. You were at the Sorrento earlier today."

Well, crap.

"Yeah, I was," I hooked a thumb over to where Remy was speaking with another officer. "We were visiting a friend that was staying there."

"Mhmm," Hart mumbled. "Notice anything weird while you were visiting your friend?"

"Nope, can't say that I did," I answered. Weird was relative, right? I'd had a séance with a gay stoner ghost, but that wasn't particularly weird in my line of work.

"Strange, we had a sealed off crime scene that was broken into," Hart informed me.

I shrugged. "Look lady, all I can tell you is we were visiting a friend there. And we were walking by here when we heard the commotion and came to help."

"What a good Samaritan. And what about that stick on your back?" Hart pointed to my polearm.

"I'm a martial artist, just came back from a demonstration at the youth center," I explained.

"Mhmm," She grunted, writing something down in her notebook. "Do me a favor, mister..."

"Tobias, Tobias Leight," I offered.

"Mister Leight, don't leave town. I have a feeling we'll be seeing each other soon," Hart said forebodingly.

"Golly, I sure hope not," I said playfully.

Hart arched an eyebrow and then walked away without another word, returning to a group of uniformed officers. I let out a sigh of relief. The last thing I needed right now was to be caught up with the police. I'd have to be more careful from here on out. The boys in blue had caught a scent, or at least, they thought they did. If I wasn't careful, I'd wind up at the wrong end of their scrutiny.

"That looked like it went well," Remy's voice said about two inches away from me.

I yelped, surprised by their presence. I hadn't noticed them approaching. Remy chuckled and playfully punched me in the shoulder. I winced. I felt sore and drained from my encounter with that strange creature.

"Oh, sorry," Remy said.

I shook my head. "I'm okay. Just a little sore."

"So what do we do now?" Remy asked.

"Well, like I said, I think I might know someone who can give me a clue or two about what that ugly ass thing was. But you're not gonna like where I'm going,"

Remy raised an eyebrow.

"I have to pay a visit to Light Haven," I explained.

Remy scowled at me. "Seriously?"

"I know, I know. You don't care much for the Mystic Order. Trust me, neither do I. They're a bunch of suspicious old coots all wrapped up in politics. I get it. Hell, a few years ago, they were debating executing me,"

"Executing you?"

Oops, I'd never told Remy about my introduction into the world of magic. They didn't know about my experience with the Fallen angel Azazel and my supposed destiny to be his vessel to destroy the world.

"Never mind that. A story for another time," I redirected.

"Well, you do owe me a date," Remy pointed out. "If you're up to it, maybe you can tell me more about it. Let's say, tomorrow night?"

I considered that for a moment. It was technically doable, but I was worried about our current predicament. There was a killer on the loose. A killer who'd now seen me face to face. That made things far more dangerous. But Remy was looking at me with that determined look, and I had a feeling that they weren't taking no for an answer.

"Fine," I relented. "Dinner, tomorrow night."

Remy beamed. "I can't wait!"

With that settled, we made our way back to the old, rundown apartment complex where I'd parked the Bee. I took Remy home because they wanted nothing to do with a visit to Light Haven, the Mystic Order's headquarters. I considered heading straight to the local entrance to Light Haven but decided against it. Even now, I was no good at dealing with the Mystic Order or its higher-ups.

So instead, I decided to head home first. I wanted some backup for my visit and the only person I knew who could effectively deal with Mystic Order BS was my uncle. I just hoped he was feeling up to it.

Chapter 8

After dropping Remy off and swinging through a drive-thru, I finally made it back to the apartment. The apartment was dark, which wasn't unusual. My uncle tried to get to bed earlier than usual nowadays due to his vampiric condition. Bishop had yet to succumb to the full effects of the infection thanks to the powers of mental discipline and specially-made elixirs.

I threw away my trash and headed for the garage to take a look around. No sign of my uncle, which I'd expected. Then something on the worktable caught my eye. It was a small bottle filled with a pale blue liquid. My eyes widened with realization. It was Bishop's anti-vampire elixir. If this bottle was here and still full, there was a strong chance that he hadn't taken his dose tonight.

I narrowed my eyes, instinctively reaching over my shoulder for my polearm. I didn't draw it just yet, but I wanted to be ready. I grabbed the elixir bottle and crept back into the house, keeping my head on a swivel. The living room and kitchen seemed to be clear, and I didn't notice anything else suspicious in the garage. That left the rooms upstairs.

As quietly as I could, I began to take slow steps up the stairs. I avoided the squeaky stair and finally made it to the top. First, I wanted to check Bishop's room. It was the first door on the right from the stairs. I gave the knob a try. It didn't budge. The door was locked. Had he locked himself inside? The knob had a keyhole on it, so it was also possible he'd locked it from the outside.

I was about to unlock it with my lockpicking cantrip when I noticed something else. The door to my bedroom was cracked open. Moonlight leaked through and bathed the hallway in an eerie blue-ish light. Something about the sight tickled my instincts. I crept closer to my door, preparing myself for what I might find.

I steeled my nerves and in one swift movement, I charged through the door. My head swiveled side to side, taking in every detail I could. My room was absent of life, as if no one had been in there all day. I chuckled at my paranoia. Odds are, Bishop had taken his daily dose, and the dose I'd found was meant for tomorrow. That made way more sense.

I turned around to find a figure in the doorway. The moonlight lit up their features in a way that made them seem far more sharp and severe. It took me a moment to realize that it was Bishop.

"Unc?" I approached him cautiously, holding out a placating hand. "You feeling okay?"

That's when I noticed his eyes. They had a faint red glow to them. He stared at me with a hunger in his eyes. I gulped, all too aware that I was cornered in a room with a hungry wizard-turned-vampire. Bishop didn't breathe. He didn't move, except for those eyes. They tracked me like a predator tracking prey. I felt my grip tighten on the potion I'd found.

"Bishop, why don't we go downstairs so you can take your potion?" I said, one hand slowly moving to my polearm. My hands felt clammy, and I wasn't feeling too confident that I could move fast enough to counter if he decided to jump me.

Using only my thumb and forefinger, I wiggled the cork out of the potion bottle. It made a popping sound, and that's all it took to set Bishop off. He let out an inhuman growl and lunged at me. I dropped and rolled out of the way, careful to keep the potion as upright as possible. I rose with a twisting motion, arming myself with my polearm and aiming it at my uncle.

Bishop stood hunched over in the spot where I'd been only a second before, breathing hard. His body twitched and convulsed slightly every other second and I could hear him sniffing the air as he laid his eyes on me once more.

"Bishop, I need you to calm down," I said as quietly and calmly as I could, as if I were speaking to a wild animal. Which, in a way, I sort of was.

My uncle wasn't having any of it. He hissed again and lunged for me. On reflex, I swung at him with my polearm, striking him in the side of the head and sending him crashing into my closet. I had to be fast, I dropped my polearm and moved towards him.

"*Duro*," I whispered. The hardening spell immediately took effect, giving my skin the strength of steel. It wasn't much, but it should stop him from sinking his teeth into my flesh. If he drank human blood, I wasn't sure if there would be any going back.

My strike had stunned the older wizard, but it wouldn't keep him down for long. I crossed the room quickly, pinning Bishop to the ground before he could gather himself. He was still groggy and I wasted no time. I held his head back so his mouth was open and poured the potion down his gullet before he could offer any more resistance.

The elixir's effects were almost immediate. The strange red glow in his eyes faded away and his features seemed to soften up a bit, though his skin was still paler than it'd been before he was infected. I got off him and sat beside him, dropping my hardening spell as I did.

After a few minutes, he began to stir. Bishop groaned as he sat up. "Ugh, what hit me?"

"Sorry, you didn't give me much of a choice," I said. "I hit you upside the head with my polearm, so you're gonna have one gnarly headache for a little while."

Realization flashed in his eyes as he put everything together. "I fell asleep on the couch, forgot to take my potion."

"Yeah I noticed," I scoffed.

"Are you okay?" Bishop asked me.

"Well you got my heart pumping, but otherwise, yeah I'm alright," I said. Then I remembered another detail. "Where's the dog?"

"Right before I went full-on vamp, I locked him in my room," Bishop coughed. "Hit him with a minor sleeping spell so he wouldn't take too much noise and draw my attention."

"Smart move. If you two got into it, we might not have an apartment anymore." I chuckled. "Listen, I had come home because I was looking to bring you as backup for my next stop, but if you're not feeling up to it I can go alone."

"Where are you headed?"

"Light Haven," I said. "I wanted to consult someone on our killer. I'm all but certain it's a fae, probably Unseelie."

"Ah, so I'm guessing you want to speak to Fachnan," Bishop deduced.

Fachnan was a member of the High Elders of the Mystic Order and the leading expert on all things dark and spooky, including the Unseelie fae. He'd been under the thrall of a warlock in a scheme to shove a Fallen angel into my head. Ever since, we'd come to a bit of an understanding. Neither of us particularly liked the other, but we were cordial.

"Yeah, if anyone knows what this thing is, it'll be him," I said.

Bishop nodded. "Good thinking. Give me a few minutes to freshen up and gather myself, and I'll come along."

I raised an eyebrow. "Are you sure?"

"Yeah, I'm okay," Bishop assured me. "Sorry, I should've been more on top of this,"

"Don't apologize, it's not your fault," I shook my head. "We're both okay, and that's all that matters."

With that settled, Bishop rose to his feet and headed to his room. Once he was ready to go, we'd be paying a visit to Light Haven. Hopefully our efforts there would yield some kind of clue as to what the hell we were dealing with.

***

Our drive down to Pike's Place was quiet and uneventful, which was just as well. I'd already had enough excitement for the night and was looking forward to a nice and simple visit to Light Haven. I parked in a nearby parking lot, locked the car, and then Bishop and I headed for the secret entrance.

Light Haven had hundreds, if not thousands, of secret entrances scattered across the world. Seattle's was located in one of its most famous, and most disgusting, landmarks. That being the infamous Gum Wall. The Gum Wall has a whole history behind it that I won't get into, but it's pretty neat, if I do say so myself.

The Gum Wall was covered in dried up bits of chewing gum. While its original purpose had long since

come to an end, the tradition still kept on. Mostly
through the efforts of tourists. I approached the germ-
ridden brick wall and pressed specific pieces of gum as
if they were buttons on a control panel. It'd taken me a
bit of time to remember the exact combination, but
years of practice had ingrained it into my brain.

As I pressed the final gum wad in the sequence, a
rectangle of light carved itself into existence and slowly
melted into a glowing doorway. I wiped my hand on my
jeans and walked through with my uncle close behind
me.

As we stepped through, the blinding light gave way
to a pristine room that was crowded with wizards
coming and going from Light Haven. The United States
Portal Nexus was a large, rectangular room with doors
lining the walls. Each door had the name of a city
emblazoned in gold lettering. You could be in Seattle
one minute and New York the next, so long as you
could find the right door in the mild chaos.

Wizards of all shapes and sizes bustled around.
Some wore classic-style cloaks, while some wore more
modern clothing. I even saw one guy wearing one of
those big coats, I think they're called dusters, rush
through a door labelled "Chicago". I couldn't imagine
wearing a coat like that during the summer; I was
struggling enough with my bomber jacket.

"So, where can we find Fachnan at this time of night?" I asked.

"Well, for Fachnan, it's probably early morning," Bishop noted. "He's always been an early riser. There's a fair chance we can find him in his personal chambers."

A memory flashed in my mind. I'd visited Fachnan's personal quarters once before, years ago. I'd suspected him of colluding with a Fallen angel and decided to search his personal estate in Ireland. He had a portal in his room that led there, much like the various doors in the Portal Nexus.

"Alright, I hope you know how to find his room then," I said. "Because I still can't navigate this place reliably."

Bishop smiled, leaning on his staff as he began walking. "Come on then, we have a fair bit of walking to do."

Light Haven was a truly strange place, and even now I didn't totally understand how the place worked. Its hallways seemed to constantly shift and change. You'd rarely take the same route twice. There was the occasional map that could assist you by highlighting the path you needed, but it was a pain in the ass just to find one.

Having an expert like Bishop lead the way was much easier, and I was very thankful to have him around. He navigated the strange halls as if it was just a normal building, a skill that he insisted I would pick up with time. Yeah, right.

After about twenty minutes of walking and listening to our footsteps echo against the tile floor, we finally arrived at Fachnan's quarters. It was a stark contrast to the aesthetic of the rest of Light Haven. Where Light Haven was clean, bright and modern, the door leading to Fachnan's quarters was rustic, dark, and ancient. It was made of an old-looking dark oak that gave off a sinister air. The door was decorated with intricate carvings that gave the door a weird sense of depth.

Bishop raised a fist to knock on the door. Right before his knuckles made contact, the door opened slightly, a green eye shaded by a mop of ginger hair peeked through. Upon recognizing us, Fachnan opened the door fully.

His red hair had grown out a bit, almost looking shaggy. His emerald green eyes were as piercing as ever. His expression made it seem as though he was judging you or trying to size you up. He wore all-black formal attire, only missing the tie to complete the set. There was an air of arrogance that emanated from him. To most, he'd seem like a simple douchebag. And yes, he was a douchebag, but there was no doubt in my mind he was on the side of the angels.

"Wizard Bishop, Wizard Tobias, to what do I owe this unexpected visit?" Fachnan asked, his Irish accent unable to hide the flat tone in his voice.

"Oh please, can we not with the titles and stuff?" I pleaded.

Fachnan smirked slightly. I wasn't a big fan of Mystic Order politics or formalities, and he knew it. While he was an ally, he still enjoyed antagonizing me a bit whenever he could.

"We have a killer in Seattle," Bishop said bluntly. "Something unlike anything we've seen before. We were hoping you could help us identify it, and perhaps how to kill it."

There was a glint in Fachnan's eyes. The prospect of an unknown killer that only he could identify seemed to excite him. He stepped to the side and extended his arm invitingly.

"Please come in. It seems we have much to discuss," Fachnan said.

We went inside. Fachnan's quarters had changed since I'd last seen them. It still looked like a chamber from an old castle, with dark, carved stone walls and mounter candelabra. There had once been a bed in here, but it was gone. His computer desk now sat in the center of the room, the monitors off to the side so he didn't have to look over them when speaking to visitors. There were two chairs for visitors to use, but they didn't exactly look comfortable. To my right, several filing cabinets stood. No doubt they held information on all sorts of Order business and mystical creatures. To the left was another desk, littered with notes and various trinkets; most likely, they were magical artifacts of one flavor or another.

Fachnan sat at the center desk and invited us to do the same. Bishop and I sat down and I quickly realized that I was right, the chairs were not very comfortable at all. Fachnan steepled his hands and rested his face against them.

"So, what can you tell me about this mysterious killer of yours?" Fachnan asked, clearly intrigued.

"Tobias has been taking the lead on our work lately, so I'll let him explain," Bishop said.

Oh, right. I was used to Bishop always doing the talking whenever it came to dealing with the Mystic Order. But he'd taken a backseat ever since he'd become infected. I cleared my throat nervously as I struggled to collect my thoughts.

"Well, it's been feeding on random people, reducing them to mummified corpses," I began to explain. "When I finally tracked the thing down it looked like..." I floundered as I tried to find the words. "Actually, do you have some paper and a pen?"

Fachnan nodded and pulled out a pad of paper and a cheap pen. I took it and began doodling the creature I saw from memory. I wasn't an artist or anything, but I got the general idea across. By the time I was done, I'd drawn up a passable depiction of the creature I'd fought. I handed it to Fachnan and gave him a few minutes to look it over.

"Hmph," Fachnan grunted.

"Hmph? What does hmph mean?" I asked.

"Bad news is, I've never seen anything like this thing before," Fachnan said.

"I'm hoping you have some good news to add to that," I said.

"Maybe. There's a grimoire I've been meaning to," Fachnan hesitated, choosing his next words carefully. "*liberate* from a local hag in my demesne. If anything would contain information on this creature, it'd be that book."

I already knew where this was going.

"If you can retrieve the grimoire from the hag, I should be able to glean more information on your mysterious killer," Fachnan said.

I frowned. "Not to be rude, but why don't you get the grimoire yourself?"

"Well, besides the fact that you're the one who needs the information, the hag and I have had a bitter rivalry for years now," Fachnan said. "She's laid wards down around the forest where she resides that are tailor-made to keep me away."

"Unfortunate," Bishop said. "Then, how is Tobias supposed to find the hag?"

Fachnan turned his attention to his computer and typed something in. After a few more clicks, he turned his screen to face Bishop and I. The screen displayed an overhead view of a castle and the surrounding landscape for what seemed like several miles. It took me a few minutes to realize the castle was probably Fachnan's. I'd never seen it from the outside, let alone from the sky.

Fachnan pointed to a forest several miles south of his estate. "This is the forest that she calls home. If you enter her forest, rest assured that she'll find you."

I gulped. "And what? I just ask her for the grimoire?"

Fachnan shook his head, brandishing a small smile. "Of course not. She will most assuredly put up a fight. Especially when the prospect of a young wizard such as yourself is on the menu."

I gulped again.

"Fear not," Fachnan assured me. "She is powerful and can manipulate her forest and surroundings, but in a direct fight, she would be hard-pressed to defeat you."

I looked at Bishop. He simply shrugged. I considered asking him to assist me but thought better of it. Bishop's strength was constantly being sapped by his body fighting the vampiric infection. I had a feeling I'd need his strength later when we finally confronted that strange creature. I'd have to handle this on my own.

"Fine, I'll go get your book from the hobo witch," I finally relented. I didn't have much of a choice.

"Wonderful," Fachnan smiled toothlessly. He spun in his chair and extended a hand to the wall. An outline of white line carved itself into the bricks and after a moment, the bricks seemed to disappear. In their place was a glowing white doorway with a light fog billowing out of it.

"Come along, Wizards Leight," Fachnan said.

Bishop and Fachnan accompanied me to the front door of Fachnan's castle. No, door was the wrong word; gate was more like it. The place was massive and looked like it came off the set of Game of Thrones or something.

"Bishop, we gotta get a castle," I suggested.

He smiled. "I'd hate to see the mortgage on this place."

"Don't remind me," Fachnan added.

I zipped up my jacket; it was much colder than it was back home. I ensured my polearm was secure on my baldric and my charms bracelet wasn't twisted up in my sleeve. I didn't want to have to worry about shaking it loose in the middle of a fight.

I looked to both of the elder wizards. "Any last-minute advice?"

"Just remember that Scáthach prefers to keep her adversaries at a distance by manipulating the environment," Fachnan began.

"So stay on your toes, keep moving, and find a way past her defenses," Bishop added. "Worst case scenario, fire is your friend. Just try not to burn down the forest."

I nodded. "Welp, I'll be back I guess." I turned and waved over my shoulder. "Don't get too bored without me."

Chapter 9

So began my long trek to the hag's forest dwelling. I know Fachnan had said the forest was several miles away, but I don't think I appreciated the distance until now. It was cold out and the grass was covered in morning dew, which had slowly but surely soaked the cuffs of my jeans. In a way, it reminded me of the weather I've always known. But I usually tried to avoid walking several miles in the cold when I could avoid it.

I made my way up to the crest of one of Ireland's many hills and sighed in relief. After nearly an hour, I was nearly there. The forest stood as a large, isolated cluster of trees. That had to be where the hag was because there was no way I could walk another hour. I started walking down the side of the hill towards the forest and prayed that I had found the right place.

I'd visited forests several times in the past, but this one was like something out of a fairy tale. Everything was so green that focusing on one thing too long started to hurt my eyes. Small orbs of light floated lazily around me as I delved into the forest. Everything was covered in a thin layer of moss that only added to the vibrant color of the forest. The place was beautiful and peaceful, I didn't understand how this could be some dark dwelling of an evil hag. Hell, I'm pretty sure I could hear the freaking birds singing.

"Fachnan must've given me wrong directions or something," I said.

That's where things went wrong, of course. Darkness crept in from every direction, drowning out the light. The lazily floating orbs suddenly darted away, disappearing into the darkness. I spun around, anticipating a sneak attack, but all I find was more dark forest.

"Wait a second," I eyed the forest in the direction I'd just come from. The forest was completely different now. I'd walked in maybe twenty feet or so, but now there was no sign of the forest's edge. I spun once again, taking in my surroundings. In every direction, I could see nothing but forest, no matter how far out I tried to look.

"Yeah, that's not good," I muttered.

The ground shifted around me, forming into hills and small cliffs. The trees twisted and changed, becoming darker and sharper. Their leaves fell away as their branches contorted into sinister claws. Roots began to slither out from under the earth, drawing nearer to me. Despite the lack of leaves to block out light from outside, the forest retained a blanket of darkness.

I grabbed my polearm and held it in a defensive position as I scanned my surroundings. I could just make out vague shapes moving around in the darkness. Glowing eyes glinted as they locked on me. Had Fachnan underestimated Scáthach? Had he unknowingly sent me into a trap?

"Scáthach, I mean you no harm," I said. I knew the hag had to be listening. "I only want the grimoire you have in your possession. Hand it over and things don't have to get ugly."

"Hmm, so that fool Fachnan can't even be troubled to steal it away himself?" A coarse, feminine voice responded. She was using some kind of magic to throw her voice. Each syllable seemed to come from a different direction.

"You're the one who warded your forest against him," I countered.

"It thinks it's clever. It thinks it's so smart, but it's the one that has wandered foolishly into my domain," Scáthach's voice taunted.

If I could keep her talking, maybe there was a chance I could pinpoint where she was hiding. It wasn't much of a plan, but what else could I do? Either way, I'd draw her out sooner or later. Hopefully, I wouldn't take too much of a beating in the meantime.

"Sorry lady, but I need that grimoire. It's on my summer reading list," I said. "Just hand it over and I won't have to turn your forest into kindling."

I heard a surge of movement from somewhere behind me. My instincts screamed and I dove to my right in order to dodge the incoming attack. There was a sound of impact as something struck the ground where I had been a moment before. I rolled away and got my feet under me, just in time to see a giant root retreating back into the darkness. So that's what Fachnan had meant. She could control the forest itself and use it to defend herself.

My go-to wind spell wouldn't be very effective here. I'd definitely have to resort to fire magic. With my charms bracelet, I could unleash controlled fire spells up to three times in a day. Anything beyond that and it would be much more difficult for me to use fire magic effectively. I weighed my options. I could stall her, but we were in the center of her domain. Her reserves would be much deeper than mine here. And I had a feeling I wouldn't be able to escape easily now that her defenses were up.

I sensed another attack coming. I looked around wildly, but I didn't spot it in time. Something hit me hard from behind, and I was sent flying forward, hitting the ground hard and tumbling. I managed to hold onto my polearm and pulled myself to my feet. As soon as I stood up, something swept my legs out from under me, and I fell hard on my ass.

"Okay, now you're starting to piss me off," I growled. I extended my polearm out in front of me and shouted, "*Hinote!*"

Flames burst forth as if my polearm was a flamethrower. Fire consumed three of the trees nearest me, providing me with light and hopefully taking out a few of her offensive options. My flamethrower spell faded away and I pulled my polearm back into a defensive position across my chest.

"I can do this all day, wicked bitch of the west," I snapped. "I'd hate to burn down your forest, but I'll do it if I have to!"

"You won't make it out of this forest alive, foolish boy!" Scáthach hissed.

"Have it your way! *Hinote!*"

My polearm spewed flames once more. I spun on the spot, consuming several more trees with fire. My surroundings were now bathed in an angry orange light. Scáthach wailed as my flames chewed through the trees. The light from the fire revealed my surroundings to me. The vague shapes in the darkness and the glowing eyes disappeared. They were just illusions, meant to scare and distract me.

"Arrogant child!" Scáthach wailed. "My trees will feed on your corpse!"

"Lady, with the amount of caffeine I drink, I wouldn't recommend it," I taunted.

The hag let out another rage-filled scream, causing the hairs on the back of my neck to stand on end. This lady was crazy and pissed, never a good combination. My instincts screamed at me to move, but I was too slow to react. Something struck me from behind and knocked me down.

I landed on my stomach and immediately tried to twist away, but something had me pinned. As I tried to rise, a hand grabbed the back of my head and smashed my face into the dirt. I turned my head to the side and spat out a clump of dirt. That's when I got my first look at Scáthach.

I never quite understood the meaning of the phrase "That's a face only a mother could love" until now. She might have been beautiful at one point in her life, but living alone in the woods had clearly not been kind to her.

Scáthach hid her potbelly and sagging breasts under a plain, ragged olive green dress. Her arms and legs were practically skin and bone and she had long, dirty nails tipping her fingers and toes. She had a large, round nose and her cheeks hung like the jowls of a bulldog. There was a wild look in her eyes, exacerbated by her lazy eye that was looking off to the side. Her hair was a wild mane of gray that seemed to stick out in every direction.

I coughed. "Lady, I know a good barber and nail salon I can recommend you if you need it."

Scáthach made a wet snorting sound and spat a loogie that landed right on my cheek. First of all, gross. Second, it seemed hardly the correct response to someone offering you grooming services. But what do I know?

"I'm going to kill you slowly and turn your bones into eating utensils," Scáthach hissed in my ear.

"Kudos," I grunted, my words slurred from my face being pinned to the ground. "As far as threats go, that's a new one." I sighed, growing exhausted of this whole ordeal. "Lady I just need your damn book and I'll be out of your hair."

"You'll have to pry it off my corpse, boy," She spat.

"I was worried it'd have to be that way," I sighed. I braced my hands against the floor and shouted, "*Kaze!*"

A burst of wind threw me four feet into the air. Scáthach lost her balance and tumbled away. I landed in a three-point stance, recovering my polearm from where it'd fallen out of my grip. I spun on my feet until I found where the hag had fallen. I aimed the tip of my polearm at her and summoned a fireball, holding it less than six inches from her face.

"Give up yet?" I said, the words somewhere between offer and threat.

"Never," She growled. Her eyes widened, something like recognition in her gaze. "You..."

"Me?"

"You are a Son of the Eclipse," Scáthach said. "You have the mark of the Fallen on your soul."

I frowned at her. "How do you—?"

"Know? I know many things, boy. And I've seen many things. You are destined for terrible, horrible things. Life holds much pain and heartache for you in the future."

Well, that wasn't ominous at all. I didn't move or say anything, hoping that the flaming ball of death I held in front of her would still be enough to motivate her to cooperate.

"You will find yourself wielding great power, child," Scáthach taunted. "But great power always comes at a terrible cost."

"Not quite how Uncle Ben put it, but I'll put it under advisement," I said. "The book. Now."

"You will get nothing from me, boy. Not while I still breathe."

I grimaced. "So be it. *Hinote!*"

My fireball burst forth into a lance of fire that engulfed the poor, crazy hag. Her screams cut into me like a blade and I knew I'd be hearing them in my nightmares for years to come.

***

I used a water spell to dowse the flames. The forest did not need to suffer because of my conflict with its former inhabitants. After wandering around for a little while, I was able to find the hag's dwelling. It was a cave that slanted down into the earth at a forty-five-degree angle, more or less. I delved deep into the cave, lighting my way with a small flame held in my hand until I found a small alcove lit by several torches. There was a cot made from hay and animal furs off to one side and the remains of a cooking fire on the other.

But what drew my attention was the leatherbound trunk tucked against the far wall. Two padlocks sealed it shut, but I made quick work of them with my polearm. I opened it up and inside found an assortment of things. There were many odds and ends that the hag had probably used in her rituals once upon a time. I pulled out what looked like a bracelet made of thin, flexible sticks or maybe roots. When I touched it, a twinge of energy like static electricity ran up my arm.

"Must be some sort of magical artifact," I surmised.

I wasn't sure what it was, but decided it might just come in handy. And hey, it wasn't like Scáthach had any use for it now. I tucked it in my back pocket and continued digging around in the chest.

Finally, I found what I was looking for. Buried under all of the junk, I found a journal bound in leather and held closed with a buckle. I unclasped it and flipped to a random page.

"Great, random gibberish," I muttered.

The writing looked like Ancient Greek or perhaps it was Latin. I had trouble distinguishing between the two. I flipped to another random page and found a detailed illustration of a red cap. They were a type of Unseelie fae, most often used as hitmen. I'd had an encounter with one in the past. They were strong despite their size and very dangerous. But more importantly, this was definitely the grimoire that Fachnan had been talking about.

I tucked the grimoire in my jacket pocket and stood up. I had the grimoire, which means I was one step closer to learning more about my mysterious murderer. Now all I had to do was get back to Fachnan's castle so he could find the information I needed.

But there was something still nagging at me. Right before I'd turn the the old hag into a briquette, she'd said some things that didn't sit right with me. She'd called me a Son of the Eclipse. To most, it would've sounded like nonsense. But it was much more significant than that.

Rumor had it, I'd been born during an eclipse. It gave me some sort of significance on a metaphysical level. But I wasn't too clear on the details, except for the fact that it apparently made me prime possession material for a Fallen angel. Specifically, the Fallen angel known as Azazel, a being I had the displeasure of encountering in the past. She'd said the Fallen had marked me, but how could she have known that? Not to mention all that crazed gibberish she'd been spouting about the future and power I'd supposedly obtain.

I'd tried my hardest to put that all in the past, but if a strange hag hiding out in Ireland had knowledge on Fallen angels and my connection to the nastiest one, then who else could possess that information or the power to gleam it just by looking at me? Ultimately, I decided that was a concern for another time. I had what I came for, now it was time to get back.

I groaned, remembering that I had one hell of a walk to make.

Wizarding may sound cool on paper, but it was rarely glamorous.

Chapter 10

Once I'd returned to Fachnan's castle, we decided to look into the grimoire I'd retrieved in the seclusion of Fachnan's office back at Light Haven. We were sitting at his desk, Bishop and I on one side, and with Fachnan on the other.

He was hunched over his desk, examining the grimoire with a strange set of glasses. At first glance, they were an ordinary set of spectacles. But upon closer inspection, there were several smaller lenses attached to the frame via rotating joints. Fachnan flipped between different colored lenses as he investigated the grimoire. He had yet to crack it open.

"I told you already," I began, slightly annoyed. I was tending to a large bruise on my chest with an icepack. "I already opened the thing. I don't think it's got any anti-theft spells or anything like that."

Fachnan peered up at me without moving his head. He looked unenthused. No, that wasn't quite right. He looked annoyed or maybe exasperated. It was pretty much his only reaction to anything I said or did. He returned his attention to the grimoire without a word.

"You did well, Tobias," Bishop remarked, changing the subject.

Bishop and I usually discussed details about my solo outings. It was a habit that had carried over from my days as an apprentice wizard, when I'd first started having to go out on my own more and more.

"Thanks, that hag was one tough cookie," I said. "A few years ago, it would've required a lot more luck to handle her on my own."

"Luck can only take you so far, but it's always welcome. You've grown stronger and smarter. Combined with your improvisational skills, you're a force to be reckoned with—even for someone as capable as that hag."

My face heated up slightly at Bishop's praise. I wasn't so good at accepting praise, even as an adult. I'd always struggled in school and things like that as a kid, so praise wasn't something I was accustomed to hearing. It was a flaw I had to actively work on.

Everyone deserves praise when they do something well, after all.

"Not to mention my innate skill to irritate anyone I want on command," I gestured to Fachnan. "Case in point."

Bishop smiled.

Finally, Fachnan unlatched the buckle binding the book and opened it up to the first page. Almost immediately upon glancing on the opening page, Fachnan frowned. He flipped between several different lenses, examining the page closer.

"Hmm," He grunted.

"Hmm? What is hmm?" I asked, his reaction sparking curiosity in me.

"Typically, the first page in a grimoire has the title and the name of its author," Fachnan explained.

"Are you saying it's not?" Bishop asked.

"It was," Fachnan emphasized. He held up the book and turned it to face my Uncle and I. "See here?"

Bishop and I leaned in to take a closer look. On the page were a few lines of text; I recognized them as the title and author. They read:

"A Guide to the Lesser Known Fae

And

Other Creatures of the Yonder

By

███████████████

The Eclipse Druid"

Two things jumped out at me, reading that. Number one, the page had been vandalized. Where the author's name should've been, there was a streak of black paint or something obscuring the words. Someone, perhaps the hag, had gone out of their way to remove the author's name from the grimoire. But what for? As a show of disrespect, perhaps. Or maybe the author had decided to hide their association with the text.

Secondly, the line of text under the blacked-out name caught my eye for two reasons. The first is the use of the word "druid." I knew what a druid was, at least in terms of Dungeons and Dragons. They were basically hippie wizards, all in tune with nature and whatnot. But I'd never seen it used in the real magical world. You had wizards, who were typically the "good guys" and made up the ranks of the Mystic Order. And you had warlocks, magic users who'd gone rogue and used their skills for selfish reasons at best and destructive reasons at worst. But I'd never heard of a druid before.

But my confusion was playing second fiddle to the little alarm bells going off in my head. Whoever or whatever this druid was, they had taken to calling themselves the Eclipse Druid. Could that mean they were like me and had been born under an eclipse? That'd make them exceptionally powerful and dangerous, right? Overall, it didn't seem important as it pertained to the here and now, so I decided to ask the more pressing questions.

"What the heck is a druid?" I asked.

Fachnan sighed, exasperation evident on his face.

Bishop leaned back in his chair. "Druids are a sort of subcategory of wizards. They have the same innate talent a wizard does, but they accumulate more by communing with nature, and by extension, the fae."

"You're saying they use fae magic?" I asked.

"That's where a lot of their magic comes from, yes," Bishop nodded. "Often, their magic is focused on healing, growth, and tending to their territory and its inhabitants. Druids can bind or contract fae to their will to use for many purposes, including combat."

I thought about that for a minute. "But wait, I thought making contracts with the fae was a big no no. What makes it okay for a druid?"

"Typically, you aren't born a druid. You can seek out one of the sídhe, the ruling class of the fae, and make a contract that binds you for a period of time or a predetermined purpose, in return they give you the power to use fae magic and control familiars. Once you've done your time or fulfilled the purpose set out for you, you are freed from the contract while keeping your druid abilities," Bishop explained, the words coming out smooth and concise.

I nodded, spacing out while staring at Fachnan's desk while I took in the information. "Wait, you said 'typically.' Are there other ways of becoming a druid?"

Bishop smiled, a twinkle in his eye telling me he'd been hoping I'd picked up on that. "There is one other way one becomes a druid. If a mortal is raised among the fae from a young age, they naturally accrue the magic that a druid would possess. The fae, as a whole, are mischievous by nature, but their idea of mischief is much different from ours. For centuries, the fae have kidnapped children from their homes and whisked them away. Usually, the child is killed, and their remains used for food or fuel for a ritual of some kind. Occasionally, the fae raise the child as their own. These children are known as changelings. These children, should they survive living among the fae, grow up to be druids, wizard or not."

"But changelings are exceptionally rare in the modern world," Fachnan added. "The Mystic Order made it very clear in the early 1900s that we would not tolerate anymore kidnappings of mortal children."

"And I assume they just went along with it," I said sarcastically.

"I said rare, not extinct. Unfortunately, many children slip through the cracks," Fachnan said. "Anyway, I believe we're getting off track. The author's name being blacked out and their being a druid is interesting but unimportant to why we needed the grimoire in the first place."

I nodded, deciding to file away the Eclipse Druid and druidry as a whole for later consideration.

"Now, let's see if we can gleam any information from this book regarding your mysterious killer," Fachnan's voice faded to a mumble as he set the book down and began flipping through pages.

After several minutes of flipping through pages and adjusting his strange multi-lensed glasses, he let out an exasperated sigh. Fachnan pushed the grimoire away from himself and lifted his glasses to rest them on top of his head. He rubbed at his eyes and let out another breath.

"What is it?" Bishop asked.

"The grimoire is written in a cipher," Fachnan explained. Its text is also split up between several different magical inks, rendering most of it invisible."

"So what, you can't read it?" I asked him.

"I can, but it's going to take some time," Fachnan explained. "First, I have to decipher the code. Then I have to piece the information together using my spectacles to view the different inks."

"How long do you need?" Bishop inquired.

"A day, at least," Fachnan said. "Maybe longer, depending on how complex the cipher actually is."

I huffed out a breath. I was hoping we'd be able to wrap this ordeal up quickly, but that didn't seem likely at this point. The killer was still at large and our information was locked behind a code by some uber paranoid druid. All we could do now was wait. I supposed I could try tracking the thing down again, but I doubted the psychic residue I'd picked up off of that finger was still present. Even if it was, I didn't think it'd hold up for another tracking spell.

"So what are we supposed to do now?" I grumbled.

"We wait," Bishop said simply. "We have to be patient, Tobias. Fachnan will get the information we need as soon as he can."

Fachnan nodded in agreement. "As soon as I have something, I'll contact you."

"Fine," I muttered.

We said our goodbyes to Fachnan as he returned his attention to the grimoire. We left the chambers, his door closing loudly behind us and began the long walk back to the Portal Nexus. As we walked in silence, something still nagged at my brain. Our mystery killer wasn't the only faerie that had made an appearance in Seattle. The cù sìth who attacked me while I retrieved Jack and then the nachtkrapp that had interrupted my late night jog.

For one reason or another, the fae were making moves in my town, and they seemed to have it out for me. I could only think of one member of the fae who'd be trying to kill me. A few years ago, a Sídhe queen known as Medb had tried to create her own army of uber vampires. We'd managed to stop her, barely. Bishop had used the Spear of freaking Destiny to banish her from the mortal world for three years and a day. And wouldn't you know it, it'd been longer than that. It seemed most likely that Medb was back and ready to enact her revenge scheme.

I wasn't completely sure, but it was a solid theory. Perhaps draining unsuspecting victims and turning them into mummified corpses was part of some scheme of hers to continue whatever power play she'd been trying to swing all those years ago. It added up, didn't it?

My strategy so far had been to gleam information from the corpses the fae killer had left behind. So far, that hadn't been working out so well. For one, the clues I was able to obtain were few and far between. Not to mention nearly useless. Plus, this strategy relied on the fae killer to appear and put people at risk. Bodies were starting to stack up, way more than I was comfortable with.

Fachnan needed time to decipher the grimoire, but there was no way I was going to sit on my hands until he found something useful. I was not known for my patience or ability to sit still.

As Bishop and I walked back towards the gateway that would take us back to Seattle, I considered our next move.

"We can't just sit and wait for Fachnan to translate the grimoire," I said.

Bishop shook his head. "Agreed, did you have a strategy in mind?"

"Is there another expert on dark and mysterious fae we can talk to?"

Bishop scratched his chin, considering the question for a moment. "Perhaps. I have a decent standing with the Spring Court of the fae. We could try paying their king a visit and see if he's willing to play ball for any information he may possess."

I raised my eyebrows at that. "You're just casually on speaking terms with a faerie king?"

Bishop shrugged. "It's not like we meet up for a beer once a week or anything like that. But I have assisted the court with some matters in the past."

"Hmph," I grunted, impressed. "So how does one get an audience with the king of the Spring Court?"

"Let me handle that." Bishop assured me.

Chapter 11

We arrived back in Seattle and headed for the car. I asked Bishop to drive so I could make a call. He got behind the wheel and rolled out of the parking lot, heading for our apartment. I dialed a number on my phone and listened to it ring.

After the third ring, a familiar voice answered. "Hello?"

"Jacob? It's Tobias," I said, happy to hear his voice.

"Oh hey Tobias," Jacob said through a yawn.

Jacob Lewis had been my best friend for years. It wasn't until a few years ago that I'd learned he was a golem, created by the Mystic Order to protect fledgling wizards who were ignorant of their power, among other things.

"Sorry, did I wake you?" I asked.

"Yeah, it's no biggie though," He grumbled. "I was just hoping I'd get to sleep in for once."

I frowned. "Wait, where are you?"

"Shibuya. There were some rogue yōkai causing trouble for some small-time wizards over here. I was sent to help out." Jacob explained. Clarity came to his voice as he spoke as he shook off the last remnants of sleep.

"Well, I hate to drag you from one crisis to another, but I could use some help over here," I said apologetically.

"It's no issue. I was heading back stateside today anyways. What's going on?"

I explained to Jacob everything that had been going on for the last day and a half, including how I'd come across Jack of the Lantern and my encounters with the fae skulking about town.

"Huh, never heard of anything that leaves mummified corpses behind," Jacob said. "Believe it or not, it's not super common. Most supernatural predators, fae or otherwise, prefer not to leave evidence of their kills."

"And thus, my problem," I admitted. "Now Bishop and I are planning to pay a visit to the Spring Court. I was hoping you'd be down to come along. I wouldn't mind having some golem muscle covering my back."

"You expecting a fight?"

"No, but I've nearly died two or three times in less than twelve hours, and it's making me jumpy."

Jacob chuckled. "Fair enough. Give me a couple hours. I'll be there soon."

"Alright, thanks man." I said.

"Later."

Before I could return the goodbye, the line clicked. No one has any common courtesy anymore. I'd give Jacob flak for it later. I stuffed my phone in my pocket and looked over at Bishop.

He'd looked worse. My uncle's skin was still pale and looked a little tight around his neck, but his eyes had a clarity that was becoming rarer for him these days.

"How ya feeling, Unc?" I asked.

Bishop rolled his neck and adjusted his grip on the steering wheel. "Besides my slip up earlier this evening, I'm feeling well. This fae killer case has me worried though. It pains me that I can't be more help."

I waved a hand dismissively. "Don't worry about it. I know how hard this vamp thing is on you. Just get your rest and save your strength for when shit goes sideways. Let me worry about the leg work."

Bishop smiled. "Thank you, nephew. We'll be home soon. Once Jacob gets here, we'll make our way to meet with the Spring Court."

***

A couple of hours later, there was a knock at the door. I rose to open the door and was greeted by Jacob. It was eerie how little he'd changed in the last few years. Jacob was tall and thick with muscle, his dark skin pulled taut around bulging biceps, triceps, and whatever other -ceps a person might have. People use words like chiseled and sculpted when describing incredible physiques, but for Jacob it was literal. He was a golem, after all. He was created to be a guardian of the weak, with all the physical prowess he needed to do so. Throw in a little bit of magic and some shapeshifting and Jacob was definitely someone you wanted on your side in a fight.

His skin was like polished bronze, his complexion always perfect. The only blemish to distract from his otherwise perfect physique was a large honker of a nose. Back in the day, I'd gotten in a fight or two with people who thought they could get away with making fun of his appearance. He used to sport a nice head of curly hair, but he'd apparently taken to shaving it.

"Buddy!" I grinned as we clasped hands and pulled each other in for a brotherly hug. Well, it was more like he pulled me into it. I couldn't pull Jacob anywhere if I tried.

"Good to see you man," Jacob said, releasing me from his grip. "Though it always seems like you're dragging me into a mess."

I scratched the back of my head. "Yeah, sorry about that," Then I added, "I hate pulling you away from your glamorous vacations disguised as missions."

"Hardy har," Jacob waved away the comment. "Just because I was staying at a glamorous five star hotel just minutes away from Shibuya's nightlife, including all the best food spots, arcades, clubs, yadda yadda yadda, doesn't mean I wasn't working."

I gave him a suspiciously amused look.

Jacob held his hands up in surrender. "Okay, so maybe I indulged a little. But it was all part of the job."

"Right," I chuckled.

I moved to the side so Jacob could come in. Bishop rose to meet him and the two shook hands.

"Jacob, always good to see you, kid." Bishop said.

"I could say the same to you, sir," Jacob said.

"You're up to speed on the current situation, right?"

"Yes sir, and ready to help," Jacob nodded. "And after all this time, I never have visited Tír na nÓg proper. Should be fun."

"Just remember, we're going on business. I need you both on full alert." Bishop said, turning to face me as he spoke.

"Yeah yeah, I know the drill." I grunted.

Bishop nodded. "Okay then, let's get moving. Tobias, you're driving."

***

I chugged the last couple of swigs from my energy drink, crushing the can as we pulled off the highway. Our destination was somewhere I'd been once before. But last time, I'd been ignorant about its connections to the realm of the fae.

Mount Rainier National Park was a beautiful place. I only wished I'd get to visit when I wasn't on the job. And for that matter, during daylight hours. I pulled into the parking lot where the visitor center was located and parked in one of the many open spots. Bishop was the first to get out of the car. He pulled a lever on his seat that pulled it forward, allowing Jacob to extract himself from the back seat. The Super Bee's backseat was not known for its spaciousness, and Jacob had to contort his body into an uncomfortable position just to fit.

I got out last and watched Jacob stretch his arms and legs to get rid of the kinks and aches. It seemed unfair that someone whose body was made from magical stone and clay could still get sore. I opened the trunk and looked through my duffel bag until I found my baldric and put it under my jacket. Then, I retrieved my polearm, which snapped magnetically to the baldric through my jacket. As I moved stuff around in the duffel, making sure I had everything, I bumped my hand against something hard and round.

"Ow!" An annoyingly loud voice cried out.

I recognized the voice immediately, pushing aside a spare change of clothes until I found the source of the complaint.

"Jack, what the hell are you doing in here?" I growled.

"It wasn't me, kid! I swear! I didn't even want to come along! I friggin' hate faeries!" Jack's glowing green flames danced frantically, matching his voice.

"I packed him in your bag," Bishop chimed in. "As annoying as he is, the pumpkin might prove useful. Plus, who knows what kind of trouble he could get himself into if we keep leaving him alone."

I let out a breath. "Fair enough,"

I reached back into the bag until I found a leather throng. I looped it around my belt and made sure it was secure, then I looped it around Jack's pumpkin. It hung a bit loosely around my waist, so that Jack was resting against my thigh. It would have to do.

Jack did not seem too pleased at his travel accommodations. He was muttering something about indignities to himself, but I decided it was best to tune him out. There were more important things to focus on. Like the distinct change in weather.

It felt much colder at the national park than it had back in the city. There was distance and time of day to consider, but even at night, Seattle had been noticeably warm. Seattle had been plagued by uncharacteristically warm weather for the last few years. Warm weather was far from unheard of in Washington, but it'd been sticking around longer than usual and increasing in temperature with each passing year.

Global warming could be partly to blame, but given all the recent fae activity, I was inclined to believe they had something to do with it. The fae had a distinct relationship with the mortal world. They were a reflection of nature itself. When there was trouble among the fae, the natural world responded in kind. Have you ever turned on the news and heard reports of increased earthquake activity or unusually powerful hurricanes? Chances are, something was going on with the fae.

There are two notable factions of faeries; Seelie and Unseelie.

The Seelie fae were closer to humans and the natural world in their appearance and overall demeanor. They were associated with sunshine, rebirth, thriving ecosystems, and the like. Don't get me wrong, the Seelie fae were still sneaky, mischievous, and dangerous, but they were more likely to sour your milk or move all your furniture one inch to the left, rather than murder you or curse your bloodline, should you piss them off.

Then there's the Unseelie fae, they represented a darker side of mankind and nature. Darkness, decay, and disease was their forte. They were also known for their tricks and such, but their idea of a practical joke was cutting your leg off or plaguing your entire village with an extremely aggressive strain of smallpox. And that was if they were in a good mood.

Luckily for us, we were off to meet with the Spring Court. The Spring Court was one of two courts that made up the Seelie fae. And with Bishop's apparent good standing with the Spring Court, I was only feeling a bit uneasy at the prospect of meeting with them.

But if we were meeting with the Spring Court, why was Mount Rainier National Park, a supposed gateway to the Spring Court's territory, so cold and foggy? The forest's edge was coated in a thick blanket of fog. Even squinting my eyes, I couldn't see past the first row of trees into the forest. Coincidence? With my luck, I doubted it.

"What do you make of this fog, Jack?" I jostled the pumpkin.

Jack's green flames dimmed slightly, as if he were squinting. "Looks spooky."

I sighed. "Any *useful* input?"

"The drastic weather difference could be due to some turmoil between the fae," Jacob suggested, scratching his chin.

"Or it could just be normal weather. Cities are naturally hotter due to all the asphalt and metal in urban areas." Bishop countered.

"Hard to see until we get Yonder-side," Jack added. "But I have a bad feeling in my stem. You should keep your eyes peeled."

I nodded. "Alright Bishop, you know where this gateway is right? Lead the way."

"Alright, let's go, boys," Bishop took off at a brisk walk to the edge of the forest.

Jacob and I exchanged a look and then followed after my uncle into the fog.

***

Our trek into the spooky forest was surprisingly uneventful. Besides the normal sounds of nature making me jump every two minutes, there wasn't a single incident where some monstrosity tried to eat my face.

My last trip to Mount Rainier wasn't nearly as relaxing. There were way more encounters with Bigfoot, a skinwalker, and a covert government shadow organization. This time around, the only thing I had to worry about was one very irritable squirrel whose tail I'd accidentally stomped on during our hike. I swear that little rodent was dropping acorns on my head for the rest of the hike.

I watched the squirrel with a look of disdain as it disappeared into the trees once more. "Remind me why we couldn't bring Scout?"

"This is supposed to be a friendly visit," Bishop said. "The fae are a jumpy and suspicious folk. How would you feel if someone strolled up to your house brandishing assault rifles and grenades?"

"Point taken,"

After an hour of hiking, we'd arrived at our destination. It was a dip in the landscape, surrounded by thick foliage on all sides. The deep, concave area was nearly clear of any and all plants and debris. It took me a moment to realize I'd been here before. The scenery looked different, especially with the thick fog obscuring our vision, but I was positive I'd been here before.

"Huh," I said intelligently.

"What's up?" Jacob asked.

"Remember that job I did for Lugh last year?"

"I think I remember you mentioning something about a skinwalker that had taken up residence around here."

"Yeah that," I confirmed. "This is the spot where we had our showdown. The skinwalker had his ritual set up here. Nutcase nearly killed me while trying to turn himself into a demigod."

"That makes sense," Bishop said. "The location, I mean. This may just look like a deep clearing in the woods. But this spot will take us straight to the heart of Spring. So there's a lot of energy flowing around here. Assuming the skinwalker isn't stupid, he probably picked this place so his ritual could piggyback on the natural confluence of energies."

"Huh, the more you know," I said. "So how do we cross over to Tír na nÓg?"

"Right, this is something we never really went over in your training," Bishop said thoughtfully. With a twist of his wrist, Bishop's staff appeared in his hand. He pointed his staff in front of him, and I could feel the tension in the air as he gathered his power. Then he said, "*Thýra...*"

Bishop drew a line in the air with his staff, starting from shoulder height and ending near his waist. At first, nothing happened. But then, a cloudy rift parted the thin air. Light shone from it as it widened into a person-sized gash in the fabric of reality. The haze and light coming from the rift completely obscured whatever was on the other side.

My eyebrows raised, impressed as I took in the feat of magic my uncle had just performed. I did my best to commit the technique to memory, in case I ever had to replicate it.

Bishop cocked his head. "Let's go."

Then Bishop stepped through the rift. I looked over to Jacob, who gestured back towards the rift.

"After you," He said.

I took a deep breath, then followed after my uncle into the unknown.

Chapter 12

My senses were overwhelmed by the sudden change in atmosphere and lighting. I felt an intense wave of vertigo wash over me as well, as if I'd stepped into a sudden change in elevation. I blinked several times, trying to clear my vision. As my surroundings became clearer, my eyes widened in awe as I took in the new sights and sounds of Tír na nÓg, the realm of the fae.

We stood on a hill covered in bright green grass. Overhead, there was a white-hot ball of light that floated high in the sky. Though sky didn't seem to be the right word. Far beyond the "sun" was pure darkness, as if we were in a cavern deep underground. A look behind me revealed a rocky cliff face covered in glowing moss that seemed to keep going up and up...and up.

Before me was a vast forest, as vibrant as the first day of spring. The deciduous trees were full of leaves in various bright shades of green that swayed in the light breeze flowing over the land. Pinks, reds, and yellows were speckled throughout the landscape as the trees and other plants beared beautiful flowers.

A pair of blue jays flitted past my head, singing their avian song as they headed back for their nest. A mother rabbit and her kittens hopped over a log as they returned to their burrow. Bumblebees buzzed loudly as they brought pollen back to their hive. It was an image of beauty and serenity.

So it really spoiled the mood when the explosions started.

Bishop, Jacob, and I exchanged alarmed looks as an unspoken understanding settled between us. There was trouble ahead. Without a word, we all surged forward. Bishop held his staff extended to his side as he ran, and I could feel him gathering power into the magical focus. On the other side of me, Jacob's hands and forearms took on a rocky texture that glowed with a faint golden-green light.

I pulled my polearm over my shoulder and gripped it with both hands as we ran. Jack, clearly a valiant spirit, screamed bloody murder and begged us to run the other way. We rushed into the forest, towards the sound of explosions and fighting. I felt the adrenaline rush through my veins, preparing me for the fight ahead of us.

It didn't take long for us to arrive on the brutal scene and I did my best to take in the details as quickly as possible. Directly in front of us, was a group clad in black and azure armor. There were a dozen or so redcaps wielding bronze axes and sickles, riding atop various horse-like fae with black coats so deep they almost looked blue and green. I recognized the horse fae as unicorns and kelpie. They all gave off an air of decay and swamp water that made my nose sting. Several ogres and their hairier cousins, known as bugganes, rampaged alongside the horsebound fae.

I watched as an ogre, ten feet tall and packed with thick, ugly muscle, hurled a boulder the size of a small car at the defending forces. I heard distressed cries and saw bloody splatters and body parts fly through the air.

The defending forces were clad in armor made up of green, purple, and silver hues. Amidst the chaos, I noticed several centaur archers who fired glowing emerald and violet energies into the invading forces, felling several redcaps and their mounts.

Two trolls, a smaller but just as ferocious relative of the invading ogres, met one of the latter in battle. The two trolls wielded large wooden clubs with wild enthusiasm. One troll leaped up towards the ogre's head while its ally ran in a linebacker's tackle.

Together, the two trolls were able to take down the ogre and beat it into a bloody pulp.

I watched as a dryad sung a beautiful melody that pierced through the sound of fighting and chaos and sent the surrounding forestry into a frenzy. Branches and vines whipped and bound the invading forces, but ultimately, the defenders were fighting a losing battle.

"What the hell am I looking at?" I shouted towards Bishop.

Bishop pointed towards the side wearing the green, purple, and silver armor. "That's the Spring Court's guard." Then he pointed towards their attackers. "And that would be an Unseelie attack squad, probably Winter."

"So hit the guys in black, simple enough!" I yelled, though it was hard to hear even my own voice with all the sounds of battle overwhelming me.

Bishop nodded, brandishing his staff and rushing to assist the Spring forces. I followed suit, gathering my power with Jacob right on my heels. My uncle was the first to act, and I felt a sudden surge of power rush into him as he skidded to a stop, shouted a word, and unleashed an eight-foot-tall plume of purple flame that rushed for the Unseelie forces.

I followed up his attack with a fireball of my own, tapping into the prepared spell structure engraved into my charms bracelet to pull it off. Though not nearly as impressive, I'd designed the fireball spell with a bit of kinetic energy and wind added to the mix.

"*Hinote!*" I shouted. The fireball struck an unsuspecting kelpie and exploded outward, sending the kelpie and its nearest allies flying in every direction, screaming in pain as the flames consumed them.

Surprised shouts and screams erupted from the Unseelie fae as our combined fire spells overtook them. But many more of the Unseelie fae were only fueled by the sudden emergence of a new enemy. The two remaining ogres turned their attention to Bishop and I, pure malice radiating from them.

Ogres were humanoid fae, thick with muscle, large distended bellies, protruding tusks, and constantly exuding a foul odor that would make a skunk blush. They were purely physical brutes who preferred to smash the problem and ask questions later. Wizards preferred to keep their opponents at a distance, especially opponents as big and strong as ogres. They could rip a man in half without breaking a sweat.

So needless to say, it was very alarming when the two ogres charged straight for us. I nearly pissed my pants, but my panic didn't last long as my best friend shouted a battle cry and sailed through the air overhead and straight into one of the ogres, the two of them tumbling down to the ground in a chaotic flurry of flying fists. That left just one ogre for my uncle and I to take down. Bishop and I had practiced various drills and maneuvers for fighting together, including the practice of taking down much larger, physically imposing adversaries.

"*Igni gladius!*" Bishop shouted as he spun down into a three-point stance. A white-hot blade of flame expanded from the tip of his staff as he spun, nearly missing me as it cascaded down and perfectly cleaved through the ogre's legs just below the knee.

The ogre screamed in pain as it crashed to the ground. But I didn't let it suffer for long. I rushed forward, stepping up and leaping off of Bishop's shoulder. As I flew towards the ogre, I activated my body-hardening spell with the appropriate trigger word. My skin and muscle became as tough as steel moments before I landed on the ogre's head, driving my fist into the back of its skull with all my might.

The ogre's ugly head exploded into a bloody mess as it stopped struggling. I nearly hurled as the rancid smell of blood and the ogre's natural odor assaulted my nostrils.

I looked up to see Jacob drive his enlarged stony fist down into the ogre's face, killing it instantly. Once we were sure we were all alive and well, we turned our attention back to the larger battle at hand.

Our arrival had sent the Unseelie fae into a panic as they scrambled to regroup and retreat. The Spring fae took full advantage of this. A volley of glowing arrows felled several redcaps. Two sídhe warriors worked in a coordinated effort to take down a buggane with silver blades.

The remaining Unseelie forces seemed to get the hint. This was a losing battle, to stay meant they would die. A few remaining redcaps, with and without fae steeds, called for a retreat. Their horses cried out as their reins were tugged back the way they came. One lone buggane ran after them on all fours, the motion reminding me much of a gorilla.

I puffed out a breath. "Man, I didn't even get to use any of my faerie jokes."

"What a shame," Jacob rolled his eyes, but I could tell his heart wasn't in it.

I heard a rush of boots and hooves beat the ground. Next thing I knew, we were surrounded by the Spring fae who we'd just gone out of our way to save. I held up my polearm across my body in a defensive stance, ready for a fight. Jacob was in a boxer's stance, ready to back me up and throw down. But I noticed my uncle was leaning on his staff, and looked far from prepared for a fight.

"Uh, uncle?" I said unsuredly.

"Stand down, boys," Bishop said sternly.

"Drop your weapons!" One of the centaurs shouted. I had a feeling he might've been someone important. His armor was more flashy and had fancy gold trimming, presumably advertising his status as some sort of general.

"And if we don't?" I shot back.

"Tobias! I said stand down!" Bishop snapped.

"Bunch of ungrateful pixies," I muttered. I glared at the centaur, but I obeyed and dropped my polearm to the ground.

"Stand aside, Loxias," A new voice said.

The centaur, presumably Loxias, sidestepped to allow the new arrival to approach. The sídhe was one of the most beautiful men I'd ever seen. Ryan Reynolds, eat your heart out. He was around 6'5", give or take an inch with perfectly pristine silver armor with green filigree patterns carved into the edges. His eyes were a piercing blue magnified even further by his copper skin. He had long blond hair that nearly went to his ankles bound by silver rings. Gripped in a metal gauntlet was a long, similarly ornate spear that seemed to flicker with green light when the light shifted over it.

"Pfft, who's this poser?" I chuckled, bumping Jacob with my elbow.

Jacob shook his head urgently, wide-eyed.

I looked at him skeptically. "What?"

Bishop cleared his throat. "Tobias, allow me to introduce you to Tam Linn, prince of the Seelie fae."

I gulped, turning my attention back to the sídhe prince. My nerves immediately took over, and my mouth was running before I realized what was happening. "Tam Linn, that faerie dude from that one book all the ladies simp over?"

I heard someone slap their forehead. I wasn't sure if it was Jacob, Bishop, or one of the other Seelie fae.

"And you are?" Tam Linn said, neglecting to answer my question. His voice was smooth like silk and flowed like music. But underneath all that grace and serenity, I detected a hint of pompous disdain for anyone he deemed lesser than him. This attitude was shared amongst many of the fae, but especially the sídhe.

I opened my mouth to speak, but Bishop beat me to it. "Tam Linn, do you not recognize me? Bishop Leight, wizard and wielder of the Spring Flame."

Tam Linn narrowed his eyes, scrutinizing Bishop. I suspected he was examining my uncle on a level other than physical. Then his face returned to a neutral state.

"Ah, Wizard Leight, it has been quite some time since you've visited our realm," Tam Linn said in a falsely pleasant tone.

I felt annoyance flash through my mind. This Tam Linn guy was rubbing me the wrong way. But I chalked it up to his sídhe heritage. The fae, as a rule, were dicks. That's just something you have to accept when you're dealing with them.

"Yes, well, there is trouble in Seattle," Bishop explained. "Fae trouble. A fae has been killing humans, and we have to put a stop to it. I was hoping I could speak with your father on the matter."

Tam Linn's eyes flashed with a dangerous look. "Are you accusing the Spring Court of these murders?"

"Far from it," Bishop held up a placating hand. "But given our close relationship, I was hoping King Oberon would lend his aid and knowledge to our efforts."

"Liar!" Tam Linn growled. He raised his spear, pointing it at my uncle. The air around the spear shimmered and crackle with energy. "You have insulted the honor and integrity of the Spring Court! I'll have your head!"

Sheesh, this guy was operating with a short fuse. I had to do something fast, otherwise Tam Linn was gonna turn us all into an extremely unappetizing shish kabob. I wracked my brain for options, but I was stumped.

"Psst, hey kid!" Jack's voice chimed in, but it sounded odd and distant.

"Jack, pipe down! Now is not the time!" I hissed back. My words came out warbled and distant as well though. I frowned at that. "Wait, what the hell is going on?"

"Just one of my tricks, kid," Jack assured. "Listen, we don't have time for you to argue or berate me. I've got an idea!"

I listened to Jack as he rambled through his very bad idea.

"Are you sure?" I asked.

"Yeah, it's your only shot," Jack said. "Otherwise, this hot head is gonna skewer all three of you before you can say 'ow!'"

"Alright, here goes nothing," I muttered. Whatever strange magic Jack had used to keep our conversation private suddenly vanished like a gelatinous weight being lifted off of my body. As Tam Linn continued to rant and corner my uncle, I stepped between them, gently but firmly pushing his spear aside.

Tam Linn looked absolutely dumbfounded. "How dare you approach me, monkey?"

"Tam Linn, prince and heir of Spring, I challenge you to a trial by combat!" I declared.

There was an audible collective gasp both from Tam Linn and his forces as well as my uncle and Jacob. I noticed several wide-eyed stares all bearing down on me. Oh boy, what the hell had Jack gotten me into?

Chapter 13

"Tobias, what the hell are you doing?" Bishop scolded.

"Something probably incredibly stupid," I said as I shed my protective bomber jacket and handed it to him.

Tam Linn had accepted my challenge to a trial by combat. The rules were simple: no weapons, no armor, no magic, and no killing. We'd only bring our wits and fists into the fight. I removed my magnetic baldric and the leather strap wrapped around Jack and handed them to Jacob.

"Don't try to outmuscle him, Tobias," Bishop advised, I could hear the apprehension in his voice. I couldn't blame him, because I was feeling just as nervous. "Tam Linn is a strong and capable warrior, you're going to have to outsmart him to win."

"We're screwed then," Jacob chuckled.

I scowled at him. "Thanks for that vote of confidence."

I took a deep breath and stepped forward into the impromptu fight ring we'd set up. The Seelie fae stood in a circle that was about twenty feet across, give or take. I'm not a mathematician, don't judge me. Tam Linn stepped into the ring. He no longer wore his armor or carried his spear, now he only wear a long-sleeve olive shirt and beige pants.

"Wizard, I will give you one last chance to back out of this fight," Tam Linn sneered.

"As if," I scoffed. "We came here in good faith and you questioned that and accused us of lying. The terms are simple, if I win, you take us to your father. If you win, you can do with us as you please. No weapons, no magic."

Tam Linn chuckled amusedly. "Little wizard boy, you are only delaying the inevitable. I've spent centuries perfecting the art of war and combat."

"Shut up and put up your dukes, you metro jerk," I growled. I entered a simple front stance, raising my fists up in front of my face.

Tam Linn let out a quick, hysteric laugh and then entered a much looser, lower stance, moving his hands around in distracting patterns. I knew this guy was going to be annoying and painful to fight, but judging from his initial stance, he wasn't taking me seriously and probably planned to show off. I could use that to my advantage.

We began circling each other, waiting for the other to make the first move. I balanced on my toes, ready to spring forward to strike or out of the way to dodge an incoming attack. Tam Linn just sneered and smirked at me the entire time, and I realized he had no plans to make the first move. Which meant it was up to me to strike first. Fine, so be it.

I bounced once, twice, and then rushed in with a jab, following it up with a right cross, and then drove my knee towards his groin. Tam Linn had been waiting for me to act, of course, so he was prepared. He deflected the jab with a simple block, then slipped passed the punch and ended up behind me. I did my best to adjust, pulling back the knee strike and twisting back into a fighting stance facing Tam Linn.

But the sídhe prince was already on the move, unleashing a flurry of jabs and elbows aimed at my face, chest, and joints. Tam Linn was fast as hell and it was all I could do not to be completely overwhelmed by his sudden outburst of attacks. I deflected several punches and did my best to roll with the strikes I couldn't, reducing their damage.

While I was distracted by his maelstrom of punches and elbows, Tam Linn suddenly dropped to the ground and swept my legs out from under me. I hit the ground hard on my back and I felt the wind rush out of me.

Tam Linn rose and swung his leg into the air, planning to come down with an axe kick. I rolled away, the heel of his foot narrowly missing me as I rose back to my feet. He refused to let up, closing in with a roundhouse kick and transitioning into a reverse roundhouse. I leaned away from the first one and caught the second one, locking it in as I stepped into Tam Linn's space, grabbing the back of his shirt, leveraging his other leg and spinning, taking him down to the ground.

I scrambled, quickly going for his neck and locking it in a rear-naked choke. Tam Linn growled and struggled against me, but it only made room for my legs to wrap around his waist. Now fully locked in, Tam Linn would be hard-pressed to break free. He started pulling against my arms and legs, my muscles straining to hold on. Tam Linn was stronger than me, but I had more leverage.

Then he changed tactics and started dropping leopard punches into my thighs and calves. I gritted my teeth as fresh spears of pain erupted in my legs. I couldn't take this punishment for long, even without proper footing or leverage, Tam Linn's strikes hurt like hell and if I gave him too much time he'd be able to do some serious damage. I didn't want to risk ruining my legs before I could choke him out. I bailed on my body lock and shoved him away, rising to my feet once more.

Tam Linn scowled at me as he collected himself. I smirked. I'd nearly submitted him and it had definitely rattled him. Tam Linn snarled as he charged straight for me and threw a sloppy right hook. I dropped my stance, so that his punch flew harmlessly over my head. I unleashed a combo of fast punches into his stomach and then tackled him around the waist, and we both hit the ground again.

The fall had stunned Tam Linn and once I'd assumed top position I started hammering blows down on his face and chest. Tam Linn raised his arms to guard his face, but that had been the plan. Once I was sure he was disoriented, I grabbed one of his arms and twisted into an arm bar. I pulled on his arm as I heaved my waist up into the air, bracing his elbow at an awkward angle.

The arm bar kept his body twisted away while cranking his arm painfully. It made it nearly impossible for him to get a solid strike on my legs or gain any leverage to pull away.

"Yield!" I growled through gritted teeth.

"Never!" Tam Linn spat back.

"Tap, damn it!" I shouted as I cranked his arm even harder. Much more and I'd bend it back the wrong way, breaking it.

Tam Linn cried out and shouted profanities. I felt his arm start to pop and crackle like cereal. Then I felt a panicked but firm tap of his palm on my leg.

I released Tam Linn's arm and rolled away. The sídhe prince grunted and growled as he pulled himself off the ground. I could see the hate in his eyes as his attendants huddled around him to make sure he was alright. Bishop and Jacob approached me, still carrying my stuff.

"You okay, Tobias?" Bishop asked.

I rubbed my legs where Tam Linn had struck them. I was sore all over, but my legs had taken some extra punishment. "Yeah I'm alright," I grunted. "I'm gonna be sore for a week, but I'll live."

"That was pretty badass, Tobias," Jacob said. "It's not often you see one of the sídhe get their ass handed to them."

I shook my head. "Pretty sure he underestimated me. Even unarmed, if he'd taken me seriously, the guy would've mopped the floor with me."

Jacob snorted. "Just take the win, man."

Bishop and Jacob handed me my things one by one and soon I was fully equipped once again. We turned our attention back to Tam Linn and his retainers. The prince donned his armor and his spear once more.

"So Tam Linn," I tried to sound confident and like my whole body didn't hurt. "I believe we had a deal?"

"Yes, I apologize for my...*unfounded* accusations." Tam Linn's body shuddered with anger and wounded pride as he spoke through gritted teeth. "My troops and I would happily escort you to my father's fortress as our guests."

"Your hospitality is noted and appreciated, Prince Tam Linn." Bishop dipped his head slightly in a sort of bow.

"Even though I had to kick his ass to get it," I muttered to Jacob.

Tam Linn's eyes flashed dangerously. "I assure you boy, if I were allowed my full resources in our fight, you would not have lived to boast."

I stepped forward to say something aggressive and ill-advised, but Bishop cut me off by holding his staff out in front of me. I looked at my uncle and then narrowed my eyes at Tam Linn. I stood up straight and took a slow, deep breath.

"Let's just go," I sighed.

Tam Linn and his troops formed a perimeter around us as we made our way to the heart of the Spring Court's power, King Oberon's fortress. My body was still shaking with adrenaline from my fight with Tam Linn. Not to mention, the prince of Spring just gave off a bad vibe. He clearly cared little for humanity, to put it lightly. I made a mental note to keep an eye on him while we were here.

Our travels through the forest yielded much of the same scenery. A world untouched by man, completely free to thrive and flourish without having to struggle against big cities, pollution and human war. There were few places on Earth where you could find somewhere this beautiful. I looked to our faerie escort. Everyone was sporting souvenirs from the battle, mostly in the form of blood-streaked armor, broken limbs, and bruises. All except Tam Linn. How very interesting.

We reached the edge of the forest and were met by stone walls crawling with tree roots and other plant life. The walls themselves extended several stories high with the only vulnerability in the defenses being the draw bridge we were approaching. The moat surrounding the walls wasn't filled with water or anything so mundane. Or maybe it was, it was hard to be sure since I couldn't see the bottom as I peered over. It only led into darkness. I got a dizzying sense of vertigo and stepped away from the edge.

Our party crossed the bridge and into the fortress, but it was more like a small city. Directly within the entrance, we found ourselves in a bustling marketplace where various fae milled about, inspecting the stalls and their wares. It reminded me of a renaissance faire I'd visited the year before.

Tam Linn and his crew led on, ignoring the common folk fae, who oohed and aahed at us as we passed.

"What are they staring at?" I whispered.

"It's not often that humans get to visit any realm of the fae," Jacob explained. "Even wizards rarely get the chance, especially not to a faerie king's center of power."

"Be on your best behavior, Tobias," Bishop added. "Any transgression here will be treated as a direct insult to King Oberon. And there's not much in this world more dangerous than an insulted faerie king or queen."

"Hey! Why am I the one getting singled out here?" I said, insulted.

Bishop gave me a look that simply said, "Really?"

We passed through multiple security gates guarded by sídhe warriors. The last gate opened to reveal the throne room of King Oberon. It was nothing like the medieval town we'd passed through before and reminded me much more of the forest we'd initially arrived in. Trees, bushes, and flowers of all colors covered the room from head to toe. A doe and her fawn grazed on some of the grass that grew from the floor. A fox slipped out of sight into a hollowed out log. There was a family of squirrels up in one of the trees, chittering away as if discussing the new arrivals.

Roots from several trees that surrounded us all gathered in one spot at the far end to form into the throne. The throne was accented with several cherry blossom growths that seemed to glow with a faint light.

Sitting on the throne was King Oberon. And let me tell you, he was not what I was expecting when I pictured a faerie king. I'd concocted images of a huge and powerful figure clad in armor and thick with muscle.

But to the naked eye, Oberon was nothing more than a boy. Physically, he looked young enough to be going into his first year of high school. His jet-black hair was tied back and contrasted starkly with his pale white skin. I don't mean "gamer who never goes outside" pale white. His skin was as white as snow. It reminded me a lot of ancient marble statues depicting heroes and gods.

He wore light green formalwear that reminded me of something from 18th century Europe, fancy coat with a lot of frills and intricate designs. Atop his head was a crown made of thorny branches. His posture suggested boredom and ambivalence to our arrival. He leaned his head on his hand, propped up by his elbow. His pure silver eyes were locked on us as we approached.

"Well well, what have we here?" The king mused.

***

King Oberon lounged on his throne as we approached. To his left, a satyr fae sat at a desk formed from the landscape, similar to the throne. The satyr was writing on parchment, reminding me of a court stenographer. I did not like our position in that parallel, but I kept my mouth shut for now.

"King Oberon," Bishop tilted his head slightly in a bow. "we are honored to be allowed an audience with you."

Oberon's mouth curled into a small smile. "Bishop Leight, what a surprise. I'm told this one," He flicked a finger at me. "bested my son in single unarmed combat."

Bishop spared a glance in my direction. "Yes, there was a dispute of honor and integrity that came from a misunderstanding. My nephew, Tobias, fought in our stead. Your son, Tam Linn, fought honorably as well."

Oberon scoffed. "My son was a fool to let his anger and pride guide his actions. I hope his actions did not offend a friend of the court."

Bishop shook his head. "Of course not. No harm, no foul."

I sputtered. *Speak for yourself, uncle. You're not the one sporting bruises and sore muscles.*

"So what brings you to my court?" Oberon asked.

I noted that the satyr was scribbling on the parchment as we spoke. So my stenographer comparison had more merit than I thought. Point to my investigative skills, I guess.

"There have been several unusual incidents surrounding the fae in Seattle, Your Majesty," Bishop explained. "An unknown, seemingly fae, entity has been killing and mummifying mortals all over my city. There are currently two bodies on record, my nephew stopped the creature from killing a third, but there very well could be more that we don't know about. In addition, two cù sìth and a nachtkrapp have also attacked my nephew since our investigation began. We came here today hoping you might have any insight to these attacks."

The satyr looked up from his parchment, his eyes flashing in recognition. The satyr knew something, I just wasn't sure what.

Oberon considered the details my uncle had shared. "Very interesting. While the cù sìth are creatures of Spring and Summer, nachtkrapp's belong to Winter. It is strange for them to be seemingly working for a common cause."

"We thought the same," Bishop confirmed.

"This unknown creature, can you describe it for me?"

"I can do you one better," I spoke up. "If you'll allow me a pen and paper, I can draw a depiction of it."

Oberon thought about it for a moment, and then nodded. He looked over to the satyr. "Very well. Puck, if you would, please."

The satyr, seemingly named Puck, looked at me. I could tell he didn't care much for me. But the satyr beckoned me over and pulled out a fresh sheet of parchment and a quill that had been freshly dipped in ink. I allowed myself to nerd out at the prospect of writing with a quill and parchment, but only for a second.

I took the quill without saying anything, not even a polite thank you. You don't express outright personal thanks to the fae. They'd see it as an admission of debt, which they could use to fuck you over in a multitude of ways.

I began drawing my crude rendition of the creature, making note of the long, knobby limbs and razor-sharp teeth. After I was done, Puck took the drawing from me and brought it to his king.

"Your Majesty," Puck said in a low, nasally voice as he offered the drawing to the king.

Oberon scrutinized the drawing without taking it from Puck. Then he made a lazy shoo-ing motion and Puck slinked back to his desk with the drawing. Then the king turned his attention back to us.

"You are positive this is the creature you encountered?" Oberon asked, directly acknowledging me.

I gulped. "Yes, Your Majesty,"

"If you did not have the confident word of Bishop Leight to back your claims, I would call you a liar, boy." Oberon said.

"Why is that?" I asked.

"The creature you have described in appearance and habits is something from tall tales. A creature, should it have ever existed, was thought extinct for centuries. Reduced to nothing but a ghost story to scare children."

"What is this creature, King Oberon?" Bishop asked.

"It has many names, spanning across every human culture," Oberon began. "Tolokoshe, Der schwarze Mann, Baboulas, Kkullas, Namahage, and Nalusa Falaya, just to list off a few. But they are all one and the same. Among the fae, this creature is known as a boggart."

"A boggart?" Bishop said, disbelief evident in his voice. "They're nothing more than a story."

"And yet one prowls your city, killing mortals for a strange purpose." Oberon shrugged.

"Wait, a boggart? You're telling me that this mysterious fae killer is—" Jacob began to say.

"The boogeyman," I said with finality, as absurd as it sounded. "We're hunting the frickin' boogeyman."

Bishop ignored us. "This boggart, what is its purpose?"

"Boggarts were creatures of deep, dark Winter. It's said they would feed on the dreams of mortals." Tam Linn spoke up. "But they rarely killed. And never to the extent that you've described."

Oberon nodded. "If I am correct and this creature is a boggart, it is acting out of character. Boggarts were said to sneak into human homes through shadows and mirrors, usually in the countryside, and feed on their dreams, replacing them with nightmares. They only killed humans if they were discovered, and would much rather use their claws and teeth. I've never heard tales of a boggart mummifying it's victims."

"M-my lord, if I may," Puck said in a small, nervous voice. "This fae activity, it could be the work of—"

Silence, Puck!" Oberon's voice boomed, shaking the room. "I grow tired of your baseless theories."

"Wait, what was he going to say?" I asked.

Bishop flashed me a warning look.

Tam Linn scoffed. "The recordkeeper has been spouting nonsense for days now."

"Well, I love me some nonsense, so if it doesn't trouble you, King Oberon, I'd like to hear what he has to say," I said.

Oberon glared at me and I felt the familiar feeling Bishop's eyes boring down on me as well, but I stood my ground.

"Very well," Oberon muttered. "Speak, Puck."

Puck stepped forward, sniffing as he worked up the courage to speak. The satyr was a small, unremarkable character. He looked like the typical depiction of satyrs you see in old art and modern television. Goat legs, small curling ram's horns, and body hair covering much of his human half.

"My King and Prince are wise to recognize the strangeness of Seelie and Unseelie fae seemingly working in unison," Puck spoke in a soft, nervous voice.

The voice of someone who was used to being told to sit down and be quiet constantly. I almost felt bad for the guy, but I focused on his words instead. "In addition, the possible involvement of a fae thought to be extinct is also concerning. There can only be one culprit."

"Foolishness," Oberon muttered.

"Who is this culprit?" Bishop asked.

"The Spring Court's druid," Puck said. "They have been missing for several days. Before they disappeared, I noticed them consulting forbidden tomes. With their powers, they have the means to command fae, regardless of their affiliation with the Seelie or Unseelie."

"You speak treasonous words, Puck," Oberon warned. "A lesser king would have your head for simply speaking them aloud. My druid has served this court faithfully for over a decade."

"If I may, Your Majesty, it's also possible that your druid was investigating the same phenomenon that we are now," Bishop suggested. I could tell he was attempting to distract the king from his annoyance with the satyr. "It would explain their disappearance, would it not? Perhaps they had reason to go into hiding."

"It is possible," Oberon agreed. "In exchange for the information I have provided, I would request that you look into their disappearance alongside your current investigation, wizard."

I laughed to myself. Sure, the king said request, but it was more of a command. I suspected the king was just being polite, out of respect for his past relationship with my uncle.

"Of course, Your Majesty," Bishop nodded. "We would be happy to look into their disappearance. It may prove fruitful to our own endeavors anyhow."

Tam Linn scoffed. "That charlatan has no value to the court, father. Why waste any of our time looking for the druid?"

Oberon's eyes flashed dangerously. "Watch your tongue, boy,"

Tam Linn shirked away from his father, but I could see the resentment. The prince did not care for the druid in any capacity. How very interesting.

"King Oberon, can you tell us the name of your druid?" Bishop asked. "It may be helpful to know the name of the person we're tasked with looking for."

"Their name is Wraith, the Eclipse Druid," Oberon said.

Jacob and I both sucked in a breath simultaneously. We exchanged a look with each other. Did Jacob recognize that name? But how?

"Your help is appreciated, Your Majesty," Bishop bowed his head. "We've learned a lot from this visit. If we learn anything of your druid, we will be sure to let you know."

Oberon nodded. "Your continued support of this Court is noted, Wizard Leight," He made a gesture to the door. "You are dismissed."

Bishop nodded and started making his way for the exit. Jacob and I exchanged another curious look before following him. It seemed as though we had a lot to talk about.

We'd barely made it outside when I heard a voice call out to us.

"Mortals, wait a moment!"

We turned to see Tam Linn jogging after us. I raised a suspicious eyebrow.

"Prince Tam Linn, what is it?" Bishop asked.

Tam Linn held out something wrapped in cloth to me. "To assist in your search for the Eclipse Druid."

I eyed the mysterious object warily, but took it. I unwrapped the cloth to reveal a stick. It wasn't anything remarkable. It was like something a child would pick up off the ground and pretend was a sword or something.

"What's this?" I asked.

"The druid's first wand," Tam Linn explained. "I understand you can use objects to track an individual linked to it."

"That's correct," Bishop confirmed. "But why help us?"

Good question. Tam Linn wasn't our biggest fan. And he seemed the rebellious type, so I didn't think he was giving us the wand for his father's benefit.

Tam Linn's expression became grave. "Because, if you find the druid, I want you to kill them."

Chapter 14

We emerged back in Mt. Rainier National Park, the night still foggy and cold. The sudden change in temperature hit me like a truck, more so than when we'd gone in. I rubbed my arms and blew out a few breaths as I tried to warm up. Bishop and Jacob seemed completely unbothered, which made me feel like a bit of a wimp.

"So, that was educational," I said.

Bishop nodded in agreement. "Seems like there's some internal struggle in the Spring Court. At least as far as the opinion of their druid goes."

"That's not all though," Jacob added. "Don't you think it's weird that we didn't talk about that Winter attack squad at all?"

"I noticed that too," Bishop agreed. "There seems to be a power struggle going on with the fae. It would explain this bipolar weather."

"What's important is now we know what kind of fae our killer is. I just wasn't expecting it to be the boogeyman of all things," I said. "Not to mention, Tam Linn gave us a direct line to the true mastermind behind the attacks."

I held up the wand that the Spring Prince had given us. Just looking at it, the stick was nothing remarkable. But I could feel a faint power thrumming beneath its surface. The wand was powerful or was meant to channel a great amount of power. Probably both, in all honesty.

"What I find interesting is the identity of this mastermind," Bishop said. "The Eclipse Druid. Ring a bell, Tobias?"

It definitely rang a bell. "The Eclipse Druid wrote that grimoire that Fachnan sent me after. I'm willing to bet it has an entry about boggarts."

"I know the king didn't want to believe that his druid may have something to do with these killings, but it's a pretty damning connection."

"That's not all," Jacob added. "I recognize the Eclipse Druid's alias, Wraith. Remember when you called me about the vampire situation a few years back?"

I nodded and urged him to continue.

"I was on a job dealing with a sídhe who'd gotten too big for his britches. He was kidnapping children with magical talent and eating them to absorb their magic," Jacob explained. "As fate would have it, a druid named Wraith was on the case as well. We worked together to defeat the sídhe and save the last kid who'd been abducted."

"Small freaking world," I muttered.

"We need to get back to the city," Bishop said. "If a rogue druid really is behind this mess, then the situation is even more serious than I initially thought."

Personally, I thought the idea of a boggart killing loads of people was already pretty serious. This change in circumstance seemed to really worship Bishop though, which made me extra nervous. It was time to come up with a game plan, before more innocent lives were lost.

We started hiking back to the car. Fatigue made each and every step a struggle. I wanted to sleep so badly. I really needed to charge my batteries, but I had a feeling the night was only just getting started. Being a wizard is cool and all, but in my experience, it was far from a glamorous lifestyle.

***

Once we'd made it back to the parking lot, my phone starting buzzing like an angry hornet's nest. I frowned and pulled it out of my pocket. My eyes widened in shock.

"Motherfucker! We were in Tír na nÓg for like two hours, three tops!" I yelled. "How the hell is it tomorrow?"

The date and time on my phone's home screen indicated that nearly twenty-four hours had passed since we'd entered the fae realm. My phone was buzzing like crazy because it had a day's worth of notifications to catch up on. Including over two dozen messages and calls from Remy.

Oh crap. We'd been planning to go on a date tomorrow night. Or tonight, I guess. How the hell had so much time passed? Had we time-traveled? No matter what had happened, all I knew was that I was seriously in the dog house now, and we weren't even together.

"You didn't tell him about the possibility of time differentials when crossing over to The World Yonder?" Jacob asked.

"We've definitely been over it before, during his training," Bishop countered. "Though a differential of almost twenty-four hours is very unlucky and something I'd been hoping to avoid."

"I am so screwed," I groaned.

"What's wrong?" Jacob asked me.

I let out an exasperated sigh. "I was supposed to have a date tonight. We hadn't ironed out the details, but it was definitely supposed to be tonight."

"With Remy?" Bishop mused.

"Uh huh," I grumbled.

"About time."

"Who's Remy?" Jacob asked.

"I'll tell you all about them on the drive home," I said. "Tobias' chances with Remy: In Memoriam." I added, muttering angrily to myself.

I unlocked the car, and we all started piling in. I texted Remy, assuring them I was all right, that I was extremely sorry for going MIA, and that I would explain everything in an hour once I was back in town. As I started the Bee, I prayed to whatever gods would listen that I hadn't royally screwed up any chances I had with my fellow barista wizard.

***

I dropped Bishop and Jacob off at the apartment and sped all the way to Remy's place. I'd only been to their place once, and it still baffled me. Remy lived in Hawthorne Hills, one of several very expensive, very fancy neighborhoods in Seattle. Though the neighborhood was relatively small, it made up for it with a diverse style of homes. No two houses were the same. Trees lined the roads, providing plenty of shade while also blending in well with Seattle's nature.

Hawthorne Hills, as the name implied, was on a large hill, so the neighborhood had beautiful views of the nearby mountains and Lake Washington. In the distance, I could even see the Space Needle, but the sight of it only stirred up bad memories nowadays.

I had no idea how the hell Remy afforded a home here on a barista's salary. I always wanted to ask, but it felt rude to ask about money. I pulled up to their house, which was positioned on the corner of one of the tree-shaded streets. The property's position allowed for an extra large backyard that would've been perfect for family barbecues, but Remy never spoke of their family. Whenever I'd asked, they'd dodged the question.

The Bee growled as I pulled up into the driveway. I said a silent prayer for myself that Remy wasn't too furious with me. But given my luck combined with the circumstances, I knew I was in for an earful.

"Not too late to turn around, y'know," Jack piped up.

I jumped in my seat and made a less than manly sound. I turned to see Jack of the Lantern sitting snugly on the passenger seat. I rubbed my eyes and let out an exasperated sigh.

"Jack, what the hell?" I growled. "I thought Bishop took you inside."

"Nah, the old wizard forgot about little old me," Jack said, his flames flickering wildly as if he were batting his eyelashes. "Looks like you're stuck with me for a little while longer."

I puffed out a breath and opened the door to get out of the car. "Just stay in the car and be quiet."

"Couldn't move if I wanted to pal. Y'know, on the account of no legs," Jack's glowing eyes flashed towards where his legs would be.

"Right, well save your breath. I need to smooth things over with Remy and then get back on this case." I told him.

"Yeah, something stinks about this whole fae mess."

"Tell me about it," I muttered.

"Well if you insist!" Jack cheered gleefully.

Recognizing my mistake, I hauled myself out of the Bee and shut the door on Jack as he began ranting. I didn't have time to listen to the pumpkin's wild theories and speculation. Despite the pumpkin's claim of vast knowledge, he'd been of little help. I decided I'd try putting him to use later. Maybe now that we had a name for our fae killer, he could drudge up some information on boggarts.

Remy's house was a cozy little two-story cottage painted white. It had a black roof and matching siding on the windows. An overhang that matched the roof protected the wraparound porch from the elements. It was one of the smaller homes in the neighborhood, but I had no doubt the place cost a pretty penny. I climbed the steps towards the front door, my shoes clopped loudly against the hardwood, no doubt announcing my presence before I could even knock. Standing at the door, I took a deep breath and rapped my knuckles three times against the door.

A few seconds passed, and then the door swung open with such force that I was worried it'd come off its hinges. Remy stood there wearing a blue tank top with stretched armholes and short black gym shorts. Their male form was glistening with sweat, and their ensemble did nothing to hide their toned, muscular form. Clearly, Remy had been finishing up a workout. It was later than most people would be working out, but Remy had the unique ability of simultaneously being an early bird and a night owl. When the hell did they sleep?

I gulped. Accidentally keeping Remy out of the loop had backfired immensely. Now, here they were, showing off their impressive physique and glistening in sweat like Crossfit athlete, and here I was, covered in scratches and bruises and generally looking like a wreck.

I put my hand up in a nervous wave. "Uh, hi,"

"Hi," Remy said coldly. They ran a hand through their hair, the baby blue streak of dyed hair dancing between their fingers. "Nice to see you're alive."

The words had no sense of sincerity or concern to them. Yep, royally screwed. Move over, Snoopy, I'm moving in.

"Remy, I'm so frickin' sorry, I can explain everything. It's been a long day for me." I began.

Remy's face contorted into a furious expression. "Oh, *you've* had a long day? I've been worried sick. First, you missed your shift at work. I covered for you, by the way. You're welcome."

"I really apprecia—"

"No, I'm not done! I blow up your phone, texting and calling all damn day, and you can't even be bothered to respond!" They yelled.

"Can we not do this outsi—"

"On top of that, you were supposed to take me out tonight! And again, I heard nothing from you!" Remy's anger had hit a crescendo, and I thought for sure I was about to get slugged.

"I'm really sorry for missing our date, Remy. If you'll let me explain, I can—"

Remy touched their fingers to their temples, their eyes wide. "Oh my God, you absolute idiot. The *date* was the least of my concerns."

"Say what now?" I said, my eyes narrowing.

"Tobias, you are a lot of things. Smart, kind, funny, strong, and you have a huge heart. But god damn it, Tobias, I didn't realize I could add dense to the list." Remy's voice had quieted down several degrees. Anger was replaced by pure bewilderment at the sheer level of idiocy I was apparently displaying. "There is a supernatural killer on the loose. I thought you were *dead*! I had half a mind to blast down your apartment door, but I didn't feel like getting blasted by the defensive wards or mauled by Scout.

That...made a lot more sense. Holy crap, Tobias. Remy's right, you are extremely dense. Here I was so worried about something as trivial as a date that I hadn't really stopped and considered just how worried Remy had been about me.

"I...am an asshole," I concluded.

I felt a tug on my shirt a moment before I realized that Remy had pulled me into a hug. In their male body, Remy was a bit taller than me, and was currently resting their cheek on my forehead. Remy squeezed me for all they were worth, and I swear I felt my back crack under their strength. Through the sweat, I felt a tear trickle against my forehead.

"I'm glad you're not dead, Tobias," Remy said, finally letting go and letting me breathe.

I smiled up at them. "Night's still young, ain't it?"

"Not funny," Remy said. "Get inside, it's late and I don't need you getting jumped by some monster."

I was about to come back with a witty retort, but I didn't. I didn't want to reignite Remy's rage, and they had a point. There was a killer boggart and possibly a druid out there somewhere cooking up who knows what. There was no need to make myself an easy target.

I'd never been inside Remy's home before. The front door led into a small entryway with a shoe rack off to the side. There was a counter on top that held a bowl for keys and other small items one might grab on their way out the door. I took off my shoes sheepishly and tucked them in one of the empty spots on the rack. I set my keys in the decorative bowl and followed after Remy towards the living room.

Remy's home was just as adorable on the inside as it was on the outside. The living room and the kitchen were attached in an open floor plan, with glass double doors on the far wall that led to the backyard. The living room, and I suspected the rest of the house, had a similar color scheme to the outside: white with black accents. The flooring was a dark hardwood that went well with the minimalist coloring.

There was a TV mounted over the brick fireplace and several knick-knacks positioned across the mantel. The couches were black leather but judging from their pristine condition, I suspected Remy didn't actually use them that often. The kitchen was in a similar condition. State-of-the-art appliances lined the marble countertops. Everything was shiny and untarnished. Remy and I talked shop about comics and video games all the time, yet there was no evidence of either in their main living space.

So according to their home, Remy didn't eat, didn't watch TV or play video games, did they even sleep? Or did they just go to and from the coffee shop? I'd have to ask them about this once I got a chance to get my head on straight. I'd had a busy day. Days, if you counted the time differential caused by my visit to Tír na nÓg.

"Sit," Remy pointed to the couch. "I'll get you some water."

"You sure? I thought they were decorative." I said.

Remy glared daggers at me. They were already annoyed with me as is. I didn't dare risk incurring their wrath further. So I sat my miserable ass down. Remy brought over a glass of water. The glass was frosty and cold to the touch. Remy must've kept some glasses in the freezer. Why had I never come inside before? Nerves and a fear of commitment, perhaps?

I sipped at the cool water and smiled. "Thank you. I don't think I've had anything non-caffeinated to drink since this morning. Or yesterday morning, I guess. Stupid faerie time zones."

"Time differentials," Remy corrected. They sat on the couch next to me, leaning their elbow against the back of the sofa to look at me.

"That's what I said," I grumbled before taking another drink. I sighed. "Again, I'm really sorry about disappearing on you. I didn't really think it through. I've just been working my ass off to make a break in this case."

"I know, Tobias," Remy nodded reassuringly.

"You haven't heard anything about any more murders or weird fae activity, have you?" I asked.

"Mmm, no, but that detective lady came by the shop looking for you," Remy said.

Detective Hart was looking for me. That couldn't be good. I'd have to work extra hard not to catch her attention. I swallowed and cleared my throat. "About what?"

Remy shook their head. "No idea, but she told me to have you call her as soon as possible."

"Oh yeah, I'll get right on that," I grunted. I shifted uncomfortably, realizing just how sore and grimy I felt. "Uh, would you mind if I borrowed your shower? I feel gross."

"Smell like it, too," Remy said with a teasing smile.

I scowled at them.

Remy cocked their head towards the hallway. "Second door on the right. Extra towels are under the sink. I'll find ya some spare clothes."

"It better not be a mini-skirt or a crop top." I said seriously as I got up.

"I only have a couple of mini-skirts, and I don't need you stretching them out. Remy said. "But I think you could pull off a crop top quite well, actually."

"I don't have half the self-confidence for it, though." I retorted, my face heating up slightly at the compliment. I played it off well by staring critically at the ceiling.

Remy shrugged, never losing the mischievous look on their face. "Shame."

I scowled at them before heading for the bathroom. I shut the door harder than I meant to, grimacing at the loud bang it made. "Sorry!" I called out to Remy.

As with everything else in the house, the bathroom used a clean white and black color scheme. The shower was a corner stall with all glass sides and a rain shower head with an extra handheld one for getting all those hard-to-reach places. There was a large assortment of soaps; I assumed each one had a designated body part. It was way more thorough than the three-in-one soap I'd been using for years. I turned the knob until the water began to give off a thick cloud of steam.

Once I was satisfied with the water's molten heat, I stripped and hopped in. The scalding water did wonders for my sore body. Unfortunately, I also discovered several scratches and rashes I'd gained from all the fighting I'd gotten up to. The hot water stung the wounds, and the sensation intensified by the heat. I winced, but after a couple of minutes, I grew used to it, and the stinging pain faded into the background. I leaned against the tile wall, letting the water wash over me. It felt like pure heaven.

I racked up Remy's hot water bill for about ten minutes before I even thought about exploring the many soap options available to me. After deciphering the archaic text on each one, I finally settled on one that I was pretty sure was meant for my body. The soap smelled like strawberries, but there was a certain familiarity with the smell that took me a few moments to place.

Then it hit me: Remy often smelled like strawberries, even after a long day of brewing coffee. Images of Remy flooded my mind, some innocently pleasant and others were definitely not safe for work. With a monumental effort of will, I jerked the shower's knob sharply to the right. Almost instantly, the water went from molten lava to arctic waters. I yelped at the sudden change, but it was the shock to my system I needed.

Now was not the time to be daydreaming. After I was sure that my mind was out of the gutter, I eased the water back to a warmer temperature. There was a knock at the door and I nearly jumped out of my skin. I took a sharp breath in and immediately waterboarded myself. A violent coughing fit overtook me and I had to brace myself to catch my breath.

"Yes?" I called out, my voice a bit rougher than normal.

"Uh, I got some clothes for you," Remy's voice called from the other side of the door.

"Uh, okay just a sec," I cleared my throat. Then I found some shampoo, did a quick scrub of my hair, and then washed it out.

As I shut off the water, I heard the concerningly familiar sound of an explosion. The house rattled under the shockwave and I nearly broke my back slipping in the shower.

"What the fuck?" Remy shouted.

Adrenaline took over. I burst out of the shower and wrenched the bathroom door open, pushing past Remy as I ran for the front door. I was still soaking wet, so I almost wiped out on the hardwood floor as I rounded the corner that led to the front of the house. I whipped the door open just in time to see an old friend.

The nachtkrapp crouched in a predatory stance on the burning, dented heap that used to be my car. Its wings were extended outwards, making it look far larger and deadlier. Even though its eye sockets were black voids, I could feel the hatred in its stare.

It let out a laughing caw as I approached the edge of the porch. My hands were up, ready to sling spells or throw punches. I was balanced on the balls of my feet, ready to spring into action or out of danger.

"Well well well, long time no see Emo Big Bird," I said through a wild grin. "Didn't think you'd show your face after I kicked your ass last time."

The nachtkrapp let out another series of caws and it took me a second to realize it was laughing at me. I let out a low growl as I stared the fae down. What the hell did it think was so funny?

A breeze swept between us and I felt a sudden rush of cold over my body. I looked down at myself. Oh, right, I was buck-ass naked. Not my finest moment.

"Laugh all you want, you overgrown turkey! It's gonna be all the more embarrassing for you when you get your ass kicked by the same guy twice in one week, especially when his dangly bits are out!" I taunted.

The nachtkrapp's face twisted in what I assumed was a glower. Its whole body flexed as it let out a battle caw and flew towards me, talons extended.

"Just when I thought I was gonna get a break," I sighed, charging forward.

The nachtkrapp let out another taunting caw as it reared back with its talons, preparing a strike.

"*Duro!*" I shouted. My body became as hard as steel as the armor spell traveled through my body. This time, I'd knock this joker's beak right off.

Right as we were about to collide, the Nachtkrapp flared its wings and suddenly ascended twenty feet into the air. It flapped its wings a couple times to get height and momentum. And then it flew off into the night.

I cast a dirty look at the sky as I dropped my armor spell. "Did I say you were a turkey? I meant a freaking chicken!" I yelled at the sky.

I looked down in time to see Remy standing in the doorway, holding their wand at the ready to assist in the fight. But instead, they were just staring at me with a sly look in their eye, apparently enjoying the show.

My face felt like it was on fire as I remembered that again, I was naked as the day I was born. Out of embarrassment and modesty, I did my best to cover up. But I was still distracted by the sudden appearance of the nachtkrapp.

"What the hell had that been about?" I muttered to myself. I looked to Remy again. "Hey, if you wanna see the show, buy tickets! Until then, can you throw me a pair of pants or something?"

"Yeah yeah yeah," Remy smirked, reaching in the doorway and grabbing a pair of black jeans. They sent them flying in the air in an underhanded throw. I caught them with one hand, still attempting to salvage what little dignity I had left.

I tugged the pants on as quickly as I could, which wasn't very quick. They were skinny jeans and thus resisted any and all attempts to actually be worn. I carefully zipped them up and then forced myself to focus on the matter at hand.

"That was the same fae that attacked me the other day," I said, starting up the train of thought.

"Well what was it doing here?" Remy asked as they hopped down the steps to stand beside me.

I looked to the crushed, still very much on fire, hunk of metal that had been my car. I sighed. "To trash my car? That doesn't seem likely. And it clearly didn't seem interested in a rematch."

Anger flooded through me. The damn fae had trashed my car. I'd busted my ass off to get this car and now it was a wreck. I didn't see a way that it could be salvaged at this point. The nachtkrapp had crushed and twisted it every which way it could.

"Man, I only had three payments left." I whispered to myself.

"Well if it wasn't here for you or to trash your car, then what? Maybe it was looking for something?" Remy asked.

My eyes widened as shock and dread set in. I rushed to the car, the flames had started to sputter out. A couple frigid wind spells did the rest of the work. I shoved my face into one of the windows, now half the size, and looked inside.

"Oh crap," I said. "It took Jack."

Chapter 15

I'd called Bishop almost immediately after the sudden appearance of the nachtkrapp and explained what happened. I opted to crash on Remy's couch for the night because I was exhausted and I didn't feel like making the journey home in the dead of night. Especially with my propensity to get attacked by nightmarish creatures every five minutes.

I fell asleep almost instantly and I was thrust into a dream filled with darkness. I found myself in the dark, mist-covered void once more. This is where our mystery killer, now revealed to be a boggart, had tried to intimidate me last time. I say tried, but the boggart had most certainly spooked me that time. But this time I was ready, I knew what it was.

"I know you're there, Freddy Krueger," I called out into the void. "I know what you are now. You don't scare me."

"The man-thing did not heed our warning," Its dry, raspy voice echoed.

"You think you're the first bad guy who tried to intimidate me?" I said. "I've tangoed with the devil and come out the other side."

"Oh we know all about the Fallen Son, child," The boggart croaked. "The master has told us all about your feats, wizard. We know what makes you tick. We know how to break you."

"Go ahead and try it, then." I growled. "Why wait? Let's do this right now. You and me, winner takes all."

"All in due time, wizard. You cannot stop us, wizard. You are but a child. The fool Lugh and his fae underlings use you as a blunt instrument in a vain attempt to disrupt our machinations." The boggart's voice echoed throughout the void, making it nearly impossible to track its movements.

I narrowed my eyes. "You keep saying we, our, and us. Who is we?"

"You will learn of us soon enough, wizard,"

The boggart's voice came from directly behind me. I whipped my head around, but there was nothing but more darkness.

The creature cackled as I looked around wildly. I tried to prepare a magical strike of fire and wind, but my body felt completely absent of magical energy. I was completely unarmed against the creature in its element.

Pain erupted in my lower back as five hot needlepoints pierced through my back. I gasped out in pain, choking on my own blood. I felt the creature bring its mouth of razor-sharp teeth next to my ear.

"You will not live to see the prophecy of the Fallen Son come to pass, wizard," The boggart rasped. "This, I promise you."

I spasmed and screamed, hurling myself off the couch onto Remy's hardwood floor. I landed on my face, heat radiating from my nose. I felt a trickle of blood run from my nostril to my lip.

I grunted, pulling myself up to a seating position. I tilted my head back and pinched my nose, letting out a sigh.

Remy came rushing into the room, wearing nothing but sweatpants, and confirmed my initial suspicions that they were way more in shape than I was. They knelt by my side, their face plastered with a look of concern.

"Tobias, are you alright?" Remy asked.

"Oh I'm great," I growled grumpily. "Just kissed your floor, that's all."

Remy shook their head, their expression going from concern to amusement. They walked into the kitchen and came back a moment later with a dishtowel that they'd dipped in water.

Remy placed the wet part of the towel to my nose, dabbing at the excess blood and stopping the flow.

"Thanks," I said, my voice coming out nasally. "And sorry. I had a bad dream."

"Let me guess, the boggart?" Remy asked.

After our visit from the Nachtkrapp, I'd brought Remy up to speed on everything we'd learned from our trip to Tír na nÓg, including our killer's identity and the possible involvement of the Spring Court's druid. Unfortunately, Remy didn't have any new information regarding the creature.

"Yup, the stupid thing paid me a visit in my sleep last night," I muttered. "Whatever game it's playing, I think there's a bigger threat behind the scenes acting as the Dungeon Master."

"The druid?"

"Maybe, I'll have to look more into this Eclipse Druid character to be sure," I said. "Which means I have another long day ahead of me."

"Well lucky for you, we're both off work today," Remy said. "So once we get the Bee taken care of, we can plan out our next move with Bishop and Jacob."

"The Bee's screwed," I said.

Remy shook their head. "I know a guy."

An hour later, a mechanic named Miguel showed up at Remy's door with a tow truck. Apparently, he was in the know about the hidden world of magic and monsters, and this wasn't the first time he had to resurrect a vehicle from death. Remy may avoid the Mystic Order like the plague, but they still had connections. Even so, I wasn't looking forward to Miguel's bill.

I'd managed to salvage my gear from the wreckage, but my gaze lingered on the spot where I'd left Jack. The nachtkrapp had gone out of its way to steal Jack, but why? Did the lantern spirit know more about this mess than he was letting on? As much as I hated to admit it, saving him was now pretty high on my list of priorities.

Remy had retained their male form for today. It only threw me off for a second, usually they swapped between their masculine and feminine bodies daily.

Maintaining one body or the other for more than a day was rare. They came out of their room wearing a black t-shirt, black leather jacket, ripped jeans, and combat boots. Their wand rested in a leather sleeve attached to their belt. I borrowed a pair of jeans and a blue t-shirt from their closet and donned my usual gear.

I glanced at the bracelet made of small tree roots that I'd taken from the hag's lair. Since I wasn't sure what it did just yet, I decided against adding it to my ensemble. I would have to get Bishop to take a closer look at it later.

I was the first outside. I pulled out my phone, preparing to call a rideshare. Remy came up behind me and gently pushed my phone down.

"We'll take mine," Remy said.

They pulled a small remote out of their pocket and pressed a button. I heard the sound of a garage opening somewhere. On the side of the house, tucked behind two large oak trees, was a one-car garage. Remy switched out the garage remote for a small key fob, clicking it twice. I heard an engine start and headlights illuminated the shaded area under the oak trees.

"Remy, you have seriously been holding out on me," I said slyly.

"Who's fault is it for never coming over?" Remy retorted, making their way towards the garage.

I followed after them. Now that I was closer, I could see Remy's vehicle perfectly. They drove a black BMW X5. Remy got in the driver's seat, and I took the passenger seat. My eyes widened as I took in the car's interior—premium brown leather seats, a full-touch display for the radio, GPS, and various other apps. It even had cupholders and heated seats. The down payment alone probably cost me a full month's work.

"Remy, after this is over, you and I gotta talk about how you afford all this," I said.

Remy grunted and shifted into drive, closing the garage behind us. I raised an eyebrow at that. Remy was not one who really spoke in monosyllabic grunts. I had a feeling I may have stumbled upon a sore spot. I cleared my throat and faced forward as we drove out of the neighborhood in silence. Smooth, Tobias, smooth.

It took about forty-five minutes to get from Remy's place back to my apartment. On the drive, I tried to tie all the random details of this case together. The killer boggart, the rogue druid, and what seemed like a brewing conflict between the fae. Oberon had completely avoided speaking about the battle we'd stumbled upon in Spring's domain.

Unseelie fae attacking Spring right before summer was about to begin was strange. The Spring and Summer fae would be at their strongest this time of year, so what was their angle? If the Eclipse Druid was behind the boggart attacks, what was their motive? The boggart was killing people, not just consuming their dreams. I grimaced, images of the boggart's victims coming back to the forefront of my mind. I hated not knowing things. Meanwhile, this boggart was going to keep on killing. I had to track it down and fast, before it killed anyone else.

I snapped back to reality just as Remy pulled into a visitor's parking spot near my apartment. I hoped Bishop had some good news for us. I was tired of spinning my wheels on this wild goose chase.

We entered the apartment and I was immediately tackled to the ground by our resident guard dog and badass hellhound Scout. I scratched his ears and neck vigorously as my dog showered me with slobbery doggy kisses.

"Ack, I missed you too boy!" I shouted, trying to push the dog off of me. After a couple more seconds, Scout finally relented and allowed me to stand. I wiped my face off with my shirt and turned my attention to the room.

Bishop and Jacob were playing chess at the dining table. They were lost in thought, and I was beginning to wonder if they'd even noticed our entrance. Right before I was going to speak up, my uncle beat me to it.

"I was wondering when you'd show up, nephew," Bishop said without looking up from the chessboard.

"Yeah well it was an eventful night," I grumbled.

Bishop grunted in agreement. "Well now that you're here, we can get moving. Fachnan called, he has something for us."

"He found something in the grimoire?" I asked.

Bishop nodded. "Once we know what he has for us, we can plan our next move. If all goes well, we can end this tonight."

I grinned furiously at that. "Rock on, let's get moving then!"

"Screw that, I'll wait here," Remy protested.

"Oh right," I hooked a thumb in their direction. "Remy is not a big fan of the Mystic Order,"

"That's no issue," Bishop said. "You can keep Jacob and Scout company. Sub in for me, if you'd like." He pointed to the half-finished game of chess.

"Please do!" Jacob pleaded. "Maybe I'll finally have a chance of winning."

"Borrow your car?" I asked Remy.

They tossed me the key fob, and I pocketed it. "'preciate it."

"Come along nephew," Bishop said.

I followed my uncle out of the apartment. We piled into Remy's spaceship of an SUV and headed for Light Haven.

The drive to Light Haven was quiet and uneventful. For the majority of the drive, Bishop sat quietly in the passenger seat, eyes closed. I knew he wasn't asleep, but shielding his now sensitive eyes from the sun. For the most part, my uncle had a handle on his case of vampirism. He'd yet to be fully transformed, so long as he didn't act on his urges to feed. Between drinking his elixirs and spending a lot of time in meditation, he had a handle on the virus that corrupted him. For now, at least. It had been three years since he had been infected.

From the Mystic Order's records, we'd learned that anyone who had tried to resist the vampiric urges lost the battle within a year without help. It was something always nagging at the back of my mind. I'd basically placed the rest of my life on hold to care for my uncle and to cover his duties as a guardian wizard.

"So, you spent the night at Remy's place," Bishop said.

There was a question hidden within the statement. Part of taking over his duties meant I'd avoided any serious dating altogether.

"Yeah but nothing happened," I said.

"Because of the nachtkrapp showing up."

"Yes—wait, no. Nothing was going to happen. I was just tired and I'd had enough excitement for the night so I didn't risk heading home."

"Mhmm," Bishop grunted.

"I'm serious," I said.

"You've been working with them for three years. You spend a lot of time together. Ever since I was cursed, you've been shirking your social life. And then when Claire left—"

"Stop," I said firmly.

"Nephew, I—" Bishop began.

"I'm fine. There's too much going on right now to worry about my love life." I grumbled. "I have enough to worry about as is."

Bishop frowned, then closed his eyes.

I turned my focus to the road once more. An image of Remy flashed across my mind once more. I made a mental effort to push it to the back of my mind. Remy was cool and amazing, but I didn't have time to dedicate to anything serious. Plus, I didn't want to risk dragging Remy into Mystic Order business. I could hardly stand it myself. I let out a breath and tried to focus on the matter at hand. I had a boogeyman to slay and a rogue druid to catch. That's what mattered. I'd worry about my personal life later.

***

Bishop and I sat across from Fachnan, who looked very pleased with himself regarding whatever he found in the grimoire. The book was open on his desk, the page displaying a detailed image of the boggart. There were several paragraphs in a language I didn't recognize next to the hand-drawn image.

"So what are we looking at here, Dexter?" I asked.

With his ginger hair and goofy magic glasses, he reminded me a lot of the cartoon character I'd spent countless Saturdays watching on TV. The joke seemed to be lost on him though, he didn't even crack a smile. Just his usual, bored expression painted his face. I looked at Bishop. He wasn't smiling at my joke either. Tough crowd.

"It took a lot of effort, but I was able to decode the grimoire's multi-layered cipher." Fachnan explained. "As you've already learned for yourselves, your killer is a boggart. I wouldn't have believed it myself, but between this grimoire and your account of King Oberon's suspicions, it seems to be true."

"What can you tell us about boggarts, Fachnan?" Bishop asked.

"More importantly, what can you tell us about how to kill it?" I added.

Fachnan considered the grimoire momentarily, then turned his attention back to us. "As you know, boggarts haven't been seen in centuries. Their existence was reduced to myth, even amongst arcane circles."

"Oberon said they're Winter fae, is that right?" I asked.

Fachnan nodded. "They were hunters and assassins for the Winter court. They fed on dreams, replacing them with nightmares, and used the energy created to fuel their own power as well as make tributes to their queen."

That was certainly interesting. So they weren't just mindless monsters. Their hunting and feeding had a greater purpose beyond survival. A theory started forming in my mind, but I held onto it while Fachnan continued.

"Boggart activity peaked during the fifth to tenth centuries, according to our records, which I had to dig deep to find in storage," Fachnan explained.

"During the Dark Ages, how appropriate," Bishop pointed out.

Fachnan nodded in agreement. "I thought so. But as civilization developed and the old ways of life faded away, boggarts had a harder time hunting. Dense populations and advanced weaponry deterred most overt supernatural activity. It's the same reason you don't see vampires hunting openly. Eventually, boggarts faded into obscurity."

"So what's with this boggart in particular?" I wondered. "It shows up after God knows how long and starts feeding. And not only is it feeding, but its killing its victims in the process."

"Yes, that would draw undue attention, obviously. Even a starved boggart would avoid killing its prey, let alone leaving evidence of the kill for us to find." Fachnan lifted a finger to his chin. "I don't believe this boggart is acting of its own free will."

"Yeah, neither do we. We were made aware that the Spring Court's druid, the very same druid who wrote this grimoire, mind you, has been missing for quite some time." I said.

"According to King Oberon, the druid has been missing for about as long as these murders have been taking place," Bishop noted.

Fachnan held his hands up matter-of-factly. "Then there you have it. Given all that we know, I'd say the Eclipse Druid is controlling this boggart."

"But what for?" I stared at the grimoire, my brain running through the possibilities. "What would a druid of the Spring Court be doing manipulating a Winter fae?"

"Think about it, Tobias," Bishop began. "The boggart gathers power for its master by consuming dreams. In this case, this boggart is overfeeding. It's leaving its victims in a mummified state. Along with dreams, blood, moisture, nutrients, and I suspect spiritual energy are being drained entirely from the boggart's victims."

I thought about it for a moment. My theory from before was beginning to coalesce. "The druid is using the boggart to gather power."

"Exactly," Fachnan nodded in agreement.

"But power for what?" I asked.

Bishop shrugged. "It doesn't matter. Best case scenario, the druid is trying to increase their own power. Perhaps to stand against their enemies, or perhaps even the entire Spring Court. We have no way of knowing how many victims the boggart has claimed."

"And the worst case scenario?"

"Better not to speculate on that," Fachnan said. "There are countless things a druid could do with a substantial amount of spiritual energy, given their unique skillset to manipulate fae creatures. It's imperative that you find this druid and put a stop to their plans before they can enact them."

Yeah, no kidding. Theoretically, the druid could absorb the collected energy into themselves. If left unchecked, the druid could become an extremely dangerous, extremely powerful god-like being. Considering we were all still alive and chaos hadn't completely consumed the natural world, I had to assume the druid had yet to enact their plans.

"We have a way of tracking down the druid, courtesy of the Spring Court's prince." Bishop said.

Fachnan scrunched his face. "Tam Linn, I never cared much for that pompous prince. I'd watch yourself in any future interactions. He's a slippery one."

"Yeah he rubbed me the wrong way. And I don't think he cared too much for the druid either." I said. I narrowed my eyes as the words left my mouth. Something about that thought tickled at the back of my mind. I shook my head. Focus, Tobias.

"Does the boggart have any weaknesses we can exploit?" Bishop asked.

"Like any other faerie, they are susceptible to iron," Fachnan explained. "But boggarts are especially susceptible to sunlight. I suspect this weakness is due to its vampiric nature. But the lore is unclear on the matter. If you can force it out during the day, that should be more than enough to kill it."

I mentally kicked myself. Of course, it was weak to iron. I couldn't believe I'd been walking around without an iron weapon. My polearm was tipped with iron, but it was nowhere near enough to kill it. There was probably something back at the apartment I could use. As for the sunlight weakness, that'd be a little trickier. As far as I could tell, the boggart had completely avoided any daytime excursions.

"Well your help is greatly appreciated, Fachnan," Bishop nodded to the dark magic expert.

"Yeah, you've been a big help," I said.

Fachnan gave us a small smile. "If there's anything else I can do, don't hesitate to ask."

"Actually, do you mind if we hold onto that grimoire? At least until this whole mess is over." I asked. "It might have some clues on how to deal with the druid as well."

Fachnan frowned, hesitating for a moment. "Very well, but I'd like it back."

"Of course," I said eagerly.

The Irish wizard closed the grimoire and passed it to Bishop. "There is a decoder key tucked inside. With it, you should be able to translate the text on your own."

"I appreciate it, Fachnan," Bishop said. "We will return the grimoire to you as soon as this is over."

"See that you do. Godspeed, Wizards Leight," Fachnan said.

***

Back at the apartment, we formulated a game plan. The boggart was a slippery thing. Even when Remy and I had confronted it, it chose to escape through a mirror rather than stand and fight. If we were able to track down the druid, we could interrupt the boggart's next feeding and cut it off before it had a chance to escape.

"Once we locate the site of the boggart's next target, I can lay down a counterspell that should prevent the boggart from slipping away into The World Yonder." Bishop explained. "Tobias will confront the creature. Remy, if you're willing, I'd like you to be Tobias' backup, should the boggart try and escape into the night. I'll be too busy keeping it sealed off from the Yonder."

Remy nodded. They were seated at the dining room table, eating a microwaveable meal. "Can do."

"And what do I do?" Jacob asked. He sat with his arms crossed on the couch.

"You and Scout will be keeping the car warm. If Tobias and Remy fail, then we'll need you to pursue. Scout should be able to track the boggart through scent." Bishop explained.

Jacob puffed out a breath. "So I'm on dog sitting duty?"

"Don't be a complainer," I jabbed.

Bishop shook his head. "In addition, you've encountered this druid before. You said you fought them, right? If the druid shows themselves, I'll need you to engage and stall them until we can all converge."

Jacob nodded. "Wraith is one tough cookie and she has plenty of tricks up her sleeve. When I first encountered her, she had a pair of vargr familiars that worked alongside her. She also uses a silver chain to channel her magic."

Vargrs were a species of wolf fae. Assuming the cù sìth and the nachtkrapp were also familiars belonging to the druid, that made for six fae familiars under her control. That meant I had to disable or kill the boggart quickly. If the Eclipse Druid could command all her familiars simultaneously, we'd be at a distinct disadvantage where numbers were concerned.

"So we gotta make sure we do this right the first time, otherwise we might be in trouble." I said.

"Exactly," Bishop agreed.

Bishop excused himself to the garage, then returned a moment later holding multiple sheathed knives. He passed one to each of us. I unsheathed the knife, examining the craftsmanship. It was a six-inch blade with a durable rubber handle. It reminded me of something that a survivalist would own.

"Simple, but effective." Jacob said, studying the blade. "It's stainless steel, I'm assuming?"

"Yes, but it has enough iron content to do the job." Bishop assured him.

"I'm not gonna lie, I'm not too experienced with using knives in combat." Remy admitted.

"Well hopefully you won't need it. But in my experience, it's better to have it and not need it than need it and not have it." I said.

In my training, Bishop had taught me how to use conventional weapons should my magic fail or become unusable for any reason. Eskrima, staffs, knives, and even swords. Swords were cool, but expensive to make. A sword had been on my wishlist for years. I'd even tried my hand at learning to wield nunchaku, but one too many accidental hits to the family jewels dissuaded me from using them.

Bishop tossed each of us a small black case, about the size of my palm. I'd spaced out thinking about how cool having a sword would be so I almost dropped the case. But after a moment of frantic juggling, I'd managed to grab it.

"Bluetooth headsets, so we can stay in touch," Bishop explained. "Now then, is everyone clear on their roles?"

We all dipped our heads in an affirmative. Scout let out an excited bark, his tail wagging happily.

"Alright then, let's do this team," Bishop said, beaming with pride.

Chapter 16

We waited until night had settled in to make our move. I took a nap, ate some food, and made sure all my tools were in good condition. Once the sun went down, we all piled into Remy's SUV. With Jacob at the wheel, we pulled off into the night.

Using the druid's wand as a focus, I performed a tracking spell. I'd linked the spell to a compass, and it led us into one of the not-so-nice neighborhoods of Seattle. It was an area made up of multiple cheap apartment buildings that had seen better days. I made a note of several shady-looking characters, but none of them screamed nefarious druid to me. Jacob parked Remy's SUV in an alley. Scout sat in the passenger seat, the hellhound was on full alert. His eyes and ears twitched at sights and sounds that only he could detect.

After patrolling the neighborhood for a half hour, we'd narrowed down the general location where the druid was lurking. The four-story apartment building was especially rundown, I made note of multiple broken windows and piled up trash around the building's perimeter. Bishop and Remy took up position on the roof of a building across the street.

"No sign of the druid," Remy's voice came from my earpiece.

"Copy that. I'm going to head in and see if I can't sniff out the boggart." I said. "Bishop, how's that counterspell coming along?"

"I'm ready. I can't activate the counterspell until you engage the boggart. Otherwise, we may scare it off and lose it." Bishop said.

"Got it. Alright, I'm going in."

I headed into the apartment building. I avoided eye contact with the front desk, instead moving purposefully to the stairs that led to the higher floors. I've found that people will generally ignore you so long as you act like you're supposed to be somewhere. So I did just that, following the compass I'd linked to my tracking spell. In addition to the compass' arrow, the device itself pulled against my grip as I homed in on my target. The spell was tracking the druid, not the boggart, so I'd eventually have to abandon it.

Once I'd climbed the stairs to the fourth floor, the compass' tugging simply ceased. I frowned, glaring down at the compass face. The arrow simply pointed north, and I no longer felt the energy of the spell. I tried to keep my breathing steady as I tapped my earpiece.

"Bad news, the spell died," I said.

"The druid may be onto us," Bishop said. "Do you feel anything?"

"Hold on,"

I closed my eyes, focusing on my mystical senses. After sifting through the random energies that existed naturally, I brushed up against something that made my skin crawl. It felt slimy and dirty. It was the same exact feeling I'd felt in my previous encounters with the boggart and its victims. I opened my eyes again, scanning the hallway.

"I think the boggart is still here, I'm gonna try to find it," I said.

"Be careful, Tobias," Remy said. I detected the concern in their voice and tried to put on a brave face, even though the boggart still gave me the heeby jeebies.

"Don't stress. I got this," I said, trying to sound confident and reassuring.

I made sure I had my polearm at the ready and began to creep down the hall, following the slimy, sickening sensation of the boggart's presence. I can't stress enough how disgusting the creature's aura felt, even though I wasn't in its immediate vicinity yet. My stomach was tingling uncomfortably and I had to fight the urge to yak.

I stopped in front of the third door down the hall. This was where the boggart's presence was strongest. I'd sneak up on the creature and hit it hard with magic, and then finish it off with the knife Bishop had given me.

"Bishop, I'm gonna need that lockdown spell in about fifteen seconds," I whispered.

"Understood," My uncle's voice crackled through the earpiece.

"Alright then, here we go," I muttered to myself.

I used a lockpicking cantrip on the apartment's door and then opened it. The door squeaked as it swung open and I stood completely still, listening for any movement. There was no sound at all, as if the apartment were completely abandoned.

The apartment itself had minimal furniture, just a single couch and a television sitting on the floor in the corner nearest street facing window. The kitchen had an older model fridge but no other appliances. To the right of the living room was a single door that I was pretty sure led to the bedroom. As I got closer, the boggart's aura became thicker. My nose was assaulted by the smell of rot.

Bingo.

With all my might, I kicked the door open and burst into the room. The boggart was crouched on top of a sleeping form. It turned to face me a second too slow.

"*Kaze!*" I shouted.

I focused the spell underneath the boggart so that it would send the creature flying into the air. It shrieked in surprise as the wind swept it off its feet. The boggart gathered its wits quickly though, and latched onto the ceiling. It surged towards me like the world's most terrifying spider and let out an otherworldly roar as it came straight for my throat.

It dropped from the ceiling, claws outstretched to slash at me. I backpedaled into the living room, avoiding the strike and preparing for a counterattack. The boggart hit the floor harder than a creature of its size and weight should have and immediately leapt for me again. I held my polearm in a defensive position across my body, catching its claws on the length of wood. It stretched its neck towards me, giving me an up close and personal look at its needle-like teeth.

"Dude, you need some serious dental work," I grunted as I struggled against the creature's surprising strength.

I pivoted, using the boggart's force against it. It slipped passed me and I lined up the shot. *"Mizu!"*

Water coalesced around the tip of my polearm and rushed forward in a thin stream. I spun my polearm, the flying blade of water mimicking its movements. I directed the water towards the back of the boggart's long, spindly legs in an attempt to hamstring it. The boggart contorted at the last moment, flipping and turning to face me once more.

I spun my polearm again, attempting to slash the water across the creature's chest. It continued to twist its body just out of reach of my attack. Its movements reminded me of a puppet or a circus contortionist. We continued the dance for several moments, neither of us gaining ground. I was tempted to use fire to try and fight the monster. But even with my charms bracelet, I didn't have the precise control of fire that I should have. In the enclosed space of the old apartment, a fire spell would kill both of us and probably send the building up in the world's largest bonfire.

Then the boggart suddenly surged forward, dodging my blade of water and slashing its claws across my stomach. I cried out in pain, staggering backwards. The boggart tackled me to the ground, knocking my polearm away and pinning my shoulders. I struggled, but the creature was simply too strong. It brought its face within an inch of mine. And then it began to feed.

My brain felt fuzzy and I couldn't get a breath in. My vision blurred as I heard a sound like rushing wind all around me. All I could see was the boggart's pale, sickly face and those dark beady eyes as darkness began to encroach on the edge of my vision.

"Tobias! Tobias, what's happening?" Jacob's voice came in from the earpiece that had somehow managed to stay in my ear.

"What do we do? Should we go in?" Remy's alarmed tone chimed in.

I gritted my teeth and for a brief moment, lucidity and focus returned to my mind. I squirmed, barely reaching the knife in its sheathe on my belt. A primal roar of challenge escaped my throat as I brandished the knife and slashed the boggart's distended belly.

I felt warm liquid gush forth and splatter my chest. The boggart whipped its head back, letting out an anguished shriek of pain. It scrambled off of me, heading back towards the bedroom. Despite my grogginess, I managed to flip onto my stomach and get my feet under me as I pursued the creature. It was heading straight for a long standing mirror. For a second, I thought it was going to escape into the

Yonder, but Bishop's spell was still in effect. The boggart smashed into the mirror, sending glass shards everywhere. It let out a distressed cry and headed instead for the window on the opposite wall of the room.

It crashed through the window, swinging one arm towards the upper edge of the window and propelling itself up towards the roof. I hastily grabbed my polearm and stuck my head out the window. The roof was two feet above the window. I gulped and took a deep breath, steeling my nerves. I hoisted myself up onto the window's edge, counted to three, and jumped. I flailed my free hand towards the roof's edge and just barely managed to get a grip on the old brick. With a grunt and a few seconds of effort, I pulled myself up to the roof.

A quick scan of my surroundings revealed the boggart was leaping from rooftop to rooftop in an attempt to get away.

"Oh man, I've always wanted to do this," I said. I was still disoriented from the creature's attempt to feed on me, but we were so close to nailing this thing.

The boggart was only two buildings away. If I hauled ass, I could catch up to it and end this once and for all. I took off at a sprint.

"It escaped to the rooftop! I'm going after it!" I shouted.

"Tobias, wait!" Bishop said in a strained voice.

Remy and Jacob voiced their protests as well, but I ignored them. There was no way I was letting the boggart escape this time. As I approached the end of the first rooftop, I noticed that the next building was almost ten feet away. Cartoons had always led me to believe that most buildings were arranged in tight-knit blocks, but a normal person would never have been able to make the jump across safely.

Luckily, I wasn't normal. I aimed my polearm at the roof under my feet. As I leapt forward I shouted, "*Kaze!*"

The conjured wind propelled me forward at an odd angle. It wasn't a perfect strategy at all. When I landed on the neighboring rooftop, I had to fall into a roll to avoid breaking an ankle. But I was able to get back to my feet quickly and continue my pursuit without losing too much speed. I kept running, repeating the process every time I went from rooftop to rooftop.

After the fifth or sixth rooftop, the boggart made a sharp turn and disappeared behind an air conditioning unit. I landed on the roof and approached the AC unit where the creature seemed to be hiding.

"All that time spent playing Assassin's Creed finally came in handy," I said in a self-satisfied way.

I whipped around, aiming my polearm where I'd last seen the boggart. I frowned. There was no sign of the monster. It was like it'd disappeared into thin air.

"Damn it! It got away!" I kicked the AC unit in frustration.

Bishop let out a curse.

"You should get back here, Tobias," Remy advised. "It may be preparing a surprise attack."

I nodded, scanning my surroundings and then turning back to the AC unit.

"Yeah, I'll head back now." I said, trying to keep the frustration out of my tone. "I almost freaking had it."

"We'll think of something else," Jacob said. "There may be a chance we can still track it down."

"Okay, I'll see you guys in a few minutes," I said.

I turned to head back the way I came and immediately stopped dead in my tracks. A figure stood in my path, wearing a cloak that was as black as pitch. The figure's hood shadowed their face in total darkness in an unnatural way.

"The Eclipse Druid, I take it?" I asked. I did my best to keep my voice calm and level. I didn't want to let on how much the stranger's arrival had spooked me.

"Who do you think you are to continually meddle in my affairs?" The figure said in a smooth, deep voice.

"I'm Batman," I growled in my best impression of Christian Bale.

Something was wrong here. Jacob had mentioned that the Eclipse Druid was a woman. But this character had a clearly masculine voice. They could be using a spell of some kind to disguise their voice, but I couldn't figure out a reason why they would.

"I was just chasing down your lost puppy," I said. "Lost sight of it, the ugly little bastard. But if you give me your number, I'll shoot you a text if I spot it again."

The stranger extended a cloaked arm towards me. I felt a surge of power and had less than a second to respond to the sudden explosion of raw power the stranger threw at me. With a frantic shout, I managed to call up a sloppy shield of kinetic energy. It sent me flying and I tumbled to the ground, stopping just short of the rooftop's edge. I'd never been hit that hard by a mortal practitioner before. Whoever this guy was, they were packing some serious heat. The haphazard shield I'd conjured had probably saved my life.

"You have no idea what you're meddling in, young wizard," The stranger said as they approached.

"Tobias? Tobias what's happening?" A voice came from the earpiece. My brain was too rattled to discern who it was.

I could hear the stranger's footsteps getting closer as they approached me. They were gathering up a dark and slippery power to attack.

"Piss off, Voldemort..." I grunted. I rolled towards the stranger, aiming my polearm and shouted, "*Hinote!*"

A ball of flame and kinetic energy exploded from my weapon. I felt the heat from the flames as the fireball detonated and forced the stranger to take a few measly steps back. Oh man, I was in some serious trouble.

I pulled myself up to my feet and took a shaky stance. Hopefully, my allies were on their way because I would not last long at all in a straight-up fight against whoever my new friend was.

"Hmph, impressive. For an amateur of course," He pronounced amateur in that pompous way a Bond villain would, emphasizing the -eur.

"That's what your mother said last night," I grunted. I mentally kicked myself, realizing I'd dissed myself as much as I had him.

"How amusing," He said. "But I grow tired of your interference in my plans, boy."

The stranger raised their arm again, gathering energy for their next attack. I prepared another shielding spell. The stranger fired a lance of sickly green energy straight for my head. I called up my shield, sidestepping as I did so. The magic lance struck, but grazed off my shield as I moved out of the attack's path. The energy lance deflected and struck the roof near my feet and the unleashed force lifted me off my feet and pushed me towards the edge of the roof nearest the street.

I had to get the hell out of here. If this kept up, this guy would reduce me to nothing but a scorchmark.

"*Págos!*" I swung my polearm. Spears made of ice formed where I swung and launched themselves at the stranger.

The ice shards shattered against an invisible wall a foot in front of the cloaked figure. I cursed, taking a nervous step back.

"I must say, you do have some talent, child," The stranger said. "If you were a few decades older, you might have proven an actual challenge. Shame you'll never get to that level."

The stranger began walking slowly towards me. I was nearly out of gas and this guy didn't even seem winded from our confrontation so far. I took another step back and my foot bumped against the ledge of the roof. At least I had a good run.

"*Igni!*"

A wall of purple flame five feet high cut off the stranger's approach. I flinched and nearly fell off the roof as my uncle appeared on the other end of the rooftop, his eyes alight with amethyst power. He held his staff out from his body, aiming the tip at the cloaked stranger. A monstrous roar pierced the night. Scout crashed onto the rooftop in his full hellhound form. Jacob and Remy leapt off of Scout's back. Jacob's arms glowed with a golden green light and Remy held their wand at the ready to attack.

The stranger observed each of my allies in turn. His shoulders shook as he let out a low, satisfied laugh.

"Another time, then," The stranger said.

"You're not going anywhere until we have some answers!" Bishop shouted. He swung his staff, preparing to attack.

Just before my uncle could attack, the stranger suddenly dropped into the floor. As the flames died, I could see a diminishing puddle of shadow. It disappeared entirely a moment later and with that, the mastermind behind the boggart attacks was gone.

"Damn it," Bishop cursed as the violet light in his eyes faded away.

"Who the hell was that guy?" Remy asked. "Was that the Eclipse Druid?"

Jacob shook his head. "I don't think so. It sounded like a man."

"Whoever he was, the guy seriously packed a punch." I said. My body sagged, and my vision blurred. I felt a rushing sensation, stopped suddenly by someone holding me up. When my vision came back into focus, I saw Remy's face as they supported me.

"You okay, Tobias?" They asked.

"Yeah, I'm alright," I held onto their shoulder and managed to right myself.

"When you stopped answering, we rushed over," Jacob said. "We assumed the boggart was giving you trouble."

"Ye of little faith," I said breathlessly. Even though technically, he was right.

"Well they're gone now," Bishop said. "We should return home so we can tend to your cuts and bruises."

"Not yet," I said. "I want to take one more look at the apartment that I found the boggart in. Maybe it left behind some sort of clue. Plus I need to check on the victim, see if they survived the attack."

"You sure that's a good idea?" Remy asked.

"Good idea or not, we should check it out," Bishop said.

I shook my head. "I'll go back in alone. No doubt the commotion caught someone's attention. Easier to get in and out if its just me."

Bishop frowned. I could see the exhaustion in his stance. He'd expended a lot of energy to catch up as quickly as he had, not to mention the wall of fire he'd conjured. Magic like that was costly for him in his current state.

My uncle tilted his head in surrender. "Very well, you get ten minutes and then we're coming in to check on you. Otherwise, we'll meet you back at the car."

"Fair enough," I said.

Scout whined in protest. Jacob scratched his muzzle to pacify the beast.

***

I returned to the apartment without drawing too much attention to myself. I'd zipped up my jacket to hide the wounds the boggart's claws had gifted me, and the front desk clerk couldn't be bothered to look up from his phone to notice me. Several tenants were peeking out from their apartments. They whispered and stared, but nobody had given me much trouble.

I shouldered my way into the apartment's bedroom and approached the bed. Even though the smell had given it away, I grimaced as I gazed upon the corpse. I'd arrived too late. Whoever this person had been in life, they were gone now. The body had been mummified just like the rest. A t-shirt and pajama shorts hung loosely off of its limbs.

The boggart had left no other signs of its presence behind. We'd just have to try the tracking spell again and hope for the best, though I definitely wasn't up to it tonight. I decided that I'd break off one of the corpse's finger like last time, in hopes that I could use it in another tracking spell or perhaps some other ritual that would cripple its ability to fight or escape.

Just as I reached for the corpse's hand, I heard the front door slam open.

"Police! Come out with your hands up!" A firm, male voice called into the apartment.

Oh crap.

"Look around! The desk clerk said he saw that guy come back up here!" The officer shouted, presumably to his lackeys.

I spun around, looking for anywhere I could possibly hide. The closet, it was a desperate move but what other choice did I have? I was winded and wounded, there was no way I'd be able to pull myself up to the roof again. As I took the first step towards the closet, the bedroom door swung against the wall and I was blinded by a bright white light.

"Freeze! Drop the weapon and put your hands where I can see them!"

"Son of a bitch..." I muttered. "Officer, I can explai—"

I felt a pinch near my collar bone and agonizing pain overtook me. I fell to the ground, my polearm rolling away uselessly. Freaking tasers. Multiple officers piled on top of me as they attempted to restrain me. As they cuffed me and lifted me to a sitting position, someone approached and kneeled in front of me.

"Well well, Mr. Leight, this is quite the surprise," Detective Hart said.

Uh oh.

Chapter 17

I sat at the metal interrogation table, tapping my fingers against the cold steel. Hart stared at me from across the table, her face painted with a tired disbelief. I'm sure the detective had heard many an outrageous tale, but probably nothing compared to mine. For awhile, no one said anything. I averted my eyes and focused on keeping the rhythm of my finger-tapping while I waited for the detective to laugh in my face. Detective Hart began scribbling something on her notebook. It looked suspiciously like "administer drug test."

I cleared my throat. "Well?"

"You certainly have an active imagination, Mr. Leight," Hart said flatly.

"Eugh, enough with the Mr. Leight crap," I grumbled miserably. "I'm twenty-one, not forty."

Hart hit me with a piercing stare. "You're in a lot of trouble here, Tobias. And instead of telling me the truth and working with us to minimize that trouble, you're telling fairy tales."

"It's not a fairy tale," I said, exasperated. I rubbed at my eyes. I had to lean down to do so, on account of the handcuffs binding me to the table.

Granted, I knew the chances that Detective Hart would have believed my story were slim. But what else was I supposed to tell her? It was either tell her the crazy truth or a mundane lie. What mortal police officer would believe it on his word alone?

"Do you have any proof of your story, Tobias?" Hart asked. "Where is this boogeyman now? Or the mysterious cloaked figure that confronted you just before we found you?"

"Trust me, if I knew, it'd solve at least one of my problems." I said.

"Your only problem," Hart jabbed the table with a finger. "is me, right here and right now."

I glared at Hart. The detective was starting to get on my nerves. Sure, it wasn't her fault. But the frustration bubbling up in my mind didn't seem to care about that. I heaved out a breath, leaning back in my chair. My eyes rose to meet hers. Maybe I'd imagined it, but there was something in the way she looked at me. Something like...doubt.

"You've been on this job for awhile right?" I asked. "I can't imagine they just hand out detective badges."

Hart shrugged. "Sure, been on the job for nearly twenty years."

I frowned at that. "Twenty years, huh? And you're only a detective?"

Hart narrowed her eyes. "We're not here to talk about me, Tobias,"

"Indulge me, detective," I said.

Hart put down her pen, leaning back and crossing her arms. "Well, if you must know. In my earlier days I had a bit of a mouth on me. There was moments of insubordination and leads I wouldn't let go."

Bingo.

"Leads? Like what?"

Hart leaned forward again. "It doesn't matter."

I let a smirk spread across my face. "You saw something, didn't you?"

Hart raised an eyebrow. "I don't follow your meaning."

I relaxed in my seat, feeling confident. "Did you know that about eighty-three percent of Amercians report having some sort of paranormal encounter?"

The detective frowned. "Sure, everyone thinks they've got a ghost in the attic. So what?"

"And the state of Washington reports that there's currently almost a thousand missing persons cases. Now, the circles I run in approximate that about half of those missing persons are completely mundane. Murders, runaway kids, people that just want to get away from it all. Things like that."

Hart snorted amusedly. "And what about the other half?"

"Take your pick, detective," I said. "There are things that dwell around in the dark, preying on humanity. I've seen them. And I think you saw something too."

The detective's face went deadly serious. There was something there, I knew there was. But whatever it was, the detective had buried it. She didn't want to think about it. And she definitely didn't want to talk about it.

Hart gathered her things and rose from her seat. She headed for the door. "Let me know when you're ready to work out a deal, Mr. Leight."

Hart knocked three times on the heavy metal door. It opened, but before she could exit, a woman walked in, pushing past the detective. I stared at the newcomer suspiciously.

The woman was tall, around 6'5", maybe 6'6". She wore a skirt suit the color of storm clouds. Her small face and thick eyebrows over wide, thin eyes told of a Japanese origin. But her olive skin and straight nose suggested that one of her parents was Greek. Most strikingly of all were her eyes. They were a striking gray that reminded me of polished silver. Her shiny black hair was kept up in a tight, neat bun. She held a small briefcase in one hand and was typing something on her phone with the other.

"Uh," I said intelligently.

I had no clue who this lady was, but Hart seemed to know her. And I had a feeling they weren't in the same book club, judging by the way Hart was trying to burn a hole in the side of the woman's head.

"Miss Ouchi," Hart said with about as much friendliness as a black mamba.

"Detective Hart," Ouchi said absently. She spoke with a Japanese accent, but it sounded like it'd been quite awhile since she'd last been to the Land of the Rising Sun. She finished whatever she was typing and tucked her phone in her coat pocket. "And this must be Tobias Leight."

"Yes," Hart growled.

"Good. If you'd uncuff him, please." Ouchi said, keeping her eyes on me.

I shivered. Those gray eyes felt like they were boring into my soul. She hadn't looked in the detective's direction once, but Hart couldn't take her eyes off of her. I had a feeling that whoever this Ouchi woman was, she had been a thorn in Hart's side for quite awhile.

"He's a suspect in a case," Hart countered.

"That you have no hard evidence to connect him to." Ouchi said. "Or is there some damning evidence that your department has yet to bring forward?"

Hart said nothing.

"I've already cleared his release with your commanding officer," Ouchi said. "So don't waste anymore of my time or that of my client."

Hart muttered a swear under her breath as she made her way over to me. She produced a small key from one of her pockets and unlocked my cuffs. I scooted back, rubbing my wrists as I rose from my seat. I gave Hart a confused look.

"Tobias, let's go," Ouchi said. "Your uncle is waiting for you."

This woman knew my uncle huh? It figured he'd have something to do with this. I crossed the room, walking past Ouchi. I stopped and turned to Hart.

"Be seeing you, Detective Hart," I gave her a mock salute.

Ouchi put a firm hand on my shoulder and ushered me out of the room. We walked down a long hallway and into the department's bullpen where many officers were typing away on their computers, organizing paperwork, or just shooting the shit with their fellow officers. On our way out, an officer at the front desk returned everything they'd confiscated, including my phone, charms bracelet, and polearm.

"Who are you?" I asked as we continued to the front door.

"Quiet," Ouchi said. "I will explain outside."

"Uh, okay," I said, once again sounding very intelligent.

I squinted my eyes as we walked through the front door. The sunlight was nearly blinding after spending several hours in an interrogation room. I saw Bishop leaning against Remy's SUV in a temporary parking spot along the main road. He didn't look too pleased. That figured. I'd gotten myself arrested after all. I'm sure he'd be even more thrilled when I told him that I'd spilled the beans about the supernatural world to a mortal. Scout sat patiently at his feet, his leash wrapped around Bishop's wrist. In reality, Scout didn't need the leash, but it helped to keep suspicious eyes away from the hellhound in disguise. He wagged his tail excitedly as I approached.

"Hey, Unc," I said, drawing out the words as I tried to sound casual. "fancy meeting you here."

Bishop grunted. "Are you okay, Tobias?"

"Never better," I said confidently. "My back's a little stiff, the hospitality here is not great. They're definitely not getting a good Yelp review from me." I knelt down to give Scout some ear scratches and ruffle his fur. He returned the favor by planting several wet dog kisses on my chin.

Bishop turned to Ouchi. "Thank you, Chlöe,"

"Chlöe?" I said, rising to face her. That hadn't been what I expected the woman's first name to be. It definitely wasn't a Japanese name. It brought more merit to my suspicions about her Greek origins.

Ouchi nodded. "Of course, always happy to help," She turned to me and held out a small business card. "If you ever are in need of my services again, Tobias,"

I took the card and read it.

Chlöe Ouchi

Attorney At Law

There was a phone number underneath and a stylized depiction of an owl. The writing and owl were etched in a reflective silver ink that seemed to disappear depending on the angle you looked at it. I frowned, looking at the woman.

"Something tells me you're not just some ordinary lawyer," I said suspiciously.

"Oh sure I am," Ouchi said with a flat, unenthusiastic smile. "But I also specialize in keeping Seattle's more unique citizens out of trouble where I can."

So she was tuned in to the supernatural world, at least in one way or another. An image of a troll sitting next to her in court came to mind. I chuckled at the idea, earning myself a frown from both Bishop and Ouchi.

"I've reviewed the details of their case against you," Ouchi began.

"You can do that?" I said, genuinely surprised. Granted, I didn't know much about lawyers interactions with the police.

"Of course," Ouchi nodded. "You can find out even more when you're me. Regardless, I wasn't bluffing in the interrogation room. All of their evidence against you is circumstantial at best. But I'd keep your head low for a few days. They're going to be keeping an eye on you."

"Well thanks," I said. "I wasn't sure how I was getting out of there without you."

"Anytime," Ouchi smiled, this time a bit more genuinely. "Now if you'll excuse me, I have other clients to attend to. Hopefully I won't be seeing you anytime soon."

Ouchi said goodbye to us and began down the sidewalk, her heels clicking against the crosswalk as she went.

I frowned, considering her as she walked away. Whoever Chlöe Ouchi was, she'd just saved my bacon. Now we could get back to business, I had a mystical murderer to catch. Bishop opened one of the back doors to let Scout into the car and got into the passenger seat of the SUV without a word. Seeing as no one else was in the car, I got in the driver's seat and merged into the early morning traffic.

After driving for about ten minutes, my uncle finally broke the silence.

"So what happened in there?" He asked.

"Well," I began. I explained to him everything that had happened while I was locked up, including my recounting of our current ordeal to Hart, trying to figure out her past, and even the extremely handsy homeless man I'd met during my brief stint in a holding cell.

"And then, Ouchi showed up," I finished.

Bishop nodded thoughtfully, eyes on the road. "Dangerous move, telling her the whole truth like that."

"Well what else was I supposed to do?" I asked. "It kept her busy didn't it? Not to mention it kept me entertained while I waited for you to bust me out."

"And if I hadn't shown up?" Bishop asked.

"That's why I was trying to get her to tell me something," I said. "She's had an encounter with the supernatural before, I'm sure of it."

"Maybe she has, but you could have easily gotten yourself locked up in an insane asylum,"

"Maybe, maybe not," I shrugged. "Regardless, now that I'm out maybe we ca—"

I slammed my foot on the brake, the tires squealing in protest as I skidded several feet. My body jerked forward from the sudden loss of momentum. I heard Scout yelp in surprise as he lost his footing on the backseat.

"Tobias, what the hell? What's wrong?" Bishop shouted.

I said nothing, I just stared ahead. I heard several honks behind me as my fellow drivers protested my sudden stop in the middle of morning traffic. It was a miracle my stunt hadn't resulted in Remy's SUV getting rear-ended. But I wasn't focused on any of that. Because ahead of me, standing at the corner of the upcoming intersection was a figure in a black cloak.

It looked different than the cloak my assailant had been wearing last night. Instead of being pure black, this cloak had silvery white designs etched around the arms, chest, and hood. But I was sure of it. It was the same person who'd attacked me last night. Maybe their other evil cloak was at the dry cleaners. But that wasn't important. I whipped my door open and leaped out of the car, running straight for the mystery man as fast as I could.

"Tobias!" Bishop yelled, but his voice was lost amongst the noises of traffic.

I heard claws clicking against the asphalt next to me. I looked down to see Scout at my heels, ears forward and eyes locked on my target. I grinned furiously. Having Scout as backup was a huge confidence booster. I leaned forward, urging myself to run faster. This joker wasn't going to get away from me again. I was sick and tired of trailing after this guy day after day. This time, I was going to take him out.

The figure's hood jerked toward me as I closed the distance, as if he'd just noticed me for the first time. In a blur of motion, they raced down the sidewalk away from me. I cursed and doubled my efforts. I couldn't remember the last time I'd ran this hard. I knew I wouldn't be able to keep it up for long. I could ride on Scout in his true form, if it weren't for the fact that we were out in broad daylight.

So I ran, ignoring the aches and pains I'd accrued over the last couple of days. My lungs burned but that didn't matter. All that mattered was I nailed this guy once and for all. I shouldered past a meandering crowd of people just as the mystery man blurred into an alley. I turned, skidding on my heels as I changed direction. Scout was matching me step for step, but I knew the hound could outpace me with ease.

"Scout, pin him down!" I said between heaving breaths.

Scout barked in response, and he suddenly shot past me into the alley. The alley was protected from the morning sunlight, making it hard to see the cloaked figure in the shade of the tall buildings on either side. But Scout's eyes were a million times better than mine and he was locked on to his target.

Right when I thought the mystery man had nowhere else to run, he did something that surprised me. Teal green energy lit up the alley like Christmas. I skidded to a stop, shielding my eyes from the bright light. Once my eyes had adjusted, I could see the figure standing at the end of the alley. But where the alley should have been, an eight-foot-tall portal swirled and pulsed like a living thing. Within the emerald haze of the portal, I could see something. It looked like a serene valley of grass. There was a building perched on a hill in the middle distance, but I couldn't identify any distinguishing details. Before I could stop him, the figure leaped into the portal. Scout was still chasing after him.

"Scout, wait!" I shouted.

But I was too late, my furry companion leaped through the portal. I cursed, realizing I was about to do something even more stupid than chasing after this guy in the first place.

"Alright, fuck it," I muttered.

I leaped forward, into the swirling mass of green energy.

"Geronimo!"

Chapter 18

Just like with the portal to Tír na nÓg, as I passed through the stranger's portal, a sudden change in atmosphere disoriented me for a few seconds. I stumbled as I landed on the soft green grass, but I shook the disorientation away. Now that we were away from the public, Scout wasted no time in transforming into his true, monstrous form. Scout let out a leonine roar that rattled my bones. The stranger stood several feet away, arms extended out by their side with their palms facing out.

"You might've gotten the jump on me last night," I said. "But I'm ready for you this time."

The stranger cocked their head to the side, as if confused by my words. I reached for my polearm, but to my surprise it wasn't mounted on my back. I gritted my teeth. In my hurry to pursue the stranger, I'd left my polearm in Remy's car. The only magical focus I had with me at the moment was my charm bracelet and it wasn't built to focus my power, only to assist me with specific spells. I'd have to make due without my weapon. At the very least, I had Scout to back me up.

"Alright, let's do this, Scout," I shouted.

Scout bellowed another colossal roar and leaped straight for the stranger. I thrust out my hand and shouted the trigger word for my wind spell. An out-of-control cyclone of wind rushed from my palm and ripped through the air towards the stranger. We had him dead to rights.

The stranger wasted no time and gathered energy around their cloaked hands. They aimed one at Scout and one at my incoming wind blast. A second before our attacks would have landed, emerald energy domes coalesced in front of their hands. Scout collided with the shield and the stranger redirected him away into the field. My wind blast clashed with the other shield. The wind exploded in every direction, the shield flashing brighter as the magic collided.

I was already on the move. My wind blast was nothing but a distraction so I could close the distance. By the time the stranger had dropped their shields, I was already upon them. I swung a right hook toward their hood. They ducked and countered with a tiger palm strike to my gut. I gasped as the wind was knocked out of me, staggering backward a few steps while I tried to get air into my lungs.

The stranger dropped their stance and swung their lead leg towards my ankles. I was swept off my feet and landed on my back hard, further making it harder to breathe. They raised their foot to stomp on my chest and I had enough clarity to realize that would hurt a whole lot. I rolled away a moment before their heavy boot stomped on the ground hard enough to kick up a cloud of dust.

I rolled up to my feet, barely managing to get a breath in. I activated the fire spell charm on my bracelet and shouted, "*Hinote!*"

A fireball the size of a beach ball flew from my open palm, the heat singing my fingertips. The stranger had no time to react, and the fireball detonated on impact. Flame and kinetic energy exploded in every direction, hurtling the stranger away.

The blowback from the explosion threatened to knock me over again, but I held my ground. I crossed my arms over my face, the enchantments on my bomber jacket protecting me from the flames. Scout let out a challenging roar and leaped through the air, landing so he stood over the stranger. Scout roared in the stranger's face, daring them to make a move.

"Call off your dog, wizard!" The stranger shouted.

I twisted my face into a confused expression. Their voice was not the same as the figure from the night before. It was higher, less gruff. I walked over to where Scout had the stranger pinned. I knelt down by their head and ripped their hood away. My eyes widened in surprise.

Instead of a middle-aged grizzled villain, looking up at me was a young woman. She looked to be older than me, but not by much. She had fair skin blemished bly a splattering of freckles across her nose and cheeks. She had striking hazel eyes and a cute button nose. Her most unique and striking feature was her snow white hair. It gave her an otherworldly appearance. And there was something about her that was strangely familiar. I couldn't put my finger on it and it was going to bug the hell out of me.

"You...are not what I was expecting," I said dumbly.

"Your skills of deduction are astounding, wizard," She scoffed.

I narrowed my eyes, still wary of the stranger. "Who are you?"

"You may call me Wraith," She said. "I am the Eclipse Druid of the Spring Court."

That made sense, I'd already assumed as much. But I scoffed at her code name. "I'm not calling you Wraith. What's your real name?"

"You think I'm so foolish as to give you my true name, wizard?"

I rolled my eyes, but her fears weren't unfounded. Magic practitioners could do a lot with a being's real name. Granted, I wasn't that competent, but she didn't know that. I glared at the druid. Not to mention, you needed a being's full name to do anything worthwhile anyhow.

"You spend too much time with the fae. Just your first name will do," I growled, trying to sound menacing. "I've got plenty of questions for you. And we're gonna start with you giving me your name."

She gave me a smoldering look before puffing out a breath. "My name is Seraphina,"

I gave her a false pleasant smile. "Nice to meet you, Seraphina. My name's Tobias. If you're done fighting with me, I'd love to have a chat."

Seraphina scoffed. "You started it."

I considered that, nodding. "Fair enough,"

I looked to Scout, and understanding passed between us. The hellhound backed off and let the druid rise from where she lay prone. Even as she stood, Scout bared his maw of mismatched fangs and let out a low, warning growl.

"Easy boy," I stood by the big dog's shoulder, patting his head in a placating manner. "Let's hear her out."

Seraphina brushed off her cloak, eyeing the hellhound warily. "I've never seen a hellhound so small. Where'd you find him?"

I shrugged. "My uncle brought him home from a trip to Hades. He's been a member of the family ever since."

Seraphina smiled. "And here I thought only druids could have familiars. But you seem to have a deep bond with the beast."

"I don't know about familiars, but he's a good boy and I give him lots of treats. Sometimes, I even splurge and get him a frappuccino." I held up my hand to cover my mouth from Scout's view. "Don't tell him, but I almost always get him decaf."

Seraphina giggled. It was a strange sound coming from someone with whom I'd been at odds only a moment before. I chuckled, allowing myself to enjoy a moment of levity after days of struggle.

The Eclipse Druid straightened and her expression became serious. And I knew it was time to get down to business. I just hoped she'd be able to shed some light on the events of the last few days.

"First question," I said, raising a finger. "What's up with all the fae that have been wreaking havoc in my town over the last few days?"

Seraphina considered the question for a moment. "Can you be a little more specific?"

"Well, right before this mess started, I was almost mauled to death by a couple cù sìth,"

"Ah, right." Seraphina jerked her head forward.

Two lupine figures shimmered into existence, flanking the druid. When they came into view, I recognized them immediately as the wolf fae that I'd encountered on my venture to retrieve an unknown magical artifact, which turned out to be Jack of the Lantern.

"These are two of my familiars, Kayror," she began, gesturing to the wolf on her left and then to her right. "And Feinoc."

The twin wolf fae let out a warning snarl. Scout answered in kind. I could feel his whole body rumbling as the growl rose from his stomach. I patted Scout reassuringly. The last thing we needed was for the pups to start tearing at each other. Seraphina placed a hand on each of the cù sìths' heads, and their growling subsided.

"They were guarding a storage cache I'd set up while I was in the city," Seraphina explained. Her eyes thinned as she made eye contact with me. "They reported to me that a bumbling wizard stole one of my more precious artifacts and confidants. What do you know about that?"

The tone in her voice suggested that she knew exactly what had been taken. Jack of the Lantern, of course. By stealing him, I'd become the pumpkin's master. But he'd neglected to mention that someone else already had a claim to him. I mentally kicked myself, dreading what I was about to admit.

"Right, Jack of the Lantern," I said hesitantly. "I may or may not have lost him."

Seraphina's eyes widened, flashing with a verdant light. "What do you mean you lost him?" Her words came out tight and clipped.

I held up my hands in a pacifying gesture. "Hey hey hey, it wasn't my fault. I got jumped by a frickin' nachtkrapp. I assumed it was another of your familiars."

She raised an eyebrow. "Why would you assume that?"

"Your buddy Tam Linn put me onto your scent," I said. I further explained about how I'd come into possession of one of her wands and how we'd used it to track her to the next location where the boggart was supposed to attack.

"After the boggart escaped, I was confronted by a man in a dark cloak." I said, gesturing to her get up. "I thought it was you in some sort of disguise. Up until right now, I had assumed you were behind the killings. But seeing as how I'm not dead yet, I'm starting to think otherwise."

Seraphina grimaced. "No, I've been tracking the boggart as well. I was researching the matter when I was attacked by one of Spring's hit squads. I managed to escape and have been trying to track down the killer. My theory was that they had something to do with the attempt on my life."

I scowled at that revelation. King Oberon and his court had made no mention of the attack against the Eclipse Druid. Was he unaware that someone had tried to kill his druid and was now trying to frame her for the dark fae activity? Something about this stank, but I couldn't quite put my finger on it.

"If the nachtkrapp isn't one of yours, then who could it belong to?" I asked.

Seraphina gave it some thought, tapping her chin with her finger while gazing at the bright blue sky. Then her face contorted with anger and realization.

"You said that the nachtkrapp stole Jack, yes?" Seraphina asked.

I nodded. "It had attacked me once before, but Scout and I chased it off. A couple of days later, it attacked again. But it didn't bother going after me. It went straight for my car where I'd left Jack."

Seraphina palmed her forehead. "You left a spirit of knowledge unattended in your car?" Her voice rose with each word.

"Yeah, in retrospect, not my best move. But you've met the guy, he's annoying as hell and just yaps whenever he gets the chance." I countered, pleading my case.

Seraphina sighed. "If what you say is true, then this is bad. Really bad."

"Why's that?"

"Because, Jack has been around for a long time. And I mean a long time," She said, emphasizing the words. "He spent his life and afterlife around many a shady character and has had plenty of time to gather and store all kinds of knowledge. Including all sorts of information on dark magic and rituals."

"So what? The nachtkrapp stole him to learn some dark magic? It's still just an oversized bird." I said.

"No, I don't think the nachtkrapp stole Jack of its own volition. I think whoever sent the nachtkrapp after you and Jack is the same person who's been using the boggart to kill all those people." Seraphina theorized. "I had my suspicions, but this all but confirms it."

"Confirms what, exactly?" I said, trying not to sound as clueless as I felt.

Seraphina sighed and looked me dead in the eye, her expression grave. "That I'm not the only druid operating in Seattle."

Chapter 19

I cracked the front door to my apartment open slowly, peering in as I did. Sure enough, Bishop, Remy, and Jacob were all sitting there. Bishop sat in his recliner, staring intently at the door as I peered through. His eyes flashed with violet power as he locked his gaze on me. I swallowed nervously, opening the door fully as I entered.

Jacob sat down on the couch, scrolling on his phone. Remy was seated at the kitchen table, flipping through a novel. When Jacob and Remy noticed me, they crossed their arms in unison and stared at me as well. Everyone looked monumentally pissed as I came inside. I had a feeling that was going to be the case, even after I'd texted Jacob that I was safe and sound.

"Hey," I said nervously, dragging out the word.

"What the hell was that?" Bishop growled.

"I can explain!" I assured them, holding up my hands in surrender.

"You'd better," Remy glared at me. "Bishop told us you ran off like the devil himself was chasing you!"

"If you'll just give me a second, I can clear everything up." I said.

Scout let out a joyful bark, running past me into the apartment. He jumped onto Bishop's lap, greeting him with a barrage of doggie kisses. Bishop chuckled, pulling the hellhound away. His expression quickly flattened again, looking towards me.

"You can't just run off like that, Tobias," Bishop scolded.

"I know, I know. If you'll just listen, I think you'll be interested in what I learned." I said. I looked back towards the open door, cocking my head forward, inviting my guest inside. Seraphina stepped past the threshold of my home, still donning her dark and mysterious druid robes.

Remy and Jacob were on their feet in an instant. Remy had their ivory wand pointed at Seraphina's head. Jacob's fists began to glow with the golden green energy that was synonymous with his power. They looked like they were ready to blow Seraphina's head off.

"What the hell?" Jacob shouted in surprise.

"Tobias, isn't this the person who attacked you last night?" Remy asked.

"Guys, guys, calm down," I said, coming between them and the druid. "This is Seraphina, the Eclipse Druid. She's a friend, I think."

"I wouldn't go that far yet," Seraphina said.

"I doubt that, Tobias," Jacob said, completely ignoring Seraphina's comment. "She tried to kill you yesterday."

I shook my head. "That wasn't her. We've had it all wrong. Seraphina isn't the bad guy here, but she knows who is. If you'd just relax for a second, she can explain everything."

I noted that Bishop hadn't risen to action like my friends had. His gaze had turned to Seraphina, a pensive look on his face. I gave him a pleading look. My uncle looked to me and then back to the druid.

"Let's hear her out," Bishop said, looking to my friends.

"Thank you," I breathed a sigh of relief.

"But be on guard," Bishop added. "For all we know, this is simply a ruse to make us let our guards down."

I groaned in annoyance.

Remy and Jacob looked to Bishop and exchanged suspicious glances. Then they seemed to finally relax, sitting back down while turning their attention to Seraphina and me. I cleared my throat, then began recounting my encounter with Seraphina and the conversation that had followed, up until the point where she had mentioned the existence of another druid in Seattle.

Once I was done, I turned to Seraphina. "I'll let you explain the rest."

"First, it's good to see you again, golem." Seraphina nodded towards Jacob.

Jacob returned the gesture, but his expression was suspicious.

"Secondly, thank you for welcoming me into your home. Especially since you had every reason to attack me on sight."

I pinched my brow. The tension in the room was practically malleable.

"As you probably already know, druids are practitioners under the banner of the fae courts. There are always two to maintain balance. One that serves the Seelie fae, and another that serves the Unseelie."

I pretended as if I knew this beforehand, nodding intelligently as I followed along.

"I've grown up in and served the Seelie courts for the last sixteen years, under the direction of King Oberon." Seraphina explained. "In that time, I've learned a lot about the inner workings of the courts and studied all manner of fae, past and present."

That number, sixteen years, nagged at the back of my brain for some reason. But I couldn't quite place my finger on it. That seemed to be a reoccurring phenomenon when it came to the Eclipse Druid, but for the life of me I couldn't figure out why.

"You wrote *A Guide to the Lesser Known Fae And Other Creatures of the Yonder*," Bishop noted.

"Yes, I used my knowledge to write the grimoire in hopes that I could educate the magical community on all the creatures that wandered the Yonder. I even included beings that were thought to be extinct or purely the stuff of legend." She said. "But about a year ago, the tome was stolen from me."

"Yeah, I retrieved it from a hag's demesne," I said. "One of the High Elders from the Mystic Order asked me to grab it for him so that we could learn about the boggart."

"Scáthach?"

I nodded.

"I said before that there are always two druids serving the courts. That hag is a long time associate of my opposite number. The druid that serves the Unseelie Courts. The Plague Druid of Winter, most know him by the pseudonym of Deimos." Seraphina said.

I shivered. Deimos, aka the Greek God of Fear. You don't pick a name like that if you're trying to come off all warm and fuzzy.

Not to mention, the Unseelie Courts were bad news. I remembered when Medb, the Autumn Queen, had nearly killed me and my friends a few years back. She was scary powerful, and if it hadn't been for my uncle banishing her with the Spear of Destiny, we'd have all been dead, and the world would be facing a nearly invincible vampire army.

"So you think this Plague Druid stole your grimoire to learn about the boggart?" Jacob asked, waving his hand.

"I know he did." Seraphina nodded. "Deimos ambushed me and made off with the grimoire. I pursued but his familiars were powerful. I was lucky to come out of the encounter alive."

"So how does Winter benefit from a druid rampaging through Seattle with his pet boggart?" Remy asked.

"Seattle?" Seraphina said in disbelief. "You really don't know?"

"Know what, exactly?" Bishop said.

"This is not the first city where Deimos has appeared with his boggart." Seraphina said gravely. "What he's done in Seattle, he's been doing in cities across the country. I've been pursuing him for months but he's managed to stay one step ahead."

A collective gasp filled the room. If what Seraphina was saying was true, then the body count was much higher than the handful that we had turned up so far. But that didn't make any sense.

"How have we not heard of this?" I said, completely baffled. "Surely the Mystic Order has known about this. And even the human population would have noticed something amiss after the boggart had ravaged a couple cities."

"The Mystic Order should have known about this," Bishop agreed. "But we're only just hearing about it now. It makes no sense."

Seraphina scoffed. "You wizards and your Mystic Order. Surely you know by now you can't trust them."

I frowned. Sure, I didn't care much for any governing body full of old, pompous coots, but outright distrust was another matter entirely.

"What are you saying, Seraphina?" Bishop asked.

"There are rumors, wizard. Of new players in this grand game." Seraphina said. "They have their claws in every facet of the supernatural world, even the Mystic Order itself. You may have already come across them without even realizing it."

An image of my dark counterpart, the fallen angel Azazel, flashed across my mind. I'm not sure what had prompted it. Was Seraphina onto something?

Bishop looked uncomfortable with the idea, his brow knit tightly across his face. Jacob seemed to be considering the possibility of a grand conspiracy as well. Remy looked like they'd rather be anywhere else. I felt bad, their life had been pretty normal before I came along. Now, they were caught right in the middle of this nonsense, and it was my fault.

"Regardless of any dark conspiracy, right now we have to worry about the issue at hand. This plague druid and whatever plans he has for this boggart." Bishop said.

"Oh it gets worse," I assured him. "You remember how Jack was stolen?"

My uncle nodded.

"Jack of the Lantern previously belonged to me, before you went out of your way to procure him from where I'd stashed him away." Seraphina said. "As a spirit of power and knowledge, he possesses information that could prove extremely dangerous in the wrong hands."

"What kind of information?" Remy asked.

"The kind that could make Deimos into a god, or the next best thing. Or he could start a global plague that makes the Black Plague look like a sunny Saturday morning. The kind that would give him the power to smite gods." Seraphina said, listing off a few grave examples.

"We think," I gestured from myself to Seraphina. "that Deimos has been using the boggart to gather life energy in order to power whatever ritual he has planned. It doesn't matter what exactly he plans to do. No matter what, it's bad news."

"The kind of bad news that could upset balance between the fae courts." Seraphina said.

"The kind that could upset the balance to the entire world." I amended.

"Same thing," Jacob said gravely. "How do we stop him?"

"Now there comes the tricky part," I said.

"We have no way of tracking down the Plague Druid." Seraphina said, dread in her voice. "My tracking spells have never been able to pin him down."

"What could stop a tracking spell from honing in on him?" Remy said.

"Many things can interfere with tracking spells. Running water, or if he were to be in a different realm, for example. But even then, the tracking spells could at least point us in a general direction." Seraphina said. "But my tracking spells have been stopped cold completely. Something is protecting him."

"Or someone," I said dramatically.

That earned me a glare from almost everyone in the room except Scout, who'd been occupying himself with an extra durable chew toy.

"To completely negate a tracking spell would require some incredibly powerful magic," Bishop said. "One of the rulers of the fae could do it. And definitely the ancient gods."

"Deimos works for Winter, right?" I said. "So let's assume that..." I trailed off as I tried to remember the name of the ruling queen of Winter.

"Mab," Jacob supplied.

"Mab," I said, as if I'd remembered it on my own. "Let's assume that Mab is the one protecting him. And that for one reason or another, she wants to throw the entire world into chaos."

"The simplest solution, and all that," Remy nodded.

"It doesn't matter who's hiding Deimos' location, we still need to figure out a way to find him before he can perform whatever ritual he's cooking up." Jacob said.

Bishop sat up straight, his eyes wide. Without a word, he stood up and hurried to the garage, where all of our various wizardly implements were kept. Apparently, my uncle had an idea. We all stood there in silence, eagerly awaiting my uncle's return. I rocked back and forth on my feet, unsure what to do with myself while everyone waited with bated breath.

After several long, agonizing minutes, Bishop returned with two two-feet long plastic tubes under his arm. He moved towards the kitchen table where Remy was seated. He opened the first tube and pulled out a large roll of paper. Tossing the tube aside and setting the other down, he began to unroll the paper, weighing down the corners with a few small, polished stones.

We all gathered around the table to see what Bishop had brought to show and tell. Laid out on the table was a large, detailed map of the United States. Layered on top of the usual landmarks and state borders were colorful lines that crisscrossed across the landscape, occasionally converging in over a dozen locations.

"Alright you got me," I said. "What am I looking at?"

"Seriously Tobias, even I know this," Remy said.

"Leylines, of course," Seraphina said under her breath.

"Yes, leylines, right. Why didn't I think of that?" I said, scratching my chin and nodding.

Jacob sighed.

"Leylines are natural currents of magic that span the globe. There are hundreds of locations where three or more leylines meet. We call these wellsprings." Bishop reminded me.

"I know," I said defensively.

"A practitioner can draw energy from leylines to augment their magic," Jacob said. "You can pull off some pretty crazy stuff by tapping into one, so I've heard."

"Yes, but it's incredibly dangerous," Bishop warned, eyeing me specifically. I swear he has no faith in me. It's not like I had a history of incredibly bad ideas or something.

"Drawing from a single leyline can allow a wizard to perform insane feats of magic, but it's incredibly draining on the body." My uncle continued. "Now imagine what a wizard or druid could do with a wellspring."

I raised my hand. "Ooh ooh, pick me!"

Bishop gave me a flat look.

"Could they, perhaps, power an extremely powerful ritual?" I asked.

"Give the boy a cookie," Seraphina muttered.

Despite my levity, the idea that Bishop had just proposed scared the crap out of me. I didn't know exactly how powerful one leyline could make a wizard's spell, but everyone else seemed pretty concerned, so I figured it would be pretty bad if someone were to perform a dangerous, forbidden ritual at a confluence of leylines.

Bishop pulled the second sheet from its tube, laying it over the first and adjusted the weighted stones accordingly. This one was a map of Seattle, several leylines snaked around the city. Sure enough, they all converged in one place.

I placed a finger on the wellspring marked on the map. "And where exactly is this?"

Jacob shook his head. "Figures you wouldn't know a thing,"

I frowned.

"That's Lumen Field, the home stadium of the Seahawks," Bishop explained.

My frown deepened. "There's a wellspring of magic at a football stadium?"

Seraphina shrugged. "It makes sense. Whether they realize it or not, mortals are naturally drawn to wellsprings. It gives the place a natural energy and excitement."

"But surely the place is locked up tight. Security cameras and guards all over the place. Would the druid really risk exposure like that?" Remy said.

"He's a megalomaniacal killer with dreams of grandeur," I said. "I doubt he's worried about being noticed by humans. And even then, he has plenty of ways to take down their security."

Bishop nodded in agreement. "However, the less prying eyes the better. That means Deimos will most likely perform the ritual in the dead of night."

"Not to mention it adds to the sinister atmosphere," I added.

"Most likely, the ritual will begin at the witching hour," Seraphina said, ignoring me. "Given all the negative association with that time, it'll lend itself well to whatever Deimos has planned."

"Agreed," Bishop said. "Everyone, get some rest. We have a long night ahead of us."

Chapter 20

Since we had several hours to kill before our confrontation with the Plague Druid, I opted for a shower and a nap. I collapsed onto my bed, completely exhausted. I'd spent all night locked up in a cold, uncomfortable interrogation room and my bed felt like it was made out of clouds and unicorn farts.

I drifted off to sleep immediately. Normally, I would've been worried about the possibility of the boggart visiting me in my dreams, but at the moment, I simply didn't care. Instead of the usual nonsensical dreams, I was prone to, my subconscious delved into my memories.

***

I was in the living room of my apartment, clad in a cheap tux. Sitting in my living room was Lugh. He'd said he wanted to talk about Medb and her nefarious plans.

"My name is Lugh." He said, introducing himself.

I frowned. "Is that name supposed to mean something to me?"

Lugh chuckled. "No. No, I suppose it wouldn't."

"Then?"

"I'm one of the Tuatha Dé Danann." Lugh explained. "I guess you could call me an Old God of Ireland. I'm here to talk to you about Medb, and the trouble she caused with my spear."

His spear? Was he talking about the Spear of Destiny?

"Medb, you guys buddies or something?" I asked.

Lugh shrugged. "Or something."

Okay, that didn't really answer my question at all.

"Medb has set something in motion. And I think you can help me stop her." Lugh said.

Oh. Oh boy, what the hell had I gotten myself into now?

I sat down across from the god and motioned for him to continue. I had a feeling it was going to be a long talk.

"I've been keeping tabs on you, Tobias," Lugh began. "Ever since that mess with Azazel."

"How do you—?" I began, then stopped myself. "You're a god, right. Mysterious ways, and all that jazz."

A satisfied smile spread across his face. "You're a quick study for someone so young."

"My teachers say I'm not applying myself as much as I should." I shrugged.

"Anyways, as I'm sure you've already surmised, a faerie queen trying to amass an army of vampires is very out of the ordinary," Lugh said. "I have reason to believe something has been set in motion. Over the last eighteen years, other strange occurrences have become more prevalent."

"For example, a fallen angel orchestrating events so that the perfect mortal vessel would be born?" I proposed.

Lugh nodded. "That's right. After thousands of years of the Fallen Son being dormant, suddenly trying to make a comeback is odd. Demons taking physical forms, even weak ones, is also highly unusual. And I'm sure I don't have to stress how odd it is for rival vampire clans to be collaborating."

"So what? You think Medb is working together with Azazel to take over the world?" I asked.

"Possibly, but these two things couldn't happen without the assistance of a third party. I suspect someone else is pulling the strings." Lugh clarified.

"Someone more badass than a faerie queen or the actual devil?"

"More badass? Maybe. More clever? Absolutely." Lugh said. "You and I are simply two pieces of a grand game of chess. And the prize is the fate of reality."

That was certainly a revelation. I knew the threats of Azazel and Medb's vampire army were world-ending threats. But if they were really just pawns in the schemes of some hidden mastermind, then I'd hate to see what other chess pieces this mysterious benefactor could deploy.

"So what the hell am I supposed to do? Why come to me? Why not my uncle or the Mystic Order itself?" I asked in quick succession. "I can barely hurl a fireball around. I'm not sure what I can do."

"You are a Child of the Eclipse, young wizard. One who was born under a solar eclipse. That event gives you potential—potential to be one of the most potent beings of your generation. Children like you are rare and dangerous. Many generations ago, it was a Child of the Eclipse who managed to seal away the Old Gods into their eternal rest."

Azazel had mentioned something about me being born under an eclipse when we'd first met. He said it made me the perfect vessel for him on Earth. Azazel, or whoever had assisted him, had engineered their very own chosen one, meant to destroy the world. Or save it, if I had anything to say about it.

"Wait, you said you were an Old God," I said. "Why aren't you sealed away?"

Lugh smiled. "Very observant of you, Tobias. In every pantheon and mythology, there is always at least one being who earns the title of Trickster. Tricksters tend to find ways to circumvent the rules. I am one such being."

"Neato," I flicked a finger gun at him. "So you're saying that I'll probably have to go up against other agents of this mastermind in his bid to take over the world."

"Not just your world, but your known universe and the World Yonder as well," Lugh reminded. "It's only a theory, but one with enough evidence to make myself and my associates very nervous."

"Associates?" I shook my head. "Nevermind, you mentioned *your* spear. You're talking about the Spear of Destiny, right? But I thought it had belonged to Odin and eventually found its way to Longinus, who used it to pierce the body of Christ?"

Lugh nodded. "All of that is true. It did originally belong to Odin, but he cast it to Earth before he was forced to sleep like the other gods. It eventually found its way to Longinus. But the Spear was not meant for mortal hands. It prolonged Longinus' life, but he eventually succumbed to its overwhelming power. I took it off his corpse, and have been wielding it ever since. But it was eventually stolen, no doubt sought after for its power. It was missing for decades, until eventually its fragments turned up here in Seattle."

"And now here we are," I gestured broadly.

"Yes, here we are," Lugh nodded. "The Spear of Destiny is one of many artifacts I believe to be instrumental in our hidden enemy's plans."

"And let me guess, the Holy Grail is another," I said, remembering the artifact's role in my encounter with Azazel and his minions.

"Exactly."

"Well, both of them are now locked up tight in the Mystic Order's vault. I can't think of anywhere safer." I said.

Lugh grimaced. "Yes, the Order. If I were you, I would keep an eye on that crowd."

I frowned. "What do you mean?"

Lugh glanced over his shoulder for a moment before turning back to me. "It would seem my time is up. I have to go now, Tobias."

"Wait a second, what did you mean I should keep an eye on the Mystic Order? What are the other artifacts?"

Lugh shook his head. "I've said more than I was supposed to. But we'll see each other again, Tobias. Until then, stay the path."

"Wait, you can't just spout some cryptic mumbo jumbo and then leave?" I rose from where I sat, reaching out for the god. But time seemed to slow and my body felt like it was made of lead.

Lugh, seemingly unbothered by the slowed passage of time, simply raised one hand and snapped his fingers.

The memory suddenly spun in all directions at once, a dark void spread over my vision. I heard someone screaming. It wasn't until the dream memory had almost faded completely that I was realized it was me.

***

There was a thud, and pain exploded at the center of my face. I let out a groan as I gathered my senses. I had fallen off of my bed and landed straight on my face. Something warm trickled past my lip. I wiped my face with my hand and found it smeared with blood. My nose hurt, so it was clear that it had broken my fall.

"Ow," I said, my voice came out nasally. I sat up and tilted my head back and pinched my nose in an attempt to slow the blood. "Can't a guy catch a break?"

There was a knock at the door. "Tobias, you okay?"

I recognized Remy's voice and let out a groan. "Yeah, I'm fine. Just had a disagreement with the floor."

Remy let themselves in, taking in the sight of my sorry ass sitting on the floor. They'd changed into their feminine form since the night before. They were wearing cargo pants that had so many pockets I was sure it was a crime somewhere in the world, as well as a tight black t-shirt that exposed about two inches of midriff. Around their waist was a tactical belt with several holsters. The holder on their left hip held their ivory wizard's wand. The holster on their right hip was empty, but was noticeably gun-shaped.

"You look like a mess," Remy smirked.

"Gee, thanks," I muttered grumpily. My face heated up as I became keenly aware that I was wearing nothing but black, form-fitting boxers.

Remy left the room, returning a moment later with a wet towel. "Here, let me help you,"

They knelt down in front of me and I moved my hand out of the way. Remy went to work on dabbing up the blood and making me look a little more presentable. I watched their face as they cleaned me up, studying the concerned expression that shaped their facial features.

Remy's eyes rose to meet mine, and I quickly darted my gaze towards the ceiling, examining the random patterns in the ceiling with a critical eye.

"Dork," Remy chuckled. "You don't have to do that you know."

"Do what?" I said, playing dumb.

"Act all tough and cool around me," Remy smiled as they wiped away a smear of blood on my cheek. "It's okay to just let yourself be normal for a few minutes."

I blushed, then scowled. "Acting? Who's acting? I am just this tough and cool."

Remy snorted. "Yeah, right."

"I am!" I protested. Then I frowned, considering my next words. "It's all just a lot, y'know? I never asked to be a wizard. And I certainly didn't ask to keep finding myself in these crazy situations."

"Yeah, you still have to bring me up to speed, y'know?" Remy said.

"Yeah I know and I will, I promise," I said. "This whole thing just got outta hand."

"I know, I don't blame you. I know you have a lot on your plate." Remy said.

I nodded. "It just feels like too much sometimes, y'know? I'm just a guy who only learned about this whole new world a few years ago. And now I'm expected to stand up against demons, vampires, and now a rogue druid? Shit's scary and I don't know how I'm going to stop the bad guys from winning."

Remy stopped what they were doing, the towel still lingering on my cheek, and gazed into my eyes. "That's what you have your friends and family for, Tobias. And me too."

For a few seconds, neither of us moved. We sat there, staring into each other's souls for an endless moment, hours before I'd risk it all again to save the world. The whole shitty world could have been exploding in that moment, and I would've been more than content to stare into their amber eyes.

My body moved without consulting my brain. I leaned forward and pushed my lips onto theirs. I heard Remy inhale sharply, but they didn't pull away. Instead, they leaned into the kiss, dropping the towel to caress my cheek. Their lips were warm and soft. The sensation of their touch sent the butterflies in my stomach into a chaotic flurry of tingles that threatened to overwhelm me. The butterflies bubbled up in my chest as a cloud of warmth and I could feel my heart threatening to beat out of my chest. Excitement radiated through me as Remy pushed harder into the kiss, leaning into me and threatening to knock me over.

The next thing I knew, I was on my back with Remy straddled on top of me, their lips still locked with mine. My hand found the small of their back as I pulled them into me, craving their touch against my skin. Remy's hands caressed my chest and my arms, their hands tracing the scars near my right shoulder, their fingers lighting a fire across my skin wherever they touched.

I'd been waiting for this moment. Man, I'd been waiting for this for so long. All I had to do was just go with it. But I let out a breath and gently pushed against Remy, urging them to stop.

Remy pulled their lips away and frowned at me. "What's wrong? Did I—?"

"No, this is on me," I said sheepishly. "It's uh, been a while for me. And if it's all the same to you, I want to take this slow."

Remy rolled their eyes, but smiled. "God, you're adorable."

Remy rose to their feet, offering me a hand. I took it and they helped me to my feet. "But after this is all said and done, you're taking me on that date."

"Wouldn't miss it for the world," I grinned.

Remy's eyes darted toward my crotch. It took me a second to realize why and I did my best to cover myself.

"Do you mind?" I growled, trying to sound intimidating.

Remy let out a throaty laugh. "Oh come on, Tobias. I've already seen you naked."

I whipped a finger towards the door, scowling.

Remy giggled, winking at me. "Come downstairs when you're decent. We have a couple hours before showtime."

Then Remy excused themselves, closing the door behind them.

I cleared my throat for no one's benefit but my own. It was time to suit up. I picked out a pair of sturdy jeans and slipped them on. Next came a shirt, and it wouldn't be an epic battle featuring Tobias Leight if I didn't wear the most out-of-place t-shirt I could find. So naturally, I picked out a hot pink t-shirt featuring Margot Robbie as Barbie plastered front and center. I found my magnetic baldric and strapped it across my chest, then put my sheepskin bomber jacket on over it.

Socks and shoes came next. Next, I slipped on three, thick metallic rings on my right hand. They were a set of magical tools I'd been working on but I had yet to test them. No time like the present, I suppose. Finally came my charms bracelet, clasped around my left wrist, and my polearm, which stuck to my back thanks to the magnetic baldric.

Standing there, fully kitted out, I couldn't help but feel like a little bit of a badass. I felt a stupid grin spread across my face.

I made my way downstairs. It seemed like everyone else was just about ready to go as well. Bishop was staring at a laptop with a scrutinizing look. He was dressed in his usual garb of jeans and a flannel button-up. His staff was nowhere in sight, but I knew he could call it up out of thin air. That was another trick I'd have to learn.

Seraphina sat on the floor, meditating in the lotus position. Jacob sat on the couch, head tilted back as he tried to catch a few more Z's. Remy was seated at the table, loading rounds into a magazine, a handgun sat on the table nearby.

"Didn't know you were strapped," I commented as I entered the room.

Scout rose from where he'd been lying near Bishop's feet and trotted over to greet me. He licked my hand, and I gave him the head scratches he was due.

"Don't worry, I've got plenty of surprises," Remy winked.

I coughed nervously, turning my attention to my uncle. "Whatcha doing there, unc?"

"Taking a look at building schematics for the stadium. I want to know every exit in the place should we need to make a speedy getaway." Bishop explained.

"How'd you get your hands on building schematics?" I asked skeptically.

Bishop shrugged, giving me a knowing look. "I know a guy."

Cryptic, as always, that was my uncle for you. I tilted my head in acknowledgment. From there, we identified all of the entry points. There were plenty of avenues we could use to get to and from the stadium pitch. So, making a getaway should things get hairy wouldn't be a problem.

"Not unless he has an army of fae watching his back," Jacob noted.

"Don't be ridiculous, the guy doesn't have an army." I shot a nervous look to Seraphina. "Right?"

She rolled her eyes. "At most, a druid can maintain a dozen familiars. But given he's going to be focused on a dangerous ritual, I suspect he'll have half as many to defend him."

"Druids need to focus to control their familiars?" Remy asked.

"That's correct," Seraphina said, rising from where she sat. "Druids need to dedicate a level of attention to commanding and reining in their familiars. The more of their familiars that they are commanding, the more divided their focus will be."

"So we hit Deimos and his familiars scatter," I said. "Easy peasy."

"It's not that simple." Bishop objected.

Of course, it wasn't. Why couldn't things ever be that simple, like in the movies? Hit the mother ship or control module, and the alien army dies instantly.

"You're right in that Deimos may temporarily lose command over his familiars, but that just leaves them to do as they wish. They could prove loyal to him and attack us anyway. They could decide to retreat. Or they could decide to run amok and attack innocent bystanders." Seraphina said.

I huffed out a breath. "So we have to take out the familiars before we deal with Deimos."

In reality, I didn't mind that too much. There was a chance I'd get to go another round with the boggart. It had managed to get away from me twice now. The same went for the nachtkrapp and whatever else Deimos had on the payroll.

"Once we've disabled the Plague Druid's familiars, I can use a banishing spell to send them back wherever they came from. That will leave Deimos defenseless and we can take him down together." Bishop said.

Seraphina scowled. "You all focus on the familiars, Deimos is mine."

Now it was my turn to scowl. I crossed my arms. "Listen, you're new to town, so I get you might not be used to how we do things. But when the big bad is about to unleash their grand master plan. We try to work together to stop them."

"I prefer to work alone," Seraphina said flatly. "I'm bringing you along as a courtesy because it is your town."

I sped across the room, getting up close and personal with Seraphina. "Oh, a courtesy?" I growled.

"That's right," Seraphina angled her head up to meet my eyes. "You've been bumbling around town for days and could barely hold your own against Deimos' familiars. It's a surprise you made it this far at all."

I growled, a rush of energy permeating through my body as my magic responded to my growing anger and annoyance with the Eclipse Druid. I clenched my fists so hard that my knuckles popped audibly. She scowled back up at me and I felt her power rising to match mine. Crackling lights danced through the air around us as our conflicting energies met.

A pulse of energy thrummed through the apartment, shaking the foundations and knocking us both off balance. I fell hard on my tailbone, grumbling all the while. I turned to see Bishop standing there with his staff.

"Enough, we don't have the time or the luxury to bicker with each other." Bishop said sternly. "Seraphina, if the Plague Druid is as dangerous as you say, then like it or not, we have to work together."

Seraphina glared at Bishop, then at me. She scoffed and then went out the front door, slamming it behind her.

"I'm gonna go check on her," Jacob said awkwardly. He made his way out the front door, following after her.

I rose to my feet, avoiding eye contact with my uncle.

"I expect better from you, Tobias," Bishop said. "By now I would have thought you'd have cooled off that hot head of yours."

"Yeah yeah," I sighed. "She can just be incredibly annoying."

"Regardless, we're going to need her. So cool it."

My uncle sat down, banishing his staff and breathing heavily. That's what really did it for me. I grimaced, reminded once more how much using magic drained Bishop's energy nowadays. He'd wasted precious energy to break us up because Seraphina and I were too heated to settle things like normal people.

I just hoped our bickering wouldn't cost us the coming battle.

I put my hands into my jacket pockets. My left hand brushed against something that I'd completely forgotten about until now. I pulled out the wooden bracelet I'd snagged from the hag's den back in Ireland. I gave it a once over, I still had no idea what it did.

"Hey uncle, can you tell me what this is?" I asked.

Bishop took the bracelet from me. His eyes glowed with a violet light as he activated his arcane senses. He turned the ring of bound twigs and roots over a couple times, occasionally bringing it up to his face to get a closer look. Then the purple light in his eyes vanished.

"Tell me again where you picked this up," He said.

"Remember that hag I had to steal the book from? It was in her hidey-hole. Thought it looked neat and it clearly had some power to it. So I snagged it." I said.

"Well it is quite interesting indeed," Bishop said. "What you have here is a portable circle."

I raised a skeptical eyebrow. "Well yeah, it is pretty small, and round."

Bishop let out a rough sigh. "No, a magic circle. As in one used in magic. Circles can be used for all sorts of things. You use one for tracking spells, remember? They can also be used for other rituals, like summoning or binding."

"Huh, pretty neat find then, huh?" I said, taking the wooden ring back.

"Indeed."

I pocketed the artifact. "Alright, time to get some grub in me before we head out. I have a bad feeling that it's going to be a long night."

"Good call," Bishop agreed.

I made myself a dinner of champions. Well, if the champions were on a budget. I made myself a plate of way too many pizza rolls and grabbed a soda from the fridge. It was going to be a long night, I figured I deserved a triple serving.

Chapter 21

We arrived at the stadium a quarter to three. I wasn't much of a sports guy, but Bishop had taken me to a few baseball games before. Stadiums were supposed to be bustling with life and energy. In the middle of the night, the place was completely abandoned. There was enough light from the streetlamps and stadium overhead, but the lingering darkness held a foreboding air. We all stood near the main entrance, staring up at the massive structure. It was incredible to look at, even as it made me feel very small.

"So, who wants to go first?" I asked.

No one answered.

I looked from left to right, staring questioningly at my allies. They all looked at me with unamused expressions.

"Fine, I had an idea, anyways," I said.

"What's that?" Jacob asked.

"I was gonna go in and talk to him." I proposed.

Again, no one said anything. Instead, they all just gave me silent, confused stares.

"What?" I said in an offended tone.

"You're just going to go in there and talk to him?" Bishop asked skeptically.

"Yeah, y'know, diplomacy."

"Deimos is not interested in talking this out," Seraphina said. "He's hell bent on his mission. We should go in hard and fast."

"That's what she said," I chuckled. No one else laughed, tough crowd. "Look Sera, it can't hurt to try."

"Don't call me Sera," She muttered.

"Plus, while I'm busy talking his ear off," I said. "You all will sneak in and surround him. If shit goes south, and we all know it will, you all can jump in while he and his mooks are focused on me."

Bishop smiled. "A decent strategy, given what we have to work with,"

"It should be me that confronts him," Sera countered.

"No offense, but you don't have the sparkling personality that I do," I wave a hand dismissively. "I can keep him talking for at least a few minutes, so you'll need to move fast."

Scout let out a yip of agreement, snuffling at my hand excitedly. I pat him on the head. Remy pushed passed Bishop and Jacob to stand next to me.

"Don't do anything stupid," Remy gave me a small smile, then stood up on their tiptoes to give me a kiss on the cheek.

I blushed for a moment, but then spread my lips into a wicked grin. "Stupid? You must have me confused for someone else." I looked to everyone else. "Give me two minutes, and then head into position. Then wait for my signal."

"What's the signal?" Jacob asked.

"You won't miss it." I said, grinning.

Seraphina didn't seem happy about this arrangement, but she didn't argue.

I walked slowly towards the building. Surprisingly enough, the front doors were unlocked. I arched an eyebrow but went inside, doing my best to focus on any out of place sounds that might betray the presence of Deimos or one of his goons. It was dark, except for dim night lights near the ceiling. They provided enough light to notice two bodies slumped near one of the food vendors. I rushed over to check on them. Judging by their uniforms, I guessed they were security guards for the stadium. I checked their pulses one at a time and it confirmed what I already knew. They were both dead.

I sighed. Clearly, this Deimos guy didn't hold much regard for human life. What were two more security guards to his master plan? Which we still didn't know anything about. All we knew was that it was extremely dangerous and that it required the essence of dozens of mortals. I thought about the memory that had resurfaced, of my conversation with Lugh three years ago. Something that the world had never seen before was starting to unfold. And I had a feeling that whatever Deimos was up to, he was somehow linked to this grand conspiracy.

I crept through the halls, following the various signs until I found a door that led to the lower levels. From there, I could access the field itself. It was the only area in the stadium with enough room for a major ritual. I tried the door, but this one was locked. I frowned, but held up a hand towards the lock.

"*Kagi,*" I whispered.

A tiny wisp of energy unlocked the door and I slunk through, closing it behind me. I took the stairs two at a time until I'd reached the lowest level. A sign on the wall pointed towards the locker room. I followed it. The empty stadium gave me the heebie jeebies.

There was no sound except for my breathing and footsteps. I'd almost feel better if some nightmarish monster lunged out of the darkness.

I found myself in the locker room. It was dimly lit like the rest of the building. If I wasn't about to confront an evil druid, I'd be enjoying the novelty of this a little more, even though I couldn't remember the last time I watched a football game. All that was left to do now was go through the final set of doors and step out onto the field.

"Alright, here goes nothing," I said. "Or everything, if I mess this up."

I pushed the last set of doors open. There was a dark tunnel with a bright light at the end of it, no doubt coming from the lights that lit the field.

"Holy crap, talk about ominous." I said, my voice echoing down the hall.

My footsteps echoed louder than before and I had no doubt that Deimos knew that I was coming. All I could do was hope that my allies hadn't found any trouble while they got into position. The bright light of the stadium blinded me as I emerged onto the field. I blinked my eyes a few times to clear my vision. I almost wished I hadn't.

Directly in the center of the field was a swirling mass of dark, purple energy. It was hard to describe, thought it reminded me of an erupting geyser of polluted water. It was huge, and I was surprised we hadn't seen its glow from the outside. I suspected the stadium lights had drowned it out. Standing at the base of the geyser was a figure in a dark cloak, presumably Deimos. It didn't seem like he'd noticed me yet. He was too focused on the ritual he was putting together.

Standing to his left was the nachtkrapp, who observed the ritual with great intrigue. To Deimos' right, stood someone I hadn't had the pleasure of meeting yet. At first glance, he looked human, but he was way too big and his proportions too bizarre. I wasn't sure what he was.

The large stranger held up one hand near Deimos, and resting in his palm, I recognized the eerie green glow of Jack of the Lantern. So Sera had been right; the crackpot spirit really knew something about the ritual Deimos was performing. If I didn't do something, Deimos would successfully perform the ritual. I took a breath.

"Time to chew ass and kick bubblegum," I said. Then I shouted. "Yo, Deimos!"

Deimos and his posse all turned to face me. The druid reached up to remove his hood, and I already wished he'd kept it on. To put it simply, Deimos looked like a zombie. His skin was gray and flaky. His eyes were shiny black orbs with no sign of humanity within.

The remnants of his hair were thin and patchy. He might've had a full head of golden blond hair at one point or another. Deimos grinned when he saw me, revealing he was missing several teeth.

I had to wonder what the hell had happened to this guy that reduced him to such a state. It looked like he'd be in great pain and agony at every moment. But judging from the way he smugly crossed his arms behind his back and waited for me to approach, his current condition didn't seem to bother him at all.

"So you've come to join me in witnessing the birth of a new era?" Deimos said. He was using a voice amplification spell to project his voice across the vast stadium.

"Not so much."I said. "I just heard *The Walking Dead* was in town, and I couldn't resist coming to check it out."

Deimos frowned, clearly not getting it.

"Or is this more of an *iZombie* situation?" I asked him. "If you eat my brain, can you remember where I left my library book? I have to return it tomorrow, and I really don't want to pay a fee."

"Did you really come to jest, young wizard?" Deimos asked me. "My plan is nearly complete. You can either swear your allegiance to me and my masters, or you can die."

"Actually, I was planning on threatening you," I said, walking slowly towards him. "But first things first, I gotta say I'm stumped. What exactly is your plan here?"

"Oh dude, this guy is a Grade A nutjob," Jack said. "I was wondering when you were gonna show up to get me out of here."

"Silence spirit," Deimos growled. Then he turned back to face me. "I know who you are Tobias Leight. I know the fate you are destined to meet. You can't avoid your destiny. Not without help, at least. Swear your allegiance to my masters, and I can assure you can forge any destiny you choose."

This all but confirmed my theory. Azazel, Medb, and now this guy, they were all connected somehow. Somewhere out there was a grand coalition that wanted to reshape or destroy the world.

"Don't worry Jack, I'm gonna get you out of here," I said, stopping ten feet away from Deimos.

"I swear I didn't tell him nothin' boss!" Jack yapped.

"Don't sell yourself short, spirit," Deimos said. "If not for you, this ritual would never have gotten off the ground. You played a big part in this grand plan."

Jack made a gulping sound. Jack was a mischievous and annoying character, but he never

screamed evil monster to me. The enchantment that
bound him forced him to obey the will of whoever
possessed his vessel. Whatever information he'd given
to Deimos, he'd had no choice in the matter.

I flicked a glance at the creature holding Jack's
pumpkin. Now that I was much closer to them, I could
get a much better look at him. He had the general build
of The Incredible Hulk—huge and muscular—but his
skin had a strange quality. I noticed cracks and
imperfections that reminded me of stone. His eyes
glowed with a faint purple light that showed no sign of
intelligence or individuality.

After racking my brain for a second, I realized
what this giant man was. Deimos' brute was a golem.
Did Deimos create him, or was he created by his
masters? Either way, it meant that Deimos and his
associates had the ability to create incredibly powerful
bruisers. I'd seen what golems could do through Jacob,
and if this guy was half as strong as my best buddy was,
I did not enjoy the thought of fighting him.

The nachtkrapp was clicking its beak eagerly,
clearly excited at the prospect of facing off with me
again. It's body shuddered with strange, twitching
motions, as if it were eager to tear my face off. It ruffled
its feathers, then turned its attention to preening
through its feathers.

I shifted nervously from foot to the other, unsure how this would go down. I noted that Deimos only seemed to have one of his familiars out in the open. The golem didn't count, as it was not controlled through normal druid magic.

"So your offer to join up with the Legion of Doom, I can't say it doesn't sound interesting. But you'll have to sell me on it a little more." I pointed towards the geyser of magical energy that flowed behind him. "You can start with your ritual. What the hell is it? Are you planning to blow up the world or something? With the energy running through the leylines under our feet, I'd say you could definitely pull it off."

Deimos chuckled, bringing out a raspiness to his voice. "Nothing so crude, young wizard. The ritual you see before you, provided by our squashy friend here, is not a bomb or anything of the sort. It's an awakening, an unlocking of a door long since sealed."

That didn't sound good. Not at all.

"You're breaking something out of magic superjail?"

"In a sense, yes." Deimos nodded. "I merely seek to right a wrong that was done many, many years ago. I wish to rebalance the scales that humanity and the fae upset so long ago."

I gritted my teeth. "And that would be?"

Deimos thrust his hands out in a grand fashion. "For generations upon generations, the gods of old have been absent from the universe. Those who helped to shape the countless worlds on both sides of the veil were imprisoned due to the hubris of lesser beings."

Oh, I did not like where this was going. Not at all.

"Tonight, I will set things right," Deimos said. "Tonight, the Old Gods will walk the Earth once again."

Chapter 22

"You're insane!" I shouted.

"What is insanity but brilliance misunderstood by weak, lesser people?" Deimos laughed. "Don't you see, Tobias? Once the Old Gods are returned to their rightful place at the tip of the pyramid, they can remake this world. Purge the impurities and the sin. The gods have been dreambound for too long. I will wake them from their slumber this night."

The idea of breaking the chains that had kept the gods bound for so long was insane. After being bound for hundreds of years, I had a feeling the gods would want to settle the score. There would be no hiding the ensuing war from humanity. And once the humans were involved, things would quickly escalate. An image of a razed Earth echoed grimly at the back of my thoughts. Deimos was trying to enact the end of days, whether he realized it or not.

"Sorry Deimos, but I can't let you do this," I shook my head. "If the gods are unleashed, it's game over. What you're talking about is a scorched Earth scenario and I can't have that. After all, the Earth is where I keep all my stuff, and I just splurged on a holographic Charizard card."

Deimos scowled at me. It quickly turned into a wild, maniacal grin. "You are but one lowly wizard, fresh from an apprenticeship. You do not scare me, wizard. And you cannot stop me."

I scoffed. "You really think I came alone?"

I reached for my polearm. As I brought it to bear, I flicked my wrist, bringing it to its full length. I spun, gathering energy into me and then thrust the polearm straight towards Deimos.

"*Kaze!*" I shouted.

A gale of wind spiraled forward. It struck Deimos like a truck, the winds reaching speeds of over 100 miles per hours. The runoff of the spell was strong enough that it caught the nachtkrapp's wings and forced it to take flight. The golem was mostly unaffected, only having to adjust its stance slightly. But to my shock,

Deimos was still standing in the same spot. He held up a shield of sickly green power that diverted the winds around him. To my dismay, the winds seemed to have no effect on the geyser of energy that bubbled behind Deimos. I had hoped that I could disrupt the ritual with my wind spell, or at the very least throw Deimos into it. Perhaps the energy would have burned him alive.

I let the wind spell die, the winds petering out to a light breeze before vanishing entirely. Deimos stood there behind his shield with a smug grin on his face.

"What a shame, Tobias," Deimos sighed. "I had hoped to bring you onboard willingly. But it seems you've yet to learn just what's at stake here."

Deimos thrust his hand forward. A shining bolt of toxic green energy surged towards me. I didn't have enough time to react. The blast hit me and sent me flying back nearly twenty feet. I took the fall well, angling myself to hit the ground in a sideways roll. I brought myself up to a kneeling position, using my polearm to help me rise. I was pleasantly surprised I hadn't lost it in the fall.

I scowled, looking up towards the stadium seats. "That was the signal, ya jerks!"

Remy landed next to me, light on their feet. They brandished their ivory wand, prepared to unleash destructive magic.

"You couldn't have shown up like ten seconds ago?" I growled.

Remy shrugged with an amused expression on their face. "You seemed like you had it under control."

"Where's everyone else?" I asked.

Remy thrust their chin forward, prompting me to take a look.

My other allies appeared from the stands, rushing the field and taking equidistant positions around Deimos and his ritual. Scout appeared somewhere to my left, close to where the nachtkrapp had been. He had already transformed into his true, bestial form and was letting out a low growl that reminded me of a sports car.

I caught a glance of Bishop in the distance, standing a ways behind Deimos' golem. His staff glowed with the bright purple energy of the Spring Flame. Ten feet to the golem's left stood Jacob. His fists were shining with the golden-green light of golem magic. I'd figured that he planned to take on the dark golem.

Finally, Seraphina descended, landing between Scout and Remy. She'd rolled up her right sleeve a few inches, and a silver chain hung from her arm. In her left hand, she held a silver rapier.

Deimos took a moment to glance at each one of my friends and family before locking onto Seraphina.

"Well Eclipse Druid, I must applaud your efforts," Deimos clapped his hands. "You've certainly done your best to amass allies against me. That's good. You'll need them."

Seraphina glowered at him. "You're a fool if you think I need them to stop you, Deimos. I insisted on coming alone, but they were very keen on helping me put you in the ground."

Deimos chuckled to himself as he spread out his arms dramatically. "You are not the only one with friends, Eclipse Druid. Meet mine."

The nachtkrapp squawked as it circled us overhead. It swooped down and landed heavily on the ground next to Deimos, flaring out its wings in an intimidation display. The dark golem passed Jack's pumpkin to his master.

"Hey be careful! I just got my stem trimmed!" Jack shrieked.

I chuckled. "Really? All you got is an oversized rat-bird and a big dumb golem?" I snuck a sideways glance to Jacob. "Uh, no offense."

Jacob cracked his knuckles, staring the other golem down. "None taken."

"Please, do you take me for a fool?" Deimos scoffed. "You are not the only one who can make an entrance."

On cue, more creatures shimmered into existence. The first to appear was a creature I recognized all too well. It reminded me of a Mogwai that had been fed after midnight, but with a much larger nose and slightly smaller ears. It had long, lanky arms and large beady eyes. Across its chest were several sheathed knives and it brandished a sharp stone axe. Atop its head, it wore its namesake, a tattered and stained red cap. The redcap snickered and sneered as it held its axe up, ready to strike.

Next, a fae horse the size of a Clydesdale materialized out of thin air next to the golem. Its fur was a deep, dark shade of green that was almost black. Instead of a mane, seaweed hung from the steed's neck. Its red eyes glowed with malice. I caught a whiff of dirty lake water as it shook its head. I recognized it from years of studying our tome on fae beings. It was a kelpie, a type of water fae that loved to drown unsuspecting victims.

A large cat-like creature shimmered into view. It was easily the size of a Great Dane but twice as thick with muscle and fur. Its fur had a metallic sheen to it, and as it bristled, I realized that it was made of small metallic needles. Its claws gleamed like steel, and its large green eyes assessed us each in turn. A cait sìth, no doubt.

Finally, the boggart appeared in all its ugly, spindly glory. It crept out of the shadows on all fours, moving around like a nightmarish spider. It locked its gaze on me immediately. That was fine with me, I was itching to go another round with the monster.

There were six dark minions and six of us. Which meant we'd each have to face off against at least one of these things before we could take a swing at Deimos.

"Okay everyone, take your pick. This party's about to get wild!" I grinned.

Deimos nodded and his minions surged forward. We responded in kind, each taking on one of Deimos' goons.

Jacob took on the dark golem obviously. Their fists clashed with earthshaking force. Bishop engaged the nachtkrapp in battle, flinging several small fire balls at its wings in hopes to ground it.

Scout and the cait sìth collided in midair, the two of them becoming a blur of flashing claws and fangs. Remy danced out of the way as the redcap lunged at them, swinging its axe at their throat. Sera kept the charging kelpie at a distance with her chain, swinging it around like a whip as it crackled with electricity.

That left the boggart to me. It leaped through the air and collided with me. We fell to the ground, scrambling for control. Our eyes locked together, and I stared the thing down with determination.

"Alright you dickless freak, you like messing with people's minds? Torturing them with nightmares? Try me on for size!" I shouted.

The boggart let out a chortling roar of challenge. My vision grew hazy, and the world began to spin as the boggart, and I plummeted into dreamland. I heard myself scream in terror as everything went black.

Chapter 23

I groaned as I peeled my eyes open from what felt like a heavy sleep. I was surprised to find myself back in my apartment. The only light came from the moon's soft glow pouring in through the window. I scanned my surroundings but could find nothing out of the ordinary. How did I get here? Where were my friends? I felt like I was missing something important.

I heard a crash from somewhere upstairs as if something or someone had fallen over. I crept towards the stairs, straining my ears to listen for any minute sound that might tell me who was fumbling about upstairs.

Hearing nothing, I took the first step up. A shiver ran up my spin and radiated through my whole body. I felt a deeply embedded sense of fear claw its way into my chest. The kind of fear only a small child could feel while alone in the dark. The kind of fear that urges you to run up the stairs after turning off the light.

The kind of irrational primal fear that despite knowing better that you were safe and sound in the comfort of your own home, there was something hiding out in the darkness, just waiting to sink its teeth into you.

I shook my head, trying to push the sensation to the back of my mind. I was home, I was safe. The apartment was protected by all kinds of wards and spells meant to defend against any manner of intruder. There was nothing that could get me here. The apartment was a bastion against evil. Even as I beat down that sense of fear, I could still feel it nagging at the back of my mind. I could feel it creeping up my back, making my skin crawl. I rubbed my arms nervously, feeling the goosebumps that had erupted along my flesh.

Another bang. I jumped, stifling a gasp.

"Hello?" I called. I tried to think of names. Who would be up there making a racket? I knew my friends. I could picture their faces and who they were to me. But their names lurked just outside of my reach.

I steeled my resolve. I'd just have to go up there myself and find out who was causing such a ruckus at this hour. I made my way up the stairs slowly and quietly, not wanting to alarm whoever it was up there. After what felt like several minutes, I realized I wasn't making much progress up the stairs. I'd only been able to progress about halfway up. I frowned, taking an experimental step up. I felt myself moving forward as I should. But the top of the stairs didn't seem to get any closer.

I gritted my teeth. Something strange was going on here. I racked my brain, trying to remember some crucial detail. Whatever it was, it continued to evade me. I leaped forward, trying to ascend several steps at once. It worked, I was closer to the top now. One more leap did the trick, and I finally reached the top. I doubled over, trying to catch my breath. Why was I so tired?

I straightened, looking around the hallway. At the end of the hall was my room. I knew that much. Next to it on the right was another room, the bathroom I think? But to my immediate right was one last room. Who did that belong to? Had there always been a room there? And why couldn't I put two simple thoughts together? I jumped as a thump came from behind the door.

"Is someone in there?" I called, my voice felt small. My words echoed strangely, as if coming from far away.

I reached for the doorknob, even as every part of me protested. My instincts screamed at me, telling me to walk away from the door. But the thought didn't seem to click in my brain. I turned the knob and pushed the door open.

A dark red glow illuminated the room, accentuating the dark shadows in the corner. The room was completely devoid of furniture—no bed, no dresser, no desk, nothing. A dark red glow illuminated the room, accentuating the dark shadows in the corner. The walls were a different story, though. The scribblings of a madman covered every inch of them. It was all nonsense, written in a dozen different languages in a sloppy scrawl. I crept into the room, examining the writing on the wall.

THIRSTY

WHY???

THE FALLEN WILL RISE

SO HUNGRY

HELP ME

And I thought I was freaked out before. What was all this? Who did this room belong to? And what had driven them to such madness?

There was a heavy thump from the closet along the far wall, and I nearly jumped out of my skin. I narrowed my eyes at the sliding door that hid the closet. I crept closer, taking a few quiet steps.

"Hello?"

There was no response.

I put my hand on the door handle and took a deep breath. With one swift motion, I slid the door all the way open. There was nothing inside, not even an old pair of shoes. I frowned at that. I was positive this was where the sound had come from. I shrugged, moving to turn and go back the way I came. Right before I began to turn, something gripped my neck like an iron vice and flung me through the air. I hit the opposite wall hard and at an awkward angle before crumpling to the ground.

My adrenaline kicked in, firing on all cylinders as I scrambled to stand and took a fighting stance. The creature standing before me renewed the dread brewing inside me and all but broke my heart.

It was a vampire of the Blood Clan, in its full vampiric form. Its skin was pale and I could see dark veins running along its body, just under the surface. Its face had been contorted into a more bat-like form, upturned spade-shaped nose, sunken red eyes, and large pointed ears. Its hair was falling out, making it look ragged and feral. The clothes it wore were in shambles, but the torn plaid button-up it wore jogged something in my memory. I knew who this vampire was. I recognized him all too well.

"Bishop..." I said breathlessly.

He had succumbed to the vampiric infection pumping through his veins. Not only that, but it had driven him mad. Bishop let out a guttural screech that no human throat should be able to produce, bearing his sharp, shining fangs at me.

He lunged at me, claws outstretched to tear me limb from limb. I rolled out of the way, flanking him. I stood behind him, fists still up and ready to defend myself. Bishop crashed into the wall and he began tearing into it with the blind rage of a savage beast. He flung a chunk of drywall to the ground, spinning to face me.

"Bishop, stop! I can help you!" I shouted pleadingly.

"You abandoned me!" Bishop screeched.

Then he lunged for me again, moving at speeds no human could match. I barely leaned out of the way as he swiped his claws at me. I sidestepped, shoving my uncle away. I watched in horror as Bishop let out an enraged shriek, turning to face me once more. His eyes glowed with a hatred I'd never seen in him before.

"How could you leave me? You were supposed to save me!" He roared.

"I didn't! And I will!" I dodged another swipe of his claws. "Bishop, this isn't right! What happened to you?"

"You left me! And I was so, so thirsty!"

Bishop lunged and this time I was too slow. He grabbed me around the neck, lifting me up and pinning me to the wall. I struggled, trying to pry his fingers off of my neck, but they were locked on tight. I tried kicking him in the chest, but it didn't seem to phase him.

"I was all alone with nothing but the thirst! Remy came looking for you one day and I couldn't take it anymore! I fed until not a drop of blood was left! But it wasn't enough! I found Jacob and I drained him dry too! I fed more and more! Men and women alike! The blood of the children was especially intoxicating! But still, it's never enough!" Bishop raved, madness driving his words. "You left me with this curse! And now we all have to suffer for it! But now that I have you, I think my thirst will finally be quenched!"

Tears stung my eyes as sorrow and rage took over. He'd killed Remy and who knew how many others. He had killed children, fed on them. The vampiric thirst for blood had driven him completely out of his mind. He'd become nothing more than a mad dog. I felt a crack somewhere deep inside my soul. There was only one way to deal with a mad dog.

"*Kaze!*" I shouted, anguish fueling the spell.

Wind erupted from every fiber of my being, blowing in every direction at once. Bishop was flung away, crashing into the closet. I fell to the ground, but managed to stay upright.

"*Kōri!*" Shards of ice began forming in the air before me, shaping themselves into sharp projectiles. I thrust my hand forward, sending the ice flying at my uncle.

Bishop screeched, rising to lunge for me again. But the ice struck first, impaling his arms, legs, and chest. One final spike struck home, hitting his heart directly. My uncle let out one final shriek, but it faded quickly. He slumped, pinned to the wall by the shards of ice that I'd summoned.

I let out a gasp, as the reality of what I'd just done sank in. I rushed to my uncle, tears streaming down my face now. I pressed my head into his chest, gripping his shirt as I let the tears fall.

"Bishop, I'm so sorry!" I wailed. "I didn't mean for this to happen!"

When I brought my eyes up to look at his face, the pain I felt doubled. He wasn't a vampire. My uncle seemed completely normal, except for the blades of ice I'd used to kill him. I stumbled back, shock and confusion overriding any sense of rationality I had left. I spun around, taking in the room once more.

The mad scribblings were gone, and so was the dark red glow that had plagued the room. The furniture was back as well. It didn't make any sense. Why had I done that? I'd killed my uncle! And for what?

"What the hell is happening!" I shouted.

"So, you finally see your true nature, Tobias," A familiar voice said.

I turned to where my uncle had been. Standing in front of my uncle's corpse was a young man. He was my age, my height, and my build. He even had my haircut, though his hair was a lighter shade of blond than mine. His eyes were the color of gold and they twinkled with mischief.

"Azazel, I should've known!" I growled, my pain and sorrow replaced with pure anger. "This is one of your tricks!"

"This is no trick, Tobias," Azazel shook his head. "In a blind rage, you killed your uncle. And do you know why? Because you're a monster. You're like me. All you're good for is causing pain to others."

Each word felt like a physical blow. No, that wasn't true. I didn't want to hurt my uncle. But he'd been driven crazy by his thirst for blood. He'd killed Remy. And he'd fed on Jacob, too. He'd drank their blood until nothing was left.

A thought slammed into my mind like a freight train. It radiated through my whole body like a shining light. Warmth spread from my fingers to my toes as something clicked. It all made sense now. I remembered how I'd gotten here and what was happening.

I slugged Azazel as hard as I could, leaning into the punch with all my weight. He stumbled and fell to the ground, facing away from me.

"You know, you almost had me for a second there," I said, trying to sound confident. But the anger and rage at what I'd just been through laced my voice with dripping malice. "But you fucked up, and you wanna know how?"

Azazel didn't turn to look at me, but his form was already melting into something else.

"Bishop said he had fed on Remy and Jacob, that he'd drained their blood and killed them. But there's just one problem with that," I grabbed Azazel's shoulder and forced him to face me. The boggart stared back at me instead. "Jacob's a golem. He doesn't have blood. Bishop couldn't have fed on him. If you're going to make a nightmare for me, maybe do your research first."

The boggart screamed at me, thrusting its claws towards my chest.

"*Hinote!*" I shouted, not caring about the consequences of unleashing my fire spell at point-blank range.

The flames consumed us both. I felt the fire searing my flesh, but I gritted my teeth and bared it. There was no way I was going to miss listening to the sound of the boggart screaming in pain as it died.

Chapter 24

I was jolted awake by the sound of a gun going off. There were three shots followed by the shriek of a dying animal. My awareness snapped back to reality, and I found myself back in the arena. Chaos had ensued all around me. My allies were all engaged with their respective opponents while the Plague Druid had returned his attention to the ritual.

To my left was the boggart, or what was left of it. The flames of my dream spell had clearly affected it more than just on a spiritual level. Its pale, smooth skin was replaced with a blackened, cracked carapace. I could make out the glowing outlines of three bullet wounds.

I turned to my right, where Remy was standing. Their gun was aimed approximately where the boggart had been crouched on my chest a moment before.

They smiled at me. "Enchanted iron rounds."

"Pretty kickass," I said with a grin. Then my eyes widened. "Behind you!"

Remy turned on the spot, raising their gun and wand over their head in a defensive block. The redcap had lunged through the air in an attempt to bury its hatchet in Remy's skull, but instead it clanged against their weapons. The redcap let out a startled cry as Remy pushed the redcap away. They fired two more shots at the airborne redcap. Supernatural strength and speed were pretty cool, but they were of little help while in freefall. Remy's aim rang true. Two glowing hot bullet holes blossomed in the redcap's chest and forehead. It fell to the ground in a useless heap.

I made a mental note that Remy was an incredible shot and that it would be wise not to piss them off. Remy offered me a hand. I took it and they heaved me to my feet.

"Thanks for the assist," I said, smiling at them.

"I think that's twice I've saved your butt now, right?" Remy smirked. "What would you do if I wasn't around?"

"I'd rather not find out," I said, scanning my surroundings. I pointed to where Deimos stood, his attention on the ritual. "Why not just put a bullet in him and we can call it a day?"

"I tried already," Remy said. "He's got some kind of shield around him. I have a feeling it's going to take a lot more oomph than a 9mm to break through."

That figured. Why couldn't these situations ever have an easy way out?

"Alright, then let's focus on whittling down his forces," I said. "Once his stooges are out of the way, we can hit him together."

"You got it." Remy nodded. They turned their attention to Scout. The hellhound and his feline opponent were circling each other in a stalemate, waiting for the other to make the first move. "I'll help the pooch."

I looked to my left. Sera had called in her two cù sìth familiars to assist her, but it didn't seem to be going too well. The kelpie's seaweed mane had extended like slimy tendrils and bound the cù sìth, holding them up in the air where they could do little to help their master. Sera was dancing around the kelpie as it charged her and tried to ensnare her as well. As she moved just out of the kelpie's reach, she slashed it with her blade, inflicting minor wounds on the beast. She used her silver chain like a whip to keep the kelpie at bay, forcefully directing it where to go.

Then I looked over to my right, where Bishop was engaged with the nachtkrapp. It had transformed into a whirlwind of shadow and feathers surrounding him. I could barely make him out in the chaos, but I caught glimpses of his purple flames as he tried to pin the avian fae down. He was struggling. Even with the elixirs he took regularly, using magic drained him more than it should nowadays since his body was devoting so much energy to keeping his vampiric infection at bay. I decided he needed my help far more than Seraphina did.

"I've got Bishop, what about you?" I asked.

"Scout looks like he needs an opening," Remy said.

"Good call," We exchanged a fist bump and ran in opposite directions.

I was sure my uncle could have easily handled the nachtkrapp if he was fighting at 100%, but he had to be more conservative with his magic. Without intervention, the nachtkrapp had a chance to wear him down. It was time to even the odds. Wind had been my friend when it came to the nachtkrapp, so I figured it'd be my best opening move.

I swung my polearm like a baseball bat and yelled, "*Kaze!*"

A huge gust of wind rushed from my right, barreling into the nachtkrapp's tornado form. The shadows shuddered and exploded to the left, now resembling a giant formless cloud. That gave Bishop the opening he needed. He aimed his staff at the cloud.

"*Igni!*"

A gout of purple flame exploded from his staff and consumed the dark cloud. The nachtkrapp screeched, and the shadows quickly surged away from the flames. The nachtkrapp might be stunned for a moment, but it wasn't down for the count just yet. I stood next to Bishop, brandishing my polearm in a defensive position.

"Any ideas on how to put this turducken down for good?" I asked.

"We need to force it back into its normal form. Otherwise, it'll be able to recover from just about anything we throw at it." Bishop explained.

As the shadows rushed back toward us, I grinned. "Is it vulnerable to light?"

"Like fire is to water," Bishop nodded.

I grinned, clenching my right hand where I wore three thick metallic rings. They were new foci I'd been working on, but I hadn't had the time to iron out the kinks yet. Here's hoping they worked how they were supposed to and I wouldn't be turned into a mushroom cloud.

I held out my hand towards the rushing nachtkrapp, then I flicked the ring on my index finger with my thumb, priming the spell I'd etched into the ring. "*Akari!*"

I squeezed my eyes shut just as light exploded from my palm. Even still my vision went from black to a pale orange color as the searing light tried to pry its way through my eyelids. I heard a pained shriek from the nachtkrapp, and something crashed into the turf to my left. I blinked my eyes, trying to ward off the dancing lights plaguing my vision.

Once my vision cleared, I saw the nachtkrapp was already rising to its feet, but I noticed the outer edges of its feathers were smoldering. It cawed angrily at me and flared its wings. It looked like it was preparing to take off into the air again, and then we'd be back at square one.

"*Gravitas!*" Bishop roared.

I felt a shift in the air. The nachtkrapp let out a startled squawk as unseen force pinned it to the earth.

I looked over my shoulder, scowling at Bishop. "Couldn't you have led with that?"

Bishop shrugged. "It's easier to use on a nonmoving target."

The nachtkrapp squawked again, clearly perturbed by its predicament.

"I guess it's time to clip your wings, Polly," I said.

"*Págos!*" I swept my polearm over the nachtkrapp.

In the blink of an eye, the nachtkrapp became encased in ice. As the ice formed, I felt Bishop releasing his gravity spell. I turned to Bishop, just in time to see him sway unsteadily. I closed the distance, catching him before he could fall over.

"You okay?" I asked.

Bishop nodded. "I'm fine, I just got a little dizzy for a second there."

I nodded. "Maybe you should fall back, I'm sure we can handle it from here."

Bishop glared at me. "Not a chance."

A cry of pain and surprise rang out. I spun as I recognized Remy's voice. They'd been flung into the air and I was just in time to see them hit the ground hard in a roll. A pained leonine roar followed suit, and Scout was sent tumbling after Remy.

The cait sìth roared triumphantly and then turned its attention to Bishop and I. It rushed us at blinding speeds, there was nearly no time to react. The cait sìth roared as it lashed out with its claws. I moved to defend with my polearm, but I already knew I wouldn't make it. I felt something shove me and I fell to the ground just as the cait sìth swiped its claws.

Bishop cried out.

A spray of blood flew from my uncle's chest and I watched him crumple to the ground.

Chapter 25

Anger flooded through me as my uncle fell to the ground in a motionless heap. The cait sìth was coming back around for another attack. I rose to face it. This dark creature of the Unseelie Court had probably just killed my uncle. Whether or not it was under the control of a druid didn't matter to me. I'd make sure it suffered.

"Hinote!" I roared. I flung fireball after fireball at the feline fae.

The cait sìth was quick on its feet, I'd give it that much. It dodged my exploding fireballs again and again. But I got the timing down. I faked it out with a weaker fireball, flinging another into the spot where it had dodged out of the way. The fireball exploded around the cait sìth and it yowled in pain as it was flung through the air, flames burning its body.

I sprinted to where it fell, flames still dancing between my fingers. I stood over the cait sìth, watching it writhe and cry out as the flames burned it. I extended my hand towards it, letting out a defiant roar. *"BURN!"*

Fire, more than I'd ever been able to call up before, exploded from my outstretched hand and consumed the cait sìth and me both in a column of flame. My flames couldn't hurt me, not so long as I channeled my magic into it, and I refused to let up. The cait sìth struggled, trying to get away, but the flames burned it all away. Fur, muscle, and bone, nothing was left as my spell faded. The lingering flames were struggling to burn, considering the artificial turf, and they would soon go out.

I was exhausted. It was all I could do not to keel over in that moment. Then I remembered Bishop. I turned back to where he lay on the ground and I ran over to him. His shirt was in tatters, and four deep gashes spread across his chest. There was blood everywhere. I tried to keep my breathing steady as panic tried to settle in.

"Scout! Remy!" I shouted, anguish shaking my words.

The ground shook as Scout covered the distance. Soon the hellhound was standing over us. I could see the concern for his master in those large eyes. Remy followed shortly after.

"Tobias, what happened to him?" Remy cried as they fell to their knees beside Bishop and me.

"That stupid cat," I growled. I felt for his pulse. It was loose and thready, but it was there. "He's still alive. I need you two to get him out of here."

"We'll get him to a hospital." Remy assured me.

The vampire form Bishop had taken in my nightmare hovered in the back of my mind. Bishop was in a delicate state, if his vampiric instincts kicked in at a hospital full of the sick and injured, the death toll would be astronomical. There was only one place we could take him where he'd have a chance at surviving with the lowest amount of potential casualties.

"No, it's too dangerous. They'd ask too many questions," I said, my words were quick and frantic, bordering on nonsensical. "Remy, you have to take him to Light Haven. Find Fachnan, he can help."

"But I—" Remy faltered. I knew they didn't like associating with the Mystic Order.

"Remy, I know I'm asking a lot from you, but we don't have any other options!" I snapped. "Promise me! Promise me you'll take him to Fachnan!"

Remy swallowed, then nodded. "Okay, we'll get him there."

I helped Remy haul Bishop onto Scout's back, and then they climbed on after.

"Wait, give me your gun. It could come in handy." Remy handed it over, checking the safety and giving me a brief rundown on how to use the weapon. I listened intently, not wanting to be screwed over by my lack of gun knowledge should I need it. I stuffed the gun into my waistband near the small of my back, double-checking that the safety was on as I did so.

"Thank you," I said, then I locked eyes with Scout. "You gotta move, boy. He doesn't have much time. Listen to Remy, and find Fachnan." I said.

Scout barked in the affirmative.

Remy and I gave each other one last look, and then Scout took off at blinding speeds. He didn't bother trying to navigate the halls of the stadium. Instead, he climbed up the stands and jumped off the outer wall. Then they were gone.

I prayed that I hadn't just doomed my uncle. But I couldn't worry about that now. Jacob was still trading blows with the larger golem. Their strikes shook the ground around them. At first glance, it looked to be an even match. But I could see that my best friend was slowing down. I had to even the odds.

I held out my outstretched palm towards the enemy golem, my thumb stretched towards the ring on my middle finger. It was going to be a tricky shot, since I didn't want to hit Jacob with the spell. Jacob leaped backward, avoiding a hammer blow by the much larger golem.

Bingo.

I flicked the middle ring. *"Fordun!"*

A wave of invisible force rolled out from the ring, hitting the ground and rushing forward. The spell's kinetic energy tore apart the turf and headed straight for the golem. If I'd designed it right, the spell would hit the golem with the force of a runaway semi-truck.

Seconds before the kinetic energy struck, Jacob leaped towards the golem, totally unaware of my incoming battering ram spell. Well, crap. Sorry buddy, this was going to hurt.

The two golems collided in a renewed flurry of punches. A second later, the kinetic energy I'd unleashed struck them both. I heard a pained cry from Jacob, the dark golem merely grunting in surprise. The battering ram spell carried them across the ruined turf of the stadium and slammed them into the wall. I rushed after them, holding my polearm out to my side so it was ready to strike.

"Jacob!" I shouted.

As the dust settled, I could make out the silhouette of a large figure pulling itself up. Definitely not Jacob. I stopped a few feet short of the hulking golem, but I didn't have time to react to its next attack. Just as the dust settled, it flung something large and heavy at me. The impact knocked the wind out of me and I hit the ground hard. The projectile rolled off of me and away somewhere behind me. I groaned as I sat up, trying to gather my senses. I turned and let out a startled cough. No wonder the golem's thrown object hadn't killed me. Because it wasn't an object at all, it was Jacob.

He struggled to his feet. I noticed multiple cracks and chipped off shards of clay. Jacob was breathing hard, his clothing had been torn in several places. Underneath his shredded shirt, my best friend was sporting a remarkable set of washboard abs. He didn't even work out. Golem or not, it just wasn't fair.

Jacob offered a hand and I took it. He hauled me off the ground with little help from my end. "You okay?"

"I should be asking you," I said. "Sorry, I was really trying to avoid hitting you with that spell."

Jacob eyed the rings I wore on my right hand. "Neat trick. Well now that I'm out of the way, maybe you could try hitting him again."

I shook my head. "Each ring only has enough juice for one spell every twenty-four hours. I was still working out the kinks before this whole shebang started. And I don't think I can produce the same effect on my own."

Jacob sniffed. "Shame. This guy's tough. Stronger than any other golem I've ever met."

"You don't think you can beat him?" I asked.

He shook his head. "Not in a straight fight. This thing's relentless, I can't get enough of a breath to trip him up with my magic. It's been a straight up brawl since this whole thing started."

The dark golem lumbered towards us. To Jacob's credit, the golem was sporting a few cracks of its own. Dark, shadowy energy seeped from the cracks. I suspected that Deimos had juiced this golem with some sort of dark fae magic, amplifying its physical abilities. It didn't seem to be in a hurry to kill us either. Or perhaps it could only move quickly in short bursts, which it saved for combat.

"If I buy you some time, can you pull off that quicksand spell?" I asked him.

Jacob nodded. "Sure, but I don't think it'll be very effective."

I cursed. He was right. The stadium's artificial turf would make Jacob's quicksand spell hardly effective.

"Okay, new plan then," I said. "You keep it busy and I'll work on slowing it down. When I say move, make yourself scarce. Otherwise you'll be caught up too."

Jacob nodded. "Deal, let's run this!"

Jacob faced the lumbering golem. He let out a bellowing battle cry and rushed to meet the golem. The golem raised a fist the size of Jacob's head and brought it down towards my friend.

Jacob brought his arms up in a crossguard at the last second, catching the blow. The collision released a shockwave that threatened to blow me away, but I held my ground. He pushed the golem away, temporarily knocking it off balance and rushed inside its guard. Jacob began unleashing strike after strike into the thing's abdomen.

The larger golem was big and that had its advantages, but it also had its downsides. Once Jacob had made it past the larger golem's reach, it would be hard-pressed to land a significant blow against him. Sure, it could grab him, but as long as Jacob kept up his assault, he could keep the golem disoriented and off balance.

Jacob was doing his part, so it was time I did mine. I slammed my polearm into the ground, gripping it tight as I closed my eyes and focused. I reached out with my magic, focusing on the water around me. The water in the air, the water underneath the ground, and the water in the stadium's pipes. This was going to be a big spell, and there was a good chance it would completely tax me. So, I had to make it count.

I felt my muscles tighten as I worked on reining the spell in. Gathering this much water from my surroundings was a monumental task. A bead of sweat broke out on my forehead as I strained against the water. Water began to flow towards me from the various hallways that led to the concession stands. It coalesced out of the very air itself, all of it gathering at the tip of my polearm. The ground broke apart as a large pipe was rendered asunder from the earth. The walls broke apart as more smaller pipes joined in, all of them releasing their water to me.

I couldn't gather as much as I wanted to, because holding that much water with nothing but my will was simply beyond me. But once I was done, I had a orb of water with a diameter of somewhere around ten feet.

I gasped for air, not realizing I'd been holding my breath in an attempt to concentrate. I really hoped this worked, because otherwise I'd ruined the stadium for nothing. I felt the spell waver as exhaustion started to set in. I had to do this now.

"Jacob, move!" I shouted.

My best friend didn't hesitate for an instant. He landed one last superpowered punch on the golem and then dove as far as he could to his right. It'd have to be far enough. I swung my staff forward, carrying the giant ball of water with it.

"*Mizu!*" I bellowed.

The ball of water surged forth, forming into a stream of water that knocked the larger golem off of its feet. The water blast pinned it to the wall. I spun my staff, directing the water into the shape I needed.

I slammed my polearm into the ground. "*Págos!*"

I dispersed as much heat as possible from the water blasting the golem. In only a few seconds, the water froze completely. The water had been mid-blast when I froze it, so the ice was in an oblong shape that looked like it could be displayed at a modern art show. The dark golem was still pinned to the wall, now trapped in the ice from the neck down. Only its head was exposed, which had been the plan.

Golems were powerful, but they had a glaring weakness. Inside their heads was a talisman that gave the golem its life and abilities. Remove the talisman, and the golem is nothing but a clay statue.

The dark golem struggled against the icy bonds, but with no leverage to lend to its strength, it was completely helpless. Now all we had to do was get the scroll inside its head.

"Jacob?" I called.

He appeared next to me. "Ah, so that was your plan,"

I nodded. Jacob was obviously very familiar with a golem's weak spot. His right hand formed into a large clay mace as he hopped onto my ice sculpture and slide towards the golem's head.

He placed a hand softly on the golem's head. "I'm sorry this happened to you, brother. May you be reborn one day, free from the chains this madman has placed on you, so you may serve your true purpose."

The golem snarled, lashing out with its teeth. Jacob pulled his hand away, raising his mace arm. Jacob brought his weapon down with all his might, shattering the golem's head. As clay dust scattered into the air, Jacob morphed his arm back to normal, reaching into the golem's remains and pulling out a tiny piece of parchment. Jacob hopped down, holding the scroll out to me.

"Do you mind, uh..." Jacob trailed off, his voice shaky.

It took me a moment to realize what he was asking. The small scroll was the golem's talisman. So long as it existed, the golem's energy and spirit wouldn't be free from Deimos' dark magic. I nodded solemnly, taking the talisman from Jacob.

"*Hinote*," I said, only putting a small effort of magic into the spell.

After a couple of seconds, the scroll burst into flames and disintegrated into ash. The fire died away, and I let the gentle breeze take the ashes away.

Jacob nodded. He didn't speak, but I could see the gratitude in his eyes. He hadn't wanted to kill the golem, but there had been no other option. I patted his shoulder, squeezing it reassuringly.

"Come on, we still have an evil druid to take down." I said, grinning.

Jacob returned the smile. "Alright."

Chapter 26

I heard the kelpie cry out. Jacob and I both swung our head towards the sound. At some point, the cù sìth had been cut free of the horse fae's seaweed tendrils. I watched in awe as Sera and her familiars worked together like a tightly knit pack of wolves. Sera whipped her chain towards the kelpie. As it struck the ground near the kelpie's hooves, it crackled with electricity, startling the equine faerie.

The kelpie reared, letting out a startled cry. While it was distracted by the sudden burst of electricity, the cù sìth moved in, slashing the kelpie's back ankles with tooth and claw. Pale blood spurted from the wounds and the kelpie stumbled as it tried to maintain balance.

The cù sìth had hamstrung it. The horse fae would barely be able to stand, let alone fight back or run away. As the kelpie stumbled awkwardly, Seraphina moved in for the killing blow. She whipped her chain again, this time ensnaring it around the beast's neck. Electricity coursed through the silver chain, paralyzing the kelpie and sending painful shocks through its body. She pulled on the chain, but instead of pulling the kelpie closer, she used the tension to vault forward, her silver rapier flashing.

The kelpie gasped. Sera landed behind the beast in a three point stance. A moment later, the kelpie's head fell to the ground. The body followed shortly after, making a loud thudding sound against the ruined turf. Seraphina flicked her wrist and the silver chain came sailing through the air, coiling around her wrist perfectly.

"Huh," I said, thoroughly impressed. "Remind me never to piss her off."

Jacob nodded. "She's good."

Seraphina turned and scowled at us. "If you boys are done staring, we have a druid to kill."

I gulped. "Right. All of his goons are dead. With the three of us, it should be no problem."

Sera frowned, looking around. "Where are the others?"

I relayed what had happened with Bishop to her, and how I'd sent Bishop, Remy, and Scout, back to Light Haven.

Sera nodded. "Good, the last thing we need to worry about is dead weight."

Anger flared in my mind. I took a step towards Seraphina. "You watch your—"

Someone placed a firm hand on my shoulder, holding me back from advancing further on Seraphina. I turned to see Jacob giving me a serious look. He shook his head. I took a deep breath and then nodded.

We all turned to where Deimos was. His attention was still on the geyser of magical energy. His hands moved in rhythmic but patternless motions. It looked like he was directing the energy, shaping it. My apprenticeship may have formally concluded, but I was still a bit of a novice.

"What exactly am I looking at?" I asked.

"Deimos said he was planning to awaken the Old Gods," Sera said. "With the leylines power, he's created a breach into the World Yonder. He'll pour all that excess energy you see back into a rift. With that done, the raw magic combined with the life energy he's collected using the boggart will stir and revitalize the gods."

"Then what happens?" I asked.

Sera shook her head. "Nothing good. The gods were sealed long ago, forced into a deep slumber by the combined efforts of humanity and the fae. They were tired of being under the gods' heel. It didn't work out so well for the humans, however. Instead of them and the fae being on equal footing, the fae treated humanity as their play thing."

"So humanity wasn't freed, just under new management," I concluded.

"Was that a Megamind reference?" Jacob asked.

I shrugged. "That movie's a classic. It gets no respect."

Sera rolled her eyes. "If we can separate Deimos from the ritual, we might be able to shut it down."

I arched an eyebrow. "Might?"

"I have no idea how far along the ritual is," Sera said. "It may be that the ritual has progressed past the point of no return."

"Then we should probably quit yappin' and start blastin'," I said, flourishing my polearm. "Jacob, you go right. Sera, take Balto and Jenna and flank his left side."

Sera pinched her eyebrows, glaring at me. I wasn't sure if she was annoyed with me calling her Sera, my nicknames for her cù sìth, me taking charge, or all of the above. Regardless, it didn't matter.

We all moved at once. Jacob formed a mace with his right arm and a shield on his left. Sera unraveled her silver chain, electricity began coursing through it once more. Her cù sìth sprinted forward, snarling eagerly. I held out my polearm to my side, ready to whack Deimos on the head.

The Plague Druid spun to face us, no doubt hearing our approach. He snarled, the expression making him look even more like a zombie. Had he been so wrapped up in what he'd been doing that he didn't notice that we'd taken out his familiars?

"Punch him in the dick!" I heard Jack shout.

"I was hoping those foolish beasts would've lasted at least a few minutes longer," Deimos growled. "Regardless, you fools can't stop what's coming."

We all ignored him, opting instead to continue our advance and prepare our attacks. Balto and Jenna sprung towards him, lips peeled back to reveal large fangs. Jenna was slightly ahead of Balto. But right before her teeth would have shredded Deimos' throat, he wrapped his fingers around her throat and squeezed. The cù sìth let out a startled cry that was quickly cut off.

The wolf fae's body went limp. Deimos swung Jenna's body with all his might and threw her at Balto. Being in mid-leap, Balto couldn't dodge the thrown corpse of his counterpart. They collided and tumbled to the ground, Jenna's body pinning Balto to the ground.

Sera cursed, but otherwise ignored her fallen hound. She whipped her chain towards Deimos from ten feet away, its length crackling with dangerous levels of electricity. Deimos caught the chain on his arm. If the deadly electricity now coursing through his veins bothered him, he didn't show it. He gripped the chain and pulled hard on it. Sera was ripped from her feet and sailed through the air towards Deimos.

She was quick to react, I'd give her that much. Already she was adjusting her body and bringing her rapier to bear, ready to strike. When she was only inches away from Deimos, she slashed with the rapier, going straight for his neck. A glowing sword made of dark green energy flashed into existence, parrying the blow that would have ended him.

"Cute," Deimos chuckled.

Sera cried out as her body suddenly went rigid. It took me a moment to realize what had happened. But somehow, he'd reversed the electric chain's power back on its wielder. Sera's back was arched at a painful angle as the electricity ravaged her body. After a moment, she went limp. Her rapier fell to the ground. Deimos clocked Jacob and I as we closed in. He swung Sera's limp form towards us, using her own chain to do it. I gritted my teeth, stopping on a dime and leaping backwards. Jacob had too much forward momentum, so there was no way his heavy golem form would've been able to perform the same maneuver. Instead, he collapsed his constructs and caught Sera, wrapping his arms around her. Deimos released the chain, and the sudden momentum change sent Sera and Jacob sprawling twenty feet away.

With his back turned, I swung my polearm as hard as I could towards Deimos' head. But his sword construct quickly flashed to intercept the blow. My eyes widened. From this angle, he shouldn't have been able to raise the sword to defend himself. I had a moment to realize that the sword itself wasn't in his hand but floating around him to defend and attack on command.

Deimos spun, extending his hand out. He shouted a word in a language I didn't recognize, but pure magical energy that matched the sword exploded from his palm and struck me. I felt my chest grow tight as the wind was knocked out of me, and I sailed through the air. I hit the ground on my back, further exacerbating my struggle to breathe.

"I applaud your efforts," Deimos made a show of bowing at the waist. "But you three are batting out of your league. Perhaps, if that older fellow hadn't been wounded, he could provide a challenge. But even he couldn't stand against the power I have been granted."

I brought myself up to a sitting position. My body hurt, inside and out. Whatever magic he'd hit me with, it was taking its toll on me. My eyes widened as I stared at Deimos. Around him, a figure seemed to form from the shadows. It towered over him, making for an imposing sight. Dark wings spread from the shadows, and I could make out the shape of a crow's head at its peak. I caught a quick glance at Jack's pumpkin where it rested on the ground. His flames were dim, but the pumpkin itself trembled under the presence of the strange shadow projection.

"What the hell is that?" I shouted in alarm.

"Deimos, you madman," Sera gasped. "You made a pact, didn't you?"

A pact? A pact with who? Or what, for that matter?

"I warned you not to cross me, Eclipse Druid. I even offered you a seat at the table." Deimos said. Another voice spoke in unison with his. It was a woman's voice, and it sounded ancient. "Instead, you chose to defy me, to cling to the ways of the fae."

"Sera? What's going on?" I shouted to her.

"He's made a pact." Sera said, offering no real explanation. She turned back to Deimos. "Mab will kill you for this."

"When I am done, Mab and all the other lords of Faerie will be powerless to stand against me," Deimos said, still speaking in a dual voice. "My brothers and sisters in arms will rule this world once more. With myself sitting atop the throne."

I had a feeling Deimos wasn't the one speaking any longer. Someone was speaking through him, using him. No doubt represented by the shadowy crow that loomed over him.

"Sera, who is that?" I said, stressing the words.

"Deimos made a pact with one of the Tuatha," Sera explained.

I racked my brain, urgently trying to remember anything I could on the Tuatha Dé Danann, Ireland's pantheon of god-like entities. I'd been studying them ever since Lugh made his presence known.

"It's the Morrígan, isn't it?" Jacob asked. "The goddess of war."

Sera nodded. "You're half right, at least. The Morrígan is represented by three goddesses. Macha, the goddess of sovereignty. Nemain, the goddess of war." She turned her attention to the crow-shaped shadow that loomed over Deimos. "And Badb, the goddess of death."

The shadow crow reared its head, crying triumphantly into the night. It flared its wings, and though they were merely shadow, they kicked up a torrent of wind that seemed intent on blowing the whole stadium away.

"I don't understand. The gods are supposed to be sealed away, that's the whole point of Deimos' ritual." I said.

"The more powerful of us can still extend our will out into the world," Badb said, using Deimos as a puppet. "I found Deimos and realized he'd be the perfect medium to exert my power unto the mortal plane once more. Like any other mortal man, he was very easy to convince. All I had to do was promise him the usual. Money, power, women, it works every time. His druid abilities were just what I needed to perform the ritual necessary to break the seal binding my brothers and sisters."

"Oh lady, you are one crazed fruit loop if you think that's going to happen." I said.

"What can you do to stop me?" Badb asked, her voice slowly overtaking Deimos. "The ritual is nearly complete. In only a few minutes, the ritual's power will shatter the seal and I can emerge into this world properly."

The druid's body was slumped, and his gaze had gone vacant. I wondered if the Plague Druid had ever truly been aware of what was happening or if Badb had been the one in control all along.

"Sweetheart, I beat down the actual devil himself in my first week as a wizard. It's been four years since then. What do you think I can do now?" I said.

The possessed druid cackled. "You're accomplishments are impressive to be sure. But I've been at this for a long time. Whether it was warring against my fellow gods or establishing my dominion over humanity. I do not care who you've bested in the past, a lowly wizard and his companions are nothing compared to what I've faced."

"Hmm, interesting," I said, scratching my chin. "You ever read *Cujo*?"

As soon as I said it, something blurred past Deimos. Blood exploded from the druid's chest. Balto the cù sìth landed near where Seraphina was pulling herself up to her feet. Jacob was missing, no longer sprawled on the ground where he and the Eclipse Druid had fallen. He burst through Badb's shadows and swung his mace hand at Deimos' head. Deimos fell to his hands and knees, Badb's projection shimmered, her connection to Deimos momentarily disrupted from Jacob's attack.

Deimos spun to his feet, hand extended towards the golem. "Die!"

A burst of dark green energy struck Jacob. He tried to raise his arm to defend himself but it was no use.

Clay shattered and exploded outward and I stared in
shock as Jacob's arm was completely destroyed by the
possessed druid's magical attack. Jacob let out a pained
shout as he crumpled to the ground.

"No!" I cried.

Chapter 27

Jacob wasn't moving, his shattered left arm in plain view for me to see. Seraphina looked from Jacob to me in shock. Balto growled, standing between Jacob and Deimos. Badb's looming form seemed to see everything but focused on nothing in particular.

"You were fools to think you could stand against me," Badb's voice slipped between Deimos' lips. "But I am not a goddess without mercy. Swear your fealty to me now, and perhaps I'll see to it that you have favorable lives in the gods' new world. I can grant you whatever you wish. Nothing is beyond my power."

The shadow crow seemed to focus on me in particular. "With my power, no ailment is incurable. You can have your uncle again, Tobias Leight, restored to his former glory."

I froze, staring at the colossal shadow. How had she known about Bishop's vampire curse? I supposed that she knew many impossible things since she was a god. Including, but not limited to, a way to cure Bishop. As of right now, Bishop was cursed to walk the earth half-turned for the rest of his days. Unless he succumbed to his baser instincts and fed on a human. The nightmare of his vampiric form emerged in my mind once more. I could cure him. I could save him. He wouldn't have to be constantly tired and in pain. He'd be able to use his magic to the fullest.

All it would cost me is the world.

Everyone always says you'd give the world for something grand and monumental. Like seeing your mother one last time. Or saving your uncle from an incurable disease. Or something as simple as seeing someone you care about smile again. Everyone thinks they'd give the world for those things right up until they're actually given the chance to do just that.

"Tobias?" Sera's voice came to me, but it sounded far away.

I stared up at Deimos and Badb. A sneer spread across the druid's lips. Badb had offered me the one thing I'd burn the world to change. I bowed my head, falling to a knee.

"Tobias?" Sera said again, alarm rising in her voice.

Then I grabbed my polearm and thrust it forward. *"Hinote!"*

A jet of searing blue flame roared from the tip of my polearm and engulfed Deimos. Badb's shadow shrieked in surprise. I let out a defiant scream, further fueling my rage and the spell alike. I kept the flames going for nearly a full minute, pouring more and more power into the spell to sustain it.

The flames began to die as my reserves hit empty. I slumped, my polearm shrinking and returning to its compact form as it fell to the ground. I glanced up at Deimos. Even through my blurry vision, I could see that he was nearly untouched.

Deimos, or Badb, I couldn't keep track anymore, slowly walked towards me. Dark energies gathered into the druid's hands. I ground my teeth. I hated how smug this guy looked. Possessed by a goddess or not, I was going to do everything I could to wipe the grin off of his face before I died.

"I've got to say, child. You're powerful, way stronger than any wizard your age should be. If you had a few decades to refine your abilities, you might've actually won this night." Badb said.

Oh great, she was going to monologue.

Badb continued to speak, but I had tuned her out. I really didn't care what she had to say. I was spent. I couldn't produce enough fire to light a candle at this point. I thought about the nearly complete ritual. Magical energy gushed from the earth like Old Faithful. Soon enough, we'd have hundreds of gods running around the planet, no doubt settling old scores after having been sealed away for countless years.

If I could just somehow throw a monkey wrench into Badb's plan, maybe the ritual would backfire somehow. At the very least, it might collapse. Rituals were delicate things. Even my tracking spell was a ritual, though a minor one by comparison. If one little thing was out of place, or if foreign magical energy was thrown into it, the spell would completely unravel.

A lightbulb went off in my head.

Ding ding ding, I had my answer. I glanced at my right hand, where I wore my spell rings. The neat thing about the rings was that I didn't need to expend any of my energy to use them. The enchantments I'd laid into them were self-sufficient, gathering ambient energy from the world around them to charge the spells I'd worked into them.

The first ring was a flashbang spell, perfect for disorienting anyone who wanted to take a crack at me. The second was a kinetic force spell, great for throwing a big punch at anything in my way, whether a brick wall, a pickup truck, or bad guys.

But for the third ring, I didn't have time to finish it. There was no specific spell in it, but the ring had still been designed to gather magical energy. Once activated, it would release raw magic all around me. All I had to do was get to the ritual.

Badb grabbed me by the jaw, forcing me to look her in the face. She growled. "Are you even listening?"

I coughed, struggling to breathe under her grip. "Hell no. I just remembered that a new season of *Power Rangers* is starting tonight, and I forgot to set the DVR."

Badb let out a shriek of rage, lifting me off the ground. I struggled against her, flailing my legs in desperate kicks into her chest. But it didn't seem to bother her.

"I am so sick of your prattling, boy," Badb hissed.

"You sound just like my 11th-grade history teacher," I choked out. "She never appreciated my humor either. But you know, it's good for one thing."

Badb raised a decrepit eyebrow.

"It makes for a really good distraction," I chuckled.

Seraphina appeared out of thin air, dropping the veil she hid under. She leaped into the air, brandishing her silver rapier and slashing it down across Badb's back. The goddess-possessed druid shrieked, dropping me to the ground. I rolled away, reaching into my left pocket where I still had the wooden ring. It was now or never.

I flung it towards Badb, siphoning the tiniest bit of energy into the ring. Luckily, it was just enough to bring the wooden ring to life. The circle fell at Badb's feet, quickly growing and expanding to encompass the goddess.

There was an inaudible snap of pressure in the air, and the twigs and roots that made up the ring began to glow with a bright green power. Badb tried to rush towards me but was instead met with an invisible barrier that lit up with luminescent energy upon collision. The goddess let out an angry scream as she fell, enraged that she had been trapped.

I sprinted past her. "Sera! Make sure she doesn't get out!"

"What the hell are you doing?" Sera asked.

"What else? Something incredibly stupid!" I shouted back.

I made my way over to the ritual, the geyser of magic rising high above me. I swore I could hear whispering voices, speaking nonsense and promises of grandeur if I freed them. I gritted my teeth, trying to block out the noise. I wasn't sure how long the wooden circle would last. I hadn't put a whole lot of energy into it. I had to do this fast.

I lifted my hand, pressing my thumb to the third and final ring, which I wore on my ring finger, funnily enough. As I did, shapes began to appear in the rushing energy of the ritual. They looked like silhouettes with glowing eyes.

I saw one of a large man with a round belly, some oblong weapon rested on his hip. As he approached, my nose caught a whiff of ozone.

Another stepped forward, this one wearing a Greek-style soldier's helmet, and he brandished a shield and spear. I heard shouts and battle cries emanating from his presence.

Finally, a third appeared. This one was much larger than the rest. It had wings and a large head, tentacles writhing around its face. I felt a sense of dread when I looked upon the final figure. I wanted to run away and hide. I smelled dirty seawater with a hint of decay.

I felt their power creep into my mind. They were all urging me to complete the ritual, to let them go free. They promised me anything I could ever want. It was very tempting, and for a moment, I let my hand fall.

A burning light in my mind seared everything away. A black void, surrounded by a thin ring of light, burned away all their promises and suggestions, leaving me alone with my thoughts again.

"Sorry fellas, flight's cancelled," I said. I held my hand up and flicked the final ring. "*Kaboom!*"

Golden light erupted from the ring in an explosion. Power surged from the ring and the magic geyser. I heard angry cries and a roar as the raw magic mixed and collided with one another. The surging energy threw me across the stadium. I swear that had to be like the fourth or fifth time today. I'd have to invest in a helmet. Though I supposed I wouldn't get the chance. As I tumbled, I realized I had been thrown way too high and was moving way too fast to survive another tumble.

I tried to activate my durability spell. But my tank was empty, I'd used the last of my reserves to empower the ring that currently held Badb at bay. The instant before I would've hit the ground, a blur of gray and green fur barreled into me, robbing me of most of my momentum and trajectory. I heard something metallic clatter away from me. I rolled across the ground, bouncing awkwardly as I did. At one point I felt a pop and my shoulder erupted into painful fire. How bad could one more dislocated shoulder really be?

Once I'd finally stopped tumbling like a weed in the desert, I turned to see that Balto the cù sìth had broken my fall. But he wouldn't have done that unless commanded to. Sera had just saved my bacon.

Balto struggled to his feet, letting out pained growls and yelps as he did. Once he stood, he kept his back left paw off the ground. It was probably broken. I felt a bit of guilt rise up in my chest. The pup and I had gotten off on the wrong foot a few days ago. Then today, I'd gotten his partner killed, and now he'd been injured.

I looked around me, trying to reorient myself. I found Sera standing a few feet away from where I'd left Badb. She had her chain and rapier ready to swing. Badb's prison crackled and whimpered. It was starting to give. Oh boy, that wasn't good. I'd sent half of our team away.

Sera only seemed to have the one cù sìth remaining, and it wasn't exactly up for a fight with an evil druid possessed by an even more evil goddess. Jacob was down for the count, and I was tapped out of magic. Not to mention, I had a newly acquired dislocated shoulder. Maybe I could flop my arm at Badb enough to distract her. Did I mention it hurt like hell?

"You miserable little worms!" Badb screeched, spittle flying from her borrowed lips.

With an exertion of shadow magic, the wooden circle's barrier finally buckled and shattered. Shards of energy that reminded me of glass flew in every direction, quickly dissipating into nothing.

Sera took a nervous step backward, but she held her weapons at the ready. There was no way she could face down a goddess on her own. The Eclipse Druid thrust her silver rapier forward and emerald green energy shot forward like a flamethrower. Badb raised a hand. A barrier of shadows coalesced in front of her, stopping the druid's attack cold.

The shadow sword reappeared and knocked Sera's rapier away. Badb surged forward towards Sera. She tried to leap away, swinging her chain in a complicated pattern in an attempt to ward the crazed goddess away. It didn't work, of course. Because at this point, why would it? The universe had it out for us.

Badb deflected the chain out of the way, grabbing the Eclipse Druid by the throat and raising her into the air. Sera let out a choked cry, but Badb only seemed to revel in it. She summoned the shadow sword and held it to Sera's throat. I stumbled forward, but exhaustion overtook me and I fell to the ground. Directly onto my hurt shoulder, of course.

"Meddling druids," Badb scoffed. "My husband was a fool to create the Order of Druidry. Like the wizards before you, you are only pretenders to the power that is rightfully ours."

Seraphina coughed. "Big talk for a bitch currently possessing a druid."

"Only a means to an end," Badb assured. She turned to face me. "You may have disrupted my ritual. But the damage has been done, wizard. The chains have been loosened. It is only a matter of time before the doors open."

"Go fuck yourself," I muttered. Very clever and witty, I know.

Badb chuckled to herself. "Your denial makes this all the more satisfying."

Then the Death Goddess turned her attention back to Sera and started squeezing. Sera tried to take in a breath, but only let out a slight choking sound. She began to struggle, but it was a losing battle. I watched the length of her chain fall and coil on the ground.

I had to do something. Anything to loosen Badb's grip. Because then maybe Sera could do something. Druids were supposed to be experts in fae magic, right? The Tuatha were no more than super-faeries. Maybe Sera could do something to cripple Badb's power.

Then I remembered.

I'd taken Remy's gun, the one loaded with enchanted iron rounds. If I could even graze the Death Goddess with a shot, I could stun her long enough to give Sera an opening. I used my good arm to reach it where I'd stowed it in my waistband.

My eyes widened. The gun was gone. I was sure I'd had it a few minutes ago. The memory of tumbling to the ground after disrupting the ritual streaked across my mind. I'd heard something clatter to the ground, but I hadn't given it much thought amid all the other distractions.

I rolled around, trying to locate the weapon, but it was nowhere to be seen. How far had it flown? It was my only chance to do something that would actually make a difference. I turned back to Badb and Sera, watching helplessly as the goddess choke the life out of the druid I'd only just met.

"Seattle PD! Put the woman down!" A voice shouted.

I whipped around, the voice had come from near the locker room tunnel.

The last person I expected to see standing there, aiming the gun at Badb, was Detective Hart. She was dressed the same as I'd seen her earlier that day. Her police badge was displayed on her belt. With all the bright fluorescent lights shining down on her, the badge shone like a beacon during what had become my darkest hour.

Badb let out a deep, throaty laugh, still holding Sera in her iron grip. "Surely you're joking. I'll give you one chance, mortal. Leave now, this matter does not concern you."

"The hell it doesn't," Hart snarled. She gestured around the arena with one finger. "Security cameras have this whole thing on camera. Breaking and entering, vandalism, assault, and attempted murder. All of those fall under my jurisdiction as a member of the Seattle Police Department."

"Detective Hart, you have no idea what you've gotten yourself into." I gasped. "You need to run!"

Hart ignored me, keeping her focus entirely on the goddess-possessed druid. "I thought it strange that a supposed wizard would bring a gun to a magic fight, then I saw this one was loaded with silver. I'm not an expert, but I've read plenty of fairy tales. How I see it, silver and psycho monsters like you don't get along."

She double-checked the safety on the gun to make sure it was ready to fire. "Last warning."

Badb rolled her eyes in an exaggerated fashion and threw Seraphina towards me. She tumbled and rolled as she hit the ground, stopping just a few feet away from me. The druid wasn't moving, but judging by the steady rise and fall of her chest, I assumed she was alive. For now, at least.

Badb floated towards Hart, gathering power as she glided forth.

"Hart! Run!" I shouted.

Badb raised her hand above her head, gathering shadows into a condensed sphere. Her body moved to fling the shadows forward and consume Hart. But a second before she could do that, three shots rang out into the night.

BAM! BAM! BAM!

Badb gasped, stopping her advance abruptly. The shadows she'd gathered slowly dissolved. The goddess looked down at her possessed body. There were two clean holes on either side of her chest. And the final had blossomed in her forehead.

Suddenly, Deimos' body began to shudder. Darkness began to pour out of every orifice, the nightmarish power of the goddess screamed as it ejected itself from the druid's body.

"No! You damned insects!" Badb screeched.

I felt her exert her will, trying to call the shadows back into her, but it was useless. It was like trying to catch a tidal wave with a plastic bucket. The darkness continued to rush out of her. The bane of the fae damaged her host body beyond repair. Iron burned the fae like acid; I could only imagine it would do the same to one of the Tuatha, especially since Badb was not here in her true form.

Badb let out a pained cry, glaring daggers at me. "This won't be the last time we meet, wizard." She turned her attention back to Detective Hart. "And you! When I return, I will come for you myself and visit torments on your body the likes of which haven't been seen in millenia!"

"Just shut up," I let out a hoarse breath. "and die."

Badb threw her head back, arms extended outward and screamed as the shadows tore her host body to shreds. They all coalesced, rising high into the sky. They formed together into a large visage of a crow and let out one final pained screech. Then the shadows dispersed completely.

Finally, the night had gone quiet. I let my head drop to the floor as exhaustion lulled me into a deep sleep.

Chapter 28

I woke up with a startled breath as memories of our latest battle came flooding back. Before I had any time to think, I reached for my magic. Splitting pain pierced my head and the magic I'd tried to call up simply faded. I cradled my head in one hand and took a moment to look around.

I was lying in Bishop's recliner back at our apartment, a blanket covered me up to my stomach. I found Seraphina lying on the couch nearby. She was no longer wearing her mysterious druid cloak. Instead, she wore a simple black tank top that showed off her broad shoulders and muscular arms. Her snow-white hair was loose, no longer bound to the confines of a ponytail. She breathed steadily as she slept. Sera was beautiful in a strange alien way. The strangeness of her only magnified by her odd hair color. But there was still something nagging at the back of my mind. Something was definitely familiar about her. I was sure I'd seen her somewhere before.

On the ground next to the couch, Balto the cù sìth lay sprawled out on the ground. The beast slept peacefully, but I watched his ears flick towards any little sound. He was still on high alert, ready to guard his master with his life.

I returned the recliner to an upright position and instantly regretted it. A wave of nausea hit me like a truck. My stomach threatened to remind me of what I'd had for dinner the night before, but I fought the urge down.

"You're awake," Someone said.

I turned and found Detective Hart standing in the kitchen. Alarm bells went off in my head. What the hell was she doing here?

She must've seen the look on my face because she held up a hand in a placating gesture.

"Relax," Hart took a sip from a mug. "I'm not here to arrest you."

I started putting the pieces together. "You saved us. And brought us back here."

Hart smiled. It was a creepy look on her, the detective who'd been hounding me for the last few days. "Hey, you could be a detective. Just don't come for my job." She gestured towards the stairs. "Your other friend, the rocky fellow missing an arm, is upstairs resting."

"I don't understand. How'd you find us?"

"I'd been keeping a detail on you since you left the precinct yesterday. I was sure you were involved with those mummy murders somehow. I figured if I followed you, sooner or later, you'd slip up." Hart explained.

"Instead, you found us in the middle of a chaotic battle of magic and monsters." I surmised.

"You really weren't kidding with that story you told, were you?" Hart asked. Clearly she was still questioning her own sanity.

"Afraid not,"

Hart nodded. "You'd better give me the whole story then."

So I did. I explained to her who Deimos was and what he and the goddess Badb had planned. I explained most of what happened to me over the last few years. I left out the parts about Azazel though, I figured bringing up the literal devil was a story for another time. I told her about the gang war between the vampire clans that had led me jumping off the Space Needle. I only gave her a brief rundown of the general idea that there was a whole other world living right alongside ours.

Hart puffed out a breath. "That is a lot to accept."

"Trust me, you don't know the half of it." I said.

"So I guess you really aren't my killer," She said.

"Nope, just a guy with phenomenal cosmic power working for minimum wage at a coffee shop," I said.

"Well, now that I know about all of this, I suppose I can't rightfully arrest you for the murders," Hart said.

"Yeah, uh, I'd really appreciate it if you didn't." I chuckled.

Hart diverted her eyes to the counter as if mulling something over. "Back at the precinct, you asked if I'd seen something."

I nodded, urging her to continue. "My second year on the job, I was responding to reports of repeated deadly assaults near a convenience store. Brutal beatdowns, if you can call them that. The victims looked as if a bear had mauled them. As luck would have it, if you can call it that, when I was checking out the alley nearby I heard a woman scream. I ran to help and what I saw changed everything I thought I knew. I thought it was a rabid dog, but it was way too big. Gray skin, large claws, pointed ears."

"Sounds like a ghoul," I said. "They're a type of undead, usually found digging up graves. But there have been cases where they develop a taste for fresher food. What happened?"

"I shot the thing, but it only seemed to piss it off. It wasn't until I grabbed the girl and headed for the street that it stopped following me. When it tried to step into the light, its skin started blistering."

I nodded. "Ghouls are related to sanguine vampires. Not even SPF 3,000 sunscreen would protect them from the sun."

"Vampires, Jesus..." Hart said.

"You did good." I said. "Most people see a ghoul and try to run faster than Speedy Gonzales. But to stand your ground and try to kill it takes guts. Don't even get me started on the Celtic God you banished last night."

Hart smiled, but I could see the uncertainty in her eyes.

"Look, strange things have been happening more and more recently. And I suspect they're going to keep happening. And it would be a lot easier to do what I do best if I didn't have to worry about the police suspecting me of every grisly murder that shows up on their desk."

"So long as I don't think you have anything to do with it, I think I can keep the SPD off of your back." Hart said. "On one condition, I want in."

"Uh, in?" I said intelligently.

Hart nodded. "If things are going to keep happening in this town, I need to be prepared to stop it. Whatever you can tell me and show me, I'd appreciate it."

I rose to my feet, unsteadily at first, and walked over to the detective standing in my kitchen. I held out my hand over the counter towards Detective Hart.

"Welcome to the madness." I said.

***

After our new partnership had been formed and I was sure I wasn't going to suddenly faint, I saw Detective Hart out the door. That left me alone with Seraphina's unconscious form. I filled a glass with water from the fridge, drank it all down, and filled the cup again. I took it with me back to the recliner and sat back, letting myself just relax. My shoulder still hurt like hell, but Hart had put it back into place while I'd been unconscious.

For a little while, I did nothing but let myself breathe and relax. I thought briefly over the events of the last few days. The boggart, the Plague Druid, and Badb. What had started as a simple murder case turned into a conflict with a maniacal Death Goddess trying to make a comeback. Nothing was ever simple, it seemed.

But there was still one question that been left unanswered. Someone within the Spring Court had wanted it to seem like Seraphina had been the one behind this. My mind first went to Tam Linn, who'd seemed all too eager to pick a fight and make the Spring Court's druid look bad. There was a chance it might even have been Oberon himself, though I couldn't figure out what reason he'd have to frame his own druid. If he wanted her out of the way, there were much simpler ways to accomplish it. He was an extremely powerful fae, after all.

The only other suspect within the Spring Court I could think of was that hothead centaur, Loxias, but that was only because I didn't like him much.

It was more likely that the culprit was someone outside of the Spring Court. Mab, perhaps? She was the Winter Queen and Deimos' direct superior. I'd never met the lady, but everything I'd read about her made her sound like one scary chick.

Medb came to mind next, the Autumn Queen. But I hadn't seen hid nor hair of her since this whole thing started, and she seemed like she'd want to make a show out of it. What all but eliminated the faerie lords from suspicion was the presence of Badb. I didn't think the lords of faerie would want anything to do with reinstating their old bosses.

"Quite the conundrum, isn't it?" A voice said.

I nearly jumped out of my seat. Sitting on a stool at the kitchen counter was Lugh, the enigmatic Celtic deity who loved to show up at inconvenient times. He looked as he always did, forest green t-shirt, maroon hoodie with a Celtic knot symbol on the front, and his rust-colored hair tied back. His eyes glowed with a faint golden light. I wondered if that's just how he always looked or if he lit them up for dramatic effect.

I steadied my breathing. "What the hell are you doing here?"

"Just checking in on my favorite wizard," Lugh placed a teabag into a mug, neither of which he'd had a moment before. "You did good work."

I scowled at him. "You couldn't have told me your deadly, chaotic aunt was in town a few days ago?"

Lugh's eyes flashed. "No, I couldn't. I told you, there are rules."

"Rules, schmules." I scoffed.

Lugh sighed and then took a sip from his tea. "You managed to banish Badb's shadow, but I'm afraid the damage she has wrought was extensive."

"Wait, so she wasn't bluffing? The seal on the Old Gods has really been weakened?"

Lugh nodded. "I'm afraid so. Even now, my brethren stir. It won't be long before they walk the earth once more."

"What can we do to stop it?" I asked him.

Lugh seemed to consider that for a moment. "I'm not sure."

My expression flattened. "You're not sure?"

"Nothing like this has happened before," Lugh said. He gestured to himself. "And obviously I averted the original sealing. It is something I will have to look into."

"Well, as soon as you figure something out, let me know." I said in a falsely pleasant voice.

Lugh nodded, oblivious to my irritation. "I will give it some thought. As soon as I know something, I will find you."

The Celtic God of Justice finished off his tea alarmingly fast and then stood from his seat. "You did well heeding my advice, by the way."

Then Lugh was gone. No flash or fanfare. One moment he was there, the next he'd vanished. I really hated when he did that.

"What the hell are you talking about!" I shouted to the empty air.

"Wha—?" A new voice rose up.

I turned to see Seraphina sitting up on the couch. Her hair was frizzy and disheveled, but it didn't detract from her beauty or the deadly power that I knew was hidden just underneath the exterior.

"You're awake," I said.

"Who the hell were you yelling at?" Sera asked.

I pointed lamely to the space where Lugh had been.

"I uh—nevermind," I shook my head. "How are you feeling?"

"Like I was nearly choked to death but an insane fae goddess," Sera said matter-of-factly.

I tilted my head at that. Sera was a straight to the point kind of gal, I could appreciate that. I recapped the last few moments of our previous evening and ended with my conversation with Hart right after I woke up. I left out any mention of Lugh. I didn't think it was wise to tell her absolutely everything just yet. I barely knew the Eclipse Druid, after all.

Sera found her druid's cloak draped over the couch nearby. She rose unsteadily as she drew it around her. The cloak seemed to move partly on its own, wrapping around the druid like a shadow. Balto whined, rising to his feet. His bad leg seemed to have healed overnight.

"You got a hot date or something?" I asked.

"No, but it's time I get back." Sera said. "I have to speak with King Oberon. He needs to know what's happened."

"Will he believe you? The whole Court seemed to think this was all your scheme." I said.

Sera nodded. "He'll have to."

I frowned. "Are you sure? There's really no rush for you to leave."

"I'm sure."

I sighed. "Fine," I found a notepad and scribbled my number down. I ripped off the sheet, folding it in half and held it out to her. "If you ever need anything."

Sera eyed the paper skeptically, then took it. The page disappeared into the sleeves of her cloak. She tilted her head, looking towards the table. "You've been uncharacteristically quiet."

I turned and saw that Jack of the Lantern was resting on the dinner table. I was getting real sick and tired of people showing up in my home.

Jack's flames sparked to life. "Hey, you're not the only one who had a long night."

"I'd say I'm glad to see you made it out okay," I said. "But I already miss the peace and quiet."

"Hey feck you too, pal," Jack spat, but there was no malice in his voice.

I smiled. "You okay? Being forced to help a psycho goddess with her evil scheme was probably a lot to deal with."

Jack shuddered. "It's no biggie, not the first time I've had to deal with some crazy bitch."

I looked to Sera, raising an eyebrow.

She scowled at the pumpkin. "Shut it before I turn you into a pie."

Jack yelped, his flames dimming slightly. Sera held her hand out, green tendrils of energy snaked out of her sleeve, grabbing the pumpkin and pulling it toward her. Jack's vessel disappeared into her sleeves.

"I'll be taking him off your hands," Sera said.

"By all means, he's been nothing but an annoying yapper since I found him," I said.

"Oh, trust me, it doesn't stop." Seraphina sighed. She found her chain and rapier resting on the floor near the couch. Those, too, disappeared into her cloak.

"How do you do that, anyway?" I asked.

"Trade secret,"

Of course, it was.

"Well, hopefully I see you soon." I said. "Maybe under better circumstances next time, though."

"Likewise, wizard," Seraphina nodded.

We shook hands. It seemed like the appropriate thing to do. I was making all sorts of new allies today. I walked Seraphina to the door. She and her faerie hound ghosted out the door. Sera looked back at me as she lifted her hood. She smiled before the darkness covered her face, which seemed impossible in broad daylight. And then she and her wolfie companion disappeared.

I had to admit, the Eclipse Druid had style. One of these days, I'd have to get her story.

***

I called Remy to check in and fill them in on everything that had happened. They did the same. They had managed to get Bishop to Light Haven, where Fachnan assisted them in getting to the Mystic Order's private medical ward. Fachnan had made Sylf, the Ljósálfar noble in charge of the Mystic Order's medical facilities, swear to secrecy when she became aware of Bishop's condition. Using Nordic elf magic and medicine, they had managed to heal his injuries, but as we already knew, there was nothing to be done about his vampire infection.

After that, I laid down on the couch. Satisfied that everyone was safe and accounted for, I let myself fall back into a deep slumber. I'd certainly earned it.

***

A few weeks went by. Bishop had healed up nicely and was allowed to return home. Scout never left his side. He never had before, unless he was with me, but now he seemed especially glued to Bishop's heels. I'd taken Jacob back to the Mystic Order so his arm could be repaired. Besides the missing arm, he was doing alright. I resumed business as usual, working at The Grind.

My car was back from the shop, good as new. It was almost like a giant faerie raven had never crushed it. It turns out that Miguel, the mechanic, was Remy's uncle. He had a minor talent for magic that he used to aid in his work as a mechanic. He assured me that The Bee would be able to take much more of a beating next time a rogue monster had a problem with it. The Bee let out a triumphant roar as I rolled it out of the shop. Remy had paid for all the damages—just another thing I loved about them. I swore to pay them back, but Remy brushed me off.

So, instead, I finally took them out on that date I promised. I finally told them about everything I'd promised to. My parents had died when I was young, and I hadn't learned about my magic until a bloodthirsty archangel came knocking on my door. Remy took it all in stride, which surprised me.

"You're not the only one with a troubled past," Remy said.

I'd asked them to elaborate, but they refused.

"Maybe another time," They said. "I think that's enough doom and gloom for one evening. I want to focus on the here and now."

I took Remy home and just before I walked back to my car, they dragged me back inside. I didn't arrive home until the following day.

***

I came home early the next morning after helping Detective Hart with an investigation that I feared spelled trouble. But I needed more information before I could do anything else to assist her.

Bishop and Scout weren't home, which I thought a bit strange, but I didn't dwell too much on it. I went to the kitchen to hunt down some breakfast.

I felt a stir in the air. I recognized the sensation. It was an early warning system that Bishop had built into the protections he'd enchanted the apartment with. Someone was outside. I narrowed my eyes at the front door.

There was a loud knock at the door like someone was trying to punch through it.

"Tobias Leight, come out now! We have the building surrounded!" A strong, masculine voice said.

I frowned. I flicked my wrist, summoning my polearm with a gust of wind and extending it to its full length as I approached the door. It figured that after a quiet few weeks, trouble would show up on my doorstep.

I opened the door and took one step outside. I stopped cold as I took in the sight before me. Over a dozen armed men wearing tactical gear were aiming assault weapons in my direction. I heard radio chatter, but nothing clear or consequential.

"Who the hell are you guys?" I growled. I twirled my polearm and slammed its end on the concrete, releasing a wave of subtle power. Just enough to show them that if they wanted a fight, they'd get one.

"Drop the stick and put your hands in the air!" A soldier said.

I narrowed my eyes, and I got a good look at their uniforms. They all wore a patch on their shoulders. The emblem consisted of two crossed swords behind a depiction of a gorgon, her snake hair flared out in all directions. Under it in big letters, was the word "Aegis."

"Everyone, stand down!" A woman's voice said.

One of the agents approached, letting their weapon hang from the strap around their shoulder. They took off their helmet and held it under their arm. It was a woman. A very specific woman. She was short, adorably so. Her golden blond hair was in a tight bun, tied low enough so that her helmet wouldn't interfere. She wasn't wearing glasses or her baggy sweaters, but I'd recognize her anywhere.

"Hey Tobias, long time no see," She said. "We have to talk."

"Hello, Claire," I said.

Author's Note

Thank you for joining Tobias and the gang in this latest installment in the Chronicles of Leight series. As always, these books wouldn't be possible without the amazing support from all my friends and family. Not to mention all of you who chose to take a chance on this silly little urban fantasy series.

To my parents, a special thank you for always supporting my dreams and aspirations. Tobias is someone who's been forming in my mind for a long time. And it's thanks to your nurturing of my creative spark.

Ashley, you work so hard to help make these books great. You read and then reread to make sure every last detail is perfect. Plus, without you, I'd probably settle on my cover designs before they're fully formed. You're always pushing to help me make these books better. And I'll never be able to thank you enough.

And then there's my Discord buddies, who get the chance to read these stories before anyone else. You all see the roughest, most unpolished versions of these stories and still see their potential!

If you enjoyed *Dreambound Fae*, please consider leaving a review on Amazon and Goodreads. Reviews are SUPER DUPER important in helping small indie authors grow. It only takes a few minutes to leave a star rating and a few words on what you thought of the book!

Oh, one last thing. I have a newsletter! In it I share updates on writing, what I'm reading, playing, and watching, and anything else I feel like rambling about. Subscribers get early previews on the next book, like early cover reveals and maybe even an early chapter or two. Oh, did I mention subscribers get a FREE ebook?Scan the QR code below to find out how to subscribe!

If you enjoyed *Dreambound Fae*, consider checking out other books by the author!

Chronicles of Leight Series

Fallen Son (Book 1)

Fang Wars (Book 2)

Gorgon's Blood (Book 0.1)

Dreambound Fae (Book 3)

Fae Moon (Book 4) *Coming Soon!*

Tales of Leight Novellas Series

Wizard Rising (Book 1)

Reading Order

Gorgon's Blood (A Chronicles of Leight Story)

Fallen Son (Chronicles of Leight Book 1)

Fang Wars (Chronicles of Leight Book 2)

Wizard Rising (Tales of Leight Novellas Book 1)

Dreambound Fae (Chronicles of Leight Book 3)

Fae Moon (Chronicles of Leight Book 4)

Coming Soon!

Tobias Leight will return...

Chronicles of Leight
Book Four

Fae Moon

Coming Soon in 2025!